SECRETS OF A SOPRANO

By

Miranda Neville

Print Edition
ISBN: 978-0-9970054-0-0

Cover art by Phatpuppy
Photography: Teresa Yeh Photography
Model: Jennie Ross
Makeup/Hair: Nadya Rutman, www.bynadya.com

BOOKS BY MIRANDA NEVILLE

The Wild Quartet series

The Second Seduction of a Lady (novella)

The Importance of Being Wicked

The Ruin of a Rogue

Lady Windermere's Lover

The Duke of Dark Desires

The Burgundy Club series

The Wild Marquis

The Dangerous Viscount

The Amorous Education of Celia Seaton

Confessions From an Arranged Marriage

Also

Never Resist Temptation

Anthologies with Maya Rodale, Katharine Ashe, and Caroline Linden:

At the Duke's Wedding

At the Billionaire's Wedding

Anthologies with Grace Burrowes, Carolyn Jewel, and Shana Galen:

Christmas In the Duke's Arms

Dancing in the Duke's Arms

Christmas in Duke Street

DEDICATION

To all my friends and relations who have shared opera performances with me, especially my father. I miss you, Papa.

CHAPTER ONE

"O Love, give me remedy
For my pain, for my sighs!
Either return my love to me
Or let me die."

The Marriage of Figaro, Act II

London, 1818

THE PLAINTIVE NOTES of the aria faded, and a profound hush fell over the theater. It took a lot to silence the carousing in the pit or the gossip of the *haut ton* in the boxes, but the new soprano had managed it. Then the audience erupted into rapturous applause such as Max had never heard in his long career as an operagoer. But then he'd never experienced such a heart-wrenching musical performance as this rendition of Mozart's reverie on lost love.

Over the years, as Maximilian Hawthorne, and more recently as Viscount Allerton, he had seen and heard many great singers and known them intimately, too. But Teresa Foscari reached inside his chest and squeezed the breath from his lungs. She stirred his emotions as only one other singer had done.

Foscari was not *her*. She couldn't be.

The theme of the aria and the genius of the singer had evoked long-forgotten suffering at love betrayed, that was all. He pushed back a churning brew of bitterness and yearning and forced himself to judge the performer objectively.

She was good, La Foscari. Better than good. A vocal artist

without peer as well as a consummate actress. And there lay the problem, immediate, practical, and nothing to do with the sorrows of his youth. He lowered his opera glasses and turned to his companion in the box at the Tavistock Theatre, London's principal—for the present—home of the operatic arts.

"We're ruined." Simon Lindo, not a man given to excessive emotion, shook his lightly grizzled head in dismay. Lindo's sentiments were aroused not by vocal virtuosity but by mundane mercenary considerations. "We're destroyed," he continued, lowering his forehead onto the upholstered railing of the box. "No one will come to the Regent while Foscari is here. That snake Mortimer will sell out every performance this season."

"Careful, Simon," Max said. "You don't want Mortimer to see you looking desperate. You can be sure he knows we're here."

Lindo raised his head and composed his features lest Bartholomew Mortimer, the lessee and manager of the Tavistock Theatre, should note the consternation on the face of his former employee and present rival.

It took a lot to upset Simon, whose years in the theatrical business had given him nerves of steel and a philosophical acceptance of adversity. But circumstances tonight justified his agitation. Lindo had sunk every penny he possessed into the brand-new Regent Opera House.

Max's anxiety was almost as great. While the loss of his own investment in the Regent would hardly leave a dent in his income, he'd poured time and energy into the venture beyond what might be expected of an aristocratic patron. Pride and ambition were at stake. His peers, many of whom swelled the packed house for Foscari's opening night, regarded his venture into the theatrical business as an eccentricity made acceptable only by his exalted social position. He cared for their opinion—a little. A great deal more important was the achievement of his goal: bringing truly great opera to London.

He looked back at the stage where Teresa Foscari, known

throughout Europe as La Divina, was taking her bow.

She was a glorious sight. Max knew heavy stage makeup and an elaborate powdered wig could disguise imperfections of face. But experience told him the sumptuous blue satin panniered gown of Mozart's Countess contained a figure worthy of the gods. No costumier's artifice could create that slender waist and magnificent bosom. The only drawback was that her allure shattered the verisimilitude of the opera's plot: no one in their right mind could believe a husband would leave the bed of this stunning creature for another woman. Every male in the audience was gaping at the full breasts, revealed by her low neckline and accentuated as she bowed in regal acknowledgment of their homage.

Not all these men, opera aficionados only by reason of fashion, could appreciate the peerless artistry of her performance, the soaring perfection of her voice. But not one was unaffected by her superb presence. There was no mystery why Teresa Foscari's fame had streaked like a comet through a dozen countries for the past ten years.

Lindo continued to bemoan their misfortune. "Look at her, Max. The men are going to be after her like flies for honey whenever she appears." He turned to his friend, his shrewd eyes narrowing. "From the look on your face I'd say you were ready to join them. I'm worried about financial ruin and all you can do is stare at her."

Max wrenched his eyes from the stage and tried to speak like a man with nothing but business on his mind. "The timing of her arrival in London is unfortunate. But the ladies will come to us. We have Edouard Delorme and he's as handsome as sin."

"You know a soprano always trumps a tenor," Lindo retorted.

"We have a soprano. An English one."

Lindo lifted his bushy eyebrows.

Miss Lucinda Johnston possessed a lovely voice and had achieved great success in the provinces and some in London. But her face, to put it kindly, was reminiscent of a bulldog. A refined, handsome, well-bred bulldog, Max told himself optimistically, likely to appeal to any patriotic Englishman.

And most unlikely to make even the most dog-loving squire forget Teresa Foscari's obvious charms.

"You're right," he said. "There's no comparison."

"One swallow doesn't make a summer," said Lindo, taking over the role of comforter since Max had relapsed into gloomy silence. "And the rest of Mortimer's company is dreadful."

"Before Foscari appeared the evening was a disaster," Max agreed. "Under-rehearsed and badly sung. Foscari can't sing every night. With adjustments of our schedule we'll at least capture the audience when she's resting."

"Though Nancy Sturridge is good. I'd have hired her if Mortimer hadn't promised her the sun and the moon."

Lindo was right, damn it, as he always was in his judgment of talent. The young woman playing Susanna, the Countess's maid, was excellent. Max had made overtures to her in a more personal way, until he heard she was on the brink of accepting an offer from the Marquess of Somerville.

But Sturridge, however commendable, didn't have the magnetism to carry a company on her slender shoulders. Foscari did, the reason Italian newspapers had proclaimed her a goddess. La Divina indeed.

Max's gaze was irresistibly drawn back to the beauty on stage. "If we had Foscari instead of Johnston our success would be assured."

Lindo understood him at once. "La Foscari? Steal her you mean? We know Mortimer pays well. And there's likely a clause or two in her contract that'll make it hard to get around."

Max shook off the objections with a casual shrug, not ready to admit any ulterior motive for approaching Teresa Foscari. "Contracts can be broken and I have a greater fortune. I'll invite her to supper and open negotiations."

The applause had finally died down and the scene continued.

Max didn't want to miss a single note of it.

"THAT WAS EVEN worse than I'd feared." Tessa collapsed onto the chaise longue and glanced with disfavor about her dingy dressing room, the best the Tavistock Theatre had to offer but far from her usual standards in either dimensions or comfort. In the auditorium the aged theater retained a semblance of its gilded splendor; backstage the rot showed.

"Thank you, Angela," she said to her maid who had hurried over to repair her stage makeup in preparation for the third act. Tessa leaned back and closed her eyes.

"The company is bad, to be sure," her friend and companion Sofie said, "but you were brilliant as ever. It's going to be another triumph." Sofie was the Austrian wife of Tessa's *répétiteur* Sempronio Montelli. Sempronio's musical coaching might be essential in the maintenance of Tessa's vocal brilliance, but Sofie's role as comforter and her constant, if sometimes bracing, support were just as important.

Tessa, who always judged musical performances with resolute honesty, waved a dismissive arm from her supine position. "Perhaps you're right. But I can't take any joy in appearing in such an inferior production. I hoped the other singers might rise to the occasion of a public performance, but they're obviously not capable. Tonight was no better than the rehearsals."

The door opened and Sempronio walked in. The rehearsal pianist had been watching the opera from the manager's box.

"I'm sorry, *cara*," he said, understanding better than Sofie how Tessa felt about the evening's musical standards. "You were *magnifica*, of course. As for the rest—" He shook the mop of curls that enhanced his resemblance to a middle-aged angel. "Susanna is good."

"Miss Sturridge sings Susanna well," Tessa agreed, her genuine admiration for the other soprano mixed with distress. She'd never become accustomed to the jealousy her own gifts aroused in others. "Unfortunately she resents me. She managed to prick me with a pin when we were dressing Cherubino. And she tried to upstage me during the finale."

"Foolish woman!" Sofie exclaimed. "Upstage La Divina indeed! As though she could! And pricking you was very unprofessional."

"I'm beginning to think there is little that is professional about the Tavistock Theatre," Tessa said, sitting up now Angela had completed her task. "What's this?" She accepted some papers from Sempronio.

"The stage porter gave them to me. From your admirers."

"Already? Let me see if there's anything promising."

While Sofie and Sempronio dissected the inadequacies of the other singers in the multilingual babble that was the common currency of their cosmopolitan group, she unfolded the notes, glancing at the signatures, looking for a particular name to leap from the bottom of a page. This was her first visit to England, her father's native land. When she had agreed to come, inevitably she had thought of the ardent young Englishman who had been her first love. Perhaps her only love. She knew he had belonged to a prominent family and her first appearance in London had attracted the avid attention of the newspapers; the cream of society would attend such an important opening at the opera house. She'd imagined him coming to see her, sorry for his desertion, eager to renew their acquaintance, still in love with her.

How foolish she was. Max Hawthorne had certainly forgotten her in eleven years. He probably never gave her a second thought after he departed Oporto without a word, leaving her shivering in a churchyard waiting to keep their appointment.

"These are both invitations to supper tonight," she said. "But of course it doesn't mean these gentlemen—" She glanced at the signatures again. "—Allerton and Somerville aren't married." Of course it didn't. She was well acquainted with the ways of the nobility all over Europe and had no reason to believe the habits of English lords were any different.

The door opened again, heralding the arrival of the florid figure of Bartholomew Mortimer, manager of the Tavistock Theatre and her current employer.

"Madame Foscari," he cried, seizing her hand and kissing it with fervent lips. Tessa withdrew it gingerly from his grasp and gave it a shake to dispel the lingering dampness from his touch. She'd had her doubts about Mortimer when he'd visited her in Paris and enticed her with guarantees of badly needed money. His repellent behavior since her arrival at the Tavistock increased her doubts about accepting his offer, however desperate her financial straits.

"You were magnificent!" the manager continued, emitting a trace of spittle in his enthusiasm. "All of London will be at your feet." He looked significantly at the correspondence in her hand. "Already the offers are coming in."

Tessa didn't like the implication of his statement. "I am anxious," she said with emphasis, "to find lucrative singing engagements to supplement my performances here. Tell me what you know of Allerton and Somerville. What kind of men are they?"

Mortimer rubbed his hands together. "Ah, *madame*! The Marquess of Somerville. A very wealthy man."

"Is he married? Does his wife host receptions?"

"A bachelor, very charming and a great patron of singers. An excellent association for you."

Tessa could imagine exactly how this charming bachelor liked to patronize singers. From the look in his eye, the oily Mortimer would be delighted to act as her pander. She'd had enough of that from Domenico, her late and unlamented husband.

"And Allerton?" she asked. "Is he, too, a great patron of singers?"

Mortimer continued to smile but his gaze shifted sideways. "I would strongly advise you to favor Somerville. A much more advantageous connection."

Sofie, who had been following the exchange in silence, chimed in. "Lord Allerton is the primary investor in the Regent Opera House and one of the richest men in England."

"He sounds an excellent connection," Tessa said. "Is *he* married?"

"Allerton's playing at running an opera house but he doesn't know what he is doing, for all his money bags. Let me remind you," Mortimer continued, leaning over her with an undercurrent of threat, "that you are promised to the Tavistock for the entire season. You should read your contract carefully."

Tessa could smell spirits on his breath and see black dots disfiguring his bulbous nose. Familiar panic clawed at her chest and she scrambled to her feet, scattering correspondence on the floor, and sidestepped the manager, eager to put some distance between them.

"We have a few minutes, my dear *madame*. I wish to discuss adding more performances to your schedule."

"You must excuse me," she said through clenched teeth, "it's almost time for the next act and I need to prepare." Even more, she needed to escape from Mortimer, whose proximity brought on the flash of heat through her body and the dizzy sensation in her head that made her want to scream.

"Not now," she ground out. She stepped backward but he followed her. "When? Tonight after the performance?"

"I shall be tired."

"I must insist."

"If you don't leave me alone now I shan't be able to sing."

Mortimer didn't budge. She had another challenging aria coming up and needed time to recover her equilibrium. Looking around wildly, she couldn't think of the words to drive him out, only of the discordant buzz in her head. Then Sofie, blessedly reliable Sofie, caught her eye and held out a teacup.

Grasping the lifeline, Tessa hurled it with all the strength she could muster. It whisked by Mortimer's ear and hit the wall behind with a satisfying crash. Her head began to clear.

"Madame Foscari! That is unnecessary! I merely wish to make an appointment for a discussion of business." She breathed deeply and reached for more ammunition. "Very well," he said, "I bid you good evening but I insist we speak soon."

Mortimer backed out of the room and Tessa collapsed onto the sofa. Angela brought her a glass of water, but her entourage knew better than to speak when she was like this. After five minutes or so Sempronio ventured to ask if she needed to test her voice. A couple of quick vocal exercises reassured her and she was calm enough to check her appearance in the mirror and make sure her wig was straight.

"I didn't mean to do that," she said with self-disgust. "I'm trying to give up melodramatic fits. Next time, Sofie, keep the china away from me."

"It doesn't matter," Sofie said. "People expect it of you. They like you for it."

Tessa didn't like herself for such behavior. What had started long ago as a means of gaining attention for a young singer, had become a habit and more recently a necessity. She wanted to stop—stop throwing things and most of all stop suffering the attacks that were soothed by the smashing of breakable objects. She'd failed at the first test.

"I'd prefer to be known for something other than throwing china."

Sofie gave her a chiding look and Tessa laughed briefly at the absurdity of the exaggeration. Still, not a single newspaper account of Teresa Foscari's extraordinary career failed to mention the flying crockery that had become part of her legend.

"Holy St. George! What a dreadful man Mortimer is." She shuddered, sinking back onto the chaise, skirts puffing out around her in a cloud of satin brocade. "Did you hear how he tried to pimp me?"

Sofie looked at her thoughtfully. "The Marquis of Somerville is said to be handsome as well as rich," she said.

"Really? How did you come about that scrap of knowledge?"

"Nancy Sturridge hopes to come under his protection." Trust Sofie, a genius at picking up backstage rumors, to know.

Tessa sighed. "Even if I were interested, which I am not, I don't need any more difficulties with Sturridge."

"She wanted to sing the Countess tonight," Sofie said. "The stage manager told me."

Why couldn't people be content with what they had? Nancy Sturridge was a natural soubrette, with the light voice and flirtatious personality that such roles required. And musically Susanna was an adorable part. Tessa had been sorry when she gave it up to graduate to the heavier role of the Countess.

"Sturridge can keep Lord Somerville and I wish her joy of him. Allerton merits further investigation."

Allerton's motives in inviting her to supper could be amorous or professional, or both. In any case, it wouldn't hurt to make him wait. "I'll tell them both I am too tired to go out tonight. Better still, you write the letters. La Divina doesn't write to just anyone, even if they are wealthy and titled. Have a footman deliver them during the fourth act. We'll keep them wondering till then."

MAX HAD NO reason to linger after the performance, but he found himself ordering his coachman to wait. Slipping around to the side of the theater, he joined the small crowd at the stage door, not his usual haunt. The men thronging the entrance were of a poorer class than the denizens of the green room where he was accustomed to meeting singers with whom he was involved. Regretting his impulse, he almost walked away, but curiosity held him.

Ever since he'd first heard of Teresa Foscari, and through all the reports of her genius and her exploits, he'd wondered. There was the name, but Teresa wasn't an uncommon one, in either France or Italy. The age was about right and the height. The hair color and features had been unidentifiable on stage. As for the voice, it would have matured in eleven years. A sense of familiarity had tugged at his senses throughout the performance, but he couldn't be certain.

A dozen times, since the end of war on the continent, he'd considered making the journey to one of the European opera houses to find out, but had resisted. He really didn't want to see her again. The heartbreak and betrayal suffered by his nineteen-year-old self were behind him. He was a grown man, for God's sake.

But suddenly he had to be sure. So he stood in the shadows of a mean alley near Covent Garden, waiting to see La Divina Foscari in the flesh.

A murmur ran through the crowd as the door opened and a woman emerged on the arm of a gentleman. An indefinable air of magic surrounded her, an aura that sent a rustle of excitement through the ranks of the waiting gallants. She wore a black velvet cloak embroidered with gold thread and trimmed with sable, more of the luxuriant fur swathing her neck to protect the golden throat from the April night air.

He couldn't see her face beyond an intriguing hint of a straight nose, but he had no trouble identifying the gentleman whose arm guided her: it was the Marquess of Somerville. While the diva settled into the waiting carriage, the marquess looked around, caught Max's eye, and winked.

Max had lost women to Somerville before. His own fortune was the greater, but the mercenary ladies of the demimonde weren't immune to the lure of high rank. And Max didn't fool himself that his dark complexion and harsh features could compete with the depraved-angel charm of Somerville's countenance.

Max was never sure if Somerville meant to torment him. If so, for the most part he failed. What Max sought in his operatic mistresses was different from the other man's uncomplicated requirements. Somerville would have no use for the combination of vocal brilliance and indefinable inner beauty that Max had found just once in his life. Whenever Somerville came out the winner in their unacknowledged contest Max moved on. There was always another opera singer willing to accept his attentions and his money.

But he'd promised Simon Lindo that he would speak to La Foscari, so he'd call on her the next day. Strictly for business reasons.

CHAPTER TWO

"The Opera House will be full this evening on account of the attractive powers of FOSCARI, who appears in London for the first time at the Tavistock Theatre."

The Morning Post

CAPTAIN JAMES STORRS, ensconced in the private sitting room of his family home, read aloud from *The Morning Post*. "*The soprano is famous for her high notes, her exorbitant fees and an artistic temperament that leads her to smash crockery when her displeasure is aroused—*"

His brother, the Earl of Storrington interrupted him to address his wife. "There's no question, Jacobin. Teresa Foscari is your cousin. Breaking china must be a family trait. We'll have to hide the Sèvres when she comes to the house."

"I don't see why you have to keep bringing that up, Anthony," the countess replied with a toss of chestnut curls. "I only once threw the good china at you, and you deserved it."

James lowered the newspaper, prepared to wait while his brother and sister-in-law indulged in the flirtatious banter that had been going on since before Anthony shocked the *ton* by marrying his pastry cook. Apparently he'd underestimated Lady Storrington's eagerness to discover all she could about her new-found cousin. "Go on, James," she said. "What else does it say?"

"*Madame Foscari, known throughout Europe as La Divina, has been delighting operatic audiences for almost a decade. Her voice and her beauty have attracted the admiration of the highest born of many lands, including, it is rumored, the intimate attentions of the Tsar of Russia and the former Emperor of France—"*

"My cousin," Jacobin interjected, "would never have the bad taste to have an affair with Napoleon!"

"What about the Tsar?" James asked. "He was our ally. Is it acceptable for your cousin to have conducted a liaison with him?"

"Quite acceptable," replied his sister-in-law. "I hear he's a very handsome man, and tall."

"Jacobin isn't attracted to short men," her own tall husband explained gravely.

"Don't be absurd, Anthony. That's not why I don't like Bonaparte. Besides, I haven't met him since I was twelve years old and far too young to be interested."

"I'm relieved to hear you won't be taking ship to St. Helena to join him."

James continued reading. "*La Divina's antecedents are mysterious. Some say she is Italian, like her late husband, a scion of a noble Venetian family. Other reports maintain that Madame Foscari is of French, Spanish or Austrian origins—*"

"And only I know the answer to that!" Jacobin said smugly. "She is half French and half English, just like me. My father and her mother, Suzanne de Chastelux, were first cousins. Their fathers were twins."

"I wish I'd known before there were twins in the family," Lord Storrington complained. "It wouldn't have been such a shock when Augustus appeared to join Felicity here."

Storrington looked over at his heir, sleeping peacefully in his mother's arms. Augustus slept a great deal, not yet recovered from the exhausting experience of sharing a womb for nine months with his elder sister. The Storringtons' infant daughter was wriggling in her father's arms. She'd already drooled on his shoulder, leaving a white mark on his otherwise pristine coat. His starched neckcloth was the worse for the efforts of her tiny hands. She was currently engaged in trying to amputate his forefinger with toothless gums while beating on his forearm with her small fist.

"I never met my cousin or her parents," Jacobin went on. "They left Paris before I was born. Papa's cousin married an Englishman, Jonathan Birkett. When the revolution came they moved to Portugal. I had forgotten about them but I was so happy to receive a letter from Tessa. And it's very exciting to discover my long-lost cousin is famous."

"How can you be sure Teresa Foscari really is Tessa Birkett?" James asked. "She might be an imposter."

Jacobin gesticulated indignantly, eliciting a squeak of complaint from her son. She soothed him and he quickly relapsed into slumber. "Why would she lie? How would anyone else even know of our connection? No James, as soon as I read her letter I felt such kinship. She even mentioned meeting my father when she was a young child. I cannot wait to make her acquaintance."

James exchanged glances with his brother and set aside his concern. Anthony would make inquiries and ascertain that Jacobin, in her delight at finding a relative to call her own, didn't fall prey to an unscrupulous charlatan. James picked up *The Morning Post* again.

"All of fashionable London will be in attendance tonight at the Tavistock Theatre to hear Madame Foscari in The Marriage of Figaro. Members of the beau monde wishing to view the phenomenon at closer quarters, must wait till next month when, it is reported, she will make her first private appearance at a soirée in the home of that ornament of society, the Honorable Mrs. Charles Sackville."

The Countess of Storrington rose to her feet, eyes ablaze. "We must leave for London at once!"

"It's too late to attend tonight's performance," her husband argued. "Even if it weren't, I doubt we could get a box."

"I don't care about tonight's performance! My cousin is not going to give her first recital at Lydia Sackville's house. Over my dead body!"

"WHO WAS THAT?" Tessa looked up from the seat of the Broadwood piano she'd hired for the duration of their London visit. "The door hasn't been still all day. I could hardly concentrate for the noise. And there's a wobble in my *mezza voce*."

Sempronio raised his eyes to the ceiling. "How many times must I tell you? You were perfect."

Tessa trusted Sempronio's assessment of her voice and she never had the least difficulty attending to her singing. Her devotion to her craft was the constant that had kept her sane through times she preferred not to remember. But distress at conditions at the Tavistock had made her edgy. She was still upset about last night's encounter with Mortimer and she couldn't stop thinking about Max Hawthorne. How foolish to dwell on an eleven-year-old affair simply because she and Max now occupied the same island.

"I've had a delightful afternoon," Sofie said, "being entertained by your callers."

"Better you than me," Tessa said, still fretful.

Sofie ignored her ill temper. "No truly. Both Somerville and Allerton are charming gentlemen though not at all happy that you refused to receive them."

"Hm, Somerville. That one is pure trouble. And he thought to impress me, ambushing me at the stage door and insisting on accompanying me home. I hope you told him the lilies he sent this morning make me sneeze."

"Allerton brought red tulips."

"I like tulips. Were other flowers delivered? Any white roses?"

"No one in London knows your favorite flower yet," Sofie said. "I shall drop a hint into a few ears."

She was being silly again. Even if Max Hawthorne still loved opera it didn't follow that he had been at the opera house last night. If he had, he wouldn't send her flowers the next day. And he certainly wouldn't remember that first bouquet of white roses with which he'd come calling on her backstage at the Oporto

Opera. There was no reason for him to connect Teresa Foscari with Tessa Birkett, none at all. And if he did, he wouldn't seek her out.

Perhaps he no longer enjoyed the opera. He'd claimed to adore it but it might have been a lie to beguile her. More than likely considering what happened later.

"Tell me about Allerton," she said, determined to be sensible. "Is he as good-looking as Somerville?"

"At first I thought not," Sofie said thoughtfully. "He's tall, very dark, straight hair, almost black eyes, sculpted features like one of those medieval Flemish portraits. At first he seems grim, but he's quite different when he smiles."

Sofie's sketch brought another man to mind, a much younger man who'd once answered to her companion's description, the man she had to stop thinking about. That man had always smiled at her.

Perhaps he lived in the country.

Or perhaps he was dead. She shouldn't care. She didn't much care. He was nothing to her, only a distant memory of a few happy weeks. Why did everything conspire to make her think of Max Hawthorne? Max Hawthorne who had not, and would not, send her white roses.

She distracted her unruly mind by teasing Sofie. "I can see you like Lord Allerton, Sofie. Sempronio had better take care."

Sofie's husband looked up and gave them a tolerant smile, then returned to his task of sorting through a pile of musical scores.

"Really," Sofie said earnestly, "he was most agreeable. He talked to me and sounded as though he were interested in what I had to say."

"Oh, oh! Sempronio. This is serious. Lord Allerton likes Sofie," Tessa teased.

"Then he has excellent taste in women," said the cherub-faced pianist, regarding his wife warmly. "And I hear his musical taste is just as good. This new opera house of his is going to be magnificent. No expense spared to make it ideal for the art."

"Very well, we are agreed," Tessa said, getting to her feet. "Allerton is a paragon and I should be singing in his company. Too bad I'm pledged to the disgusting Mortimer and the filthy Tavistock for the season. Now Sofie, are you too tired after your entertaining afternoon, or shall we go shopping? I know you're dying to see the famous Bond Street just as much as I am, even if we can't afford to buy much."

"Shouldn't you answer Lady Storrington's letter first?" Sofie asked. "It sounds like your cousin has done well for herself. A very useful connection."

"Yes, of course, cousin Jacobin. She wants me to sing at her house next week, any day I name. I wonder how much I should charge her. We could use a handsome fee right now."

"Does she get a family rate?" Sempronio asked.

"No," Tessa replied. "No family rates. We can't afford it. Holy Saint George! I don't even know how much to ask for a private recital. Let me see, what did Domenico always say? Ask for twice what you want because they will make you accept less."

"You're such a tough bargainer." The little Italian spoke with affectionate and warranted sarcasm. Domenico had also complained that she overpaid shopkeepers if he wasn't with her.

"You're right." Tessa swung around. "You shall conduct the negotiation, Sofie."

"I, Teresa? I don't know that I could. I've never had much to do with business." Before she eloped with Sempronio in Vienna, Sofie's life had been even more sheltered than Tessa's. An amateur singer of good birth and mediocre talent, she'd come to Tessa for lessons and fallen in love with the pianist.

"Then it's time you started. God knows I hated the negotiation with Mortimer. Seriously, I think you should take charge of our financial affairs."

Sofie looked alarmed. "But Teresa, I know nothing. Think of

the way I was brought up. The daughters of Austrian counts are taught nothing about managing money. I'm sorry to be so useless."

Tessa moved quickly to give Sofie a hug. "You aren't useless. You're my dearest friend. You'd think, since my father was a merchant, that I'd have some idea how to conduct business. Negotiating contracts was the one thing Domenico was good for."

And, because thinking about her late husband only made her depressed, she held out a hand to Sempronio while keeping an arm around Sofie's waist. She didn't know what she'd do without the Montellis, and Angela too. She owed them all so much.

"Sempronio," she said in a rallying tone. "How about you? Will you talk to my cousin about the fee?"

Sempronio was not to be drawn. He merely grinned and looked more like a gray-haired angel than ever. "Forget it, *cara*, I'm just a musician."

"I'll do it," blurted Sofie with a determined gulp. "I'll learn. Shall I call on Lady Storrington?"

Dear Sofie, Tessa thought, embracing her again. "Thank you, my love. I know you'll do a splendid job. Now, let's go and buy some clothes."

"We shouldn't be spending money now!" Sofie wailed.

Tessa laughed. "I can tell you're going to be very strict and that's a good thing. But Mortimer tells me every performance is sold out for the next month, and I have my cousin's and Mrs. Sackville's soirées. I think we both deserve a little treat."

CHAPTER THREE

"Madame Foscari's vocal exertions were much beyond anything we ever heard in this country before, and the public appeared so enraptured with her performance, that she sang amidst a continued scene of universal applause and admiration."

The Times

SOCIETY MUSICALES WERE hit-or-miss affairs and Max tended to avoid them. But they didn't often feature an attraction as potent as La Divina. New arrivals packed the hall of Lord Storrington's Upper Brook Street house more quickly than their predecessors could make their way up the stairs. As Max inched his way across the black and white marble floor, he was greeted by a diminutive redhead with a smile like the smallest drizzle of honey on lips that tasted only vinegar.

He kissed Lydia Sackville's hand with more enthusiasm that he usually displayed since he fully sympathized with her sentiments at being beaten by her sometimes friend and frequent rival, Lady Storrington, for the services of Teresa Foscari.

"I hear Edouard Delorme is simply marvelous, Lord Allerton," Mrs. Sackville said. "Your new venture will be a sensation."

Max would have been more gratified if he hadn't suspected her praise was heavily flavored with sour grapes.

He was one of the last arrivals and by the time he reached the top of the stairs and greeted the hosts, there was almost no one behind him.

"Will you greet the rest of our guests?" the Earl of Storrington said to his wife. "I want to have a word with Max." Leaving the countess to exchange rapturous air kisses with Lydia Sackville, he drew Max aside.

"Is it wise to leave Lady Storrington and Mrs. Sackville alone together?" Max had known Storrington for years.

The earl grinned. "I'm ready to intervene before the outbreak of open warfare."

"What can I do for you?"

"You know all about the business of singers," he said. "I'd like to know whether my wife was charged a fair price for Madame Foscari's appearance this evening." He named a sum that made Max whistle through his teeth.

"Good Lord, Storrington," he said. "That's almost twice the going rate, even for a singer of Foscari's éclat. Catalani herself doesn't earn that much for a few songs."

"I wondered," mused Storrington, "but it's no great matter. Tonight's recital made Jacobin happy and at least it's all in the family."

"Family? Are Lady Storrington and La Foscari related?"

"Their grandfathers were twins, younger sons of the Comte de Chastelux. Madame Foscari may sing for her supper but she is well born, at least on the French side."

Tessa Birkett, Max remembered, was half French. She'd also demonstrated a talent for extorting large sums of money. His stomach lurched and he was tempted to act the coward and go home.

Steady, he told himself. Tessa never said anything about a French count in the family. Drawing him in with her wiles, she was unlikely to have kept noble connections to herself.

"I suggest you keep an eye on this new-found cousin. Don't let her take advantage of your wife."

Storrington shrugged. "I won't. Thank you for the warning. Enjoy the recital. You at least will enjoy it. I'm not too fond of opera myself."

Max liked Lady Storrington and didn't wish her a grasping

harpy for a cousin. Not least among the countess's attractions, as far as he was concerned, was the faint odor of notoriety that clung to her. Although of good birth, she had lived in Storrington's house as his pastry cook and high sticklers didn't forget these things. The chaperones of well-bred virgins tended to keep their charges out of her trajectory.

Shuddering at the very idea of well-bred virgins, he congratulated himself on the unlikelihood of finding anyone overly interested in marriage—in particular his marriage—at the event. His luck was out. The first person Max spotted as he headed for the saloon was his mother.

He swore under his breath at the sight of the familiar figure in midnight-blue velvet. His eyes darted this way and that, but there was no avoiding Lady Clarissa Hawthorne in all her majesty.

"Max!" She'd been waiting for him. "I thought I'd find you here."

He kissed her on each cheek. "If you wanted to see me, Mama, you had only to send round a note."

"A mother should hardly have to summon her son to see him," Lady Clarissa said tartly. "There's no reason you shouldn't live with me. Lord knows, there's plenty of room. Then I could see you whenever I want."

Which was exactly why Max had bought his own house several years earlier. He shrugged and said nothing, awaiting her next sally with the blend of affection and exasperation she always aroused.

"I want to hear this singer everyone's talking about. I'm surprised you didn't get her. It's bad enough you're going into the theatrical business, but if you're going to do it you might at least have the best."

"I'm here to see what I can do about that," Max replied through gritted teeth. His nerves stretched to the breaking point by nearly a week of frustrated anticipation, he had even less patience than usual for dealing with his dam's invigorating personality.

"Good. And I'm here to see the Tsar's diamonds. The newspaper reports say the parure he gave Madame Foscari surpasses anything seen in England."

His mother didn't sound concerned and—eyeing her own necklace—he saw why. Tonight she was wearing the Tamworth sapphires, seven massive and flawless blue stones surrounded by diamonds. Not many monarchs in Europe had jewelry to equal her collection, and if they did they weren't liable to give it away, even to as famous a mistress as La Foscari.

He could sense other guests covertly examining his mother's adornment and giving her—and him—the enthralled attention he'd become wearily accustomed to. It had taken many years for him to accept the fact that people found the sight of the richest woman—perhaps the wealthiest person of either sex—in England fascinating. And as her only offspring he was subject to the same voracious curiosity.

As a naïve nineteen-year-old traveling in Europe, he'd been alarmed and repelled by the sycophantic fawning of others. Berlin, Vienna, Madrid: Denizens of society in each of these capitals knew all about the Hawthorne heir. It had seemed absurd to him—and still hardly made sense—that his acquaintance was desirable because the wealth of two great-grandfathers made the legendary fortune of Croesus look like a modest competence. The daughter and sole heiress of a banker had wed the heir to the earldom of Tamworth. A city fortune, whose sheer size dissipated any scent of the shop, merged with one of the country's vast landed estates to form England's greatest fortune. Max and his mother were the sole descendants of that marriage.

As far as Max was concerned it could stay that way, a sentiment his mother was far from sharing.

"Hm," she said, looking around. "A very worldly company tonight. I don't see any eligible unmarried girls to present to you." It was positively frightening sometimes how she seemed to read his thoughts.

"Since I'm not interested in meeting them, the dearth leaves me indifferent."

This was the beginning of a discussion they'd had often since, aged twenty-two, he'd flatly turned down an arranged marriage with the daughter of a duke.

"Will you come to the country with me next week?"

Max fought off irritation at her request. The one thing that tempted him into matrimony was the prospect of presenting his mother with a brood of grandchildren to divert her exhausting attention from him. She could teach them to take snuff and cheat at brag and wear tiaras at breakfast.

"The Regent Opera House opens this week, as I'm sure you're aware. I can't leave London now."

She gave him a hard look, accompanied by the poignant sigh she used to induce guilt when he failed to meet her demands. "Always opera singers," she said. "Your pursuit—for whatever reason—of Madame Foscari is inevitable. Always opera singers."

His heart missed a beat, thinking, as no doubt she was, about a particular opera singer. He couldn't help scanning the crowd, not really expecting yet still dreading to see the face he'd once known so well. Though the large saloon was thronged with the powerful, the clever, and the merely ornamental cream of the *ton*, they were all figures he'd encountered any time these ten years.

No one dared approach to pierce the golden aura that set Lady Clarissa and her son apart from other mortals and save him from his controlling parent.

"Let me escort you to a seat, Mama," he offered in desperation. "In this crowd we'd better move now if we want to be near the front."

"No thank you. I may want to leave early since my tolerance for music is limited. I can view those gemstones from a distance through my lorgnette. Something in the back row will suit me very well."

Rescue came in the unlikely form of a man who made a habit of being impressed by nothing. Under the circumstances Max was pleased to see the Marquess of Somerville threading his way effortlessly through the throng and into the Hawthorne orbit.

"Somerville," he said in his friendliest manner. "What brings you here?" As though he didn't know very well.

"To gaze on the beautiful Lady Storrington, of course. Why else?"

Lady Clarissa gave a crack of laughter. "You'll catch cold at that one, Somerville. Storrington wouldn't have married his cook if he hadn't loved her."

Somerville raised her hand to his lips. "Indeed, Lady Clarissa. That is why I only look. Besides"—Somerville was now gazing at her with his legendary blue eyes and giving Max another demonstration of his legendary technique with women—"I've found a better, and I dare hope more susceptible, object of my admiration."

Lady Clarissa actually simpered at this flattery from a man a decade younger, if not two. Max interrupted the revolting display. "Would you be good enough to find a seat in the rear for my mother? I really need to be near the stage. For professional reasons, you know."

Without giving Somerville a chance to argue, he abandoned marquess and mother and ensconced himself in the center of the second row of gilt chairs in the Storringtons' drawing room. Exactly two minutes later an immaculate figure slipped into the seat next to him.

"You owe me a favor, Max," Somerville drawled.

"I knew you'd be able to get away from my mother more easily than I, and I was right."

"And of course," the marquess continued, "you thought to steal a march on me by placing yourself closer to La Divina."

"I was rather under the impression that you were ahead of me in that particular game."

Somerville shrugged. "I don't kiss and tell, but I can assure you that the lady is, indeed, quite beautiful."

Max said nothing and tried to look as though he didn't care. Judging by the other man's knowing smile he didn't succeed.

"And after all, my dear Max, your interest is purely professional."

"WILL YOU GO out, please, and see what the audience is like?"

Sempronio withdrew his gaze from a painting of well-dressed rustics herding their sheep and looked at Tessa, surprise crinkling his normally placid face. "Are you nervous?" She rarely suffered from stage fright, and certainly not before a private recital.

"Not about the performance. Never mind, I'll look." Tessa made a final adjustment to her hair at the mirror over the fireplace. She'd decided against wearing the tiara on this occasion. The Russian necklace, bracelets and double-eagle brooch looked opulent enough against her red velvet gown, cut very low in front and lavishly trimmed with gold lace. Quite enough to announce to the London cognoscenti that Teresa Foscari was a force to be reckoned with.

The small saloon in the Storrington house led into a huge drawing room where a stage had been constructed for the occasion. The chatter of numerous voices ascended to a roar when Tessa passed into the larger room. Her view of the attendees—and theirs of her—was blocked by a screen placed to hide the doorway between the two rooms from the audience.

Briefly she closed her eyes, chiding herself for her unwonted nerves. It was unlikely he'd be here. If he was, she probably wouldn't recognize him after all this time. And if she did, what of it?

Before she could talk herself out of it, she set her eye to the slit at the fold of the screen. Almost every gilt chair was occupied and more people were standing at the back. It was always good to see a full house and this was an especially brilliant one. Under the splintered light cast by a hundred candles in cut-glass chandeliers, Tessa looked out over rich gowns and glowing jewels contrasting with the more severe tailoring of well-dressed men. Undoubtedly the cream of London society was gathered here, the very people she needed to impress if her visit to London was to meet her ambitions. But she wasn't thinking of her future or her responsibilities. Her gaze scanned well-bred faces, reddened with heat or alcohol, powdered or rouged, pretty, handsome, or commonplace beneath elaborate coiffures and fashionable crops.

Then she saw him.

Her knees trembled and she held onto the doorjamb for balance. He was older now but unmistakably the shy young man who had blushed when he brought a posy to the Oporto opera house and told her she had the voice of an angel. He had the same coal-black hair, cropped short because it wouldn't take a curl; the sharp cheekbones and hawkish nose; the olive-toned skin, once tanned to a deep bronze by the Portuguese sun but now paler in the early spring of England; the grave mouth which could broaden into a generous smile and light up an otherwise austere countenance.

It had been such a very long time. But even after eleven years, during which she'd been married and enjoyed a dazzling career, Max Hawthorne still had the ability to make her pulse race. And she bitterly resented the fact.

He wasn't smiling now. Sitting in the middle of the second row, he frowned intently at the empty stage, as though anticipating something frightful. Was he expecting her? Did he know that Tessa Birkett, the young girl he'd insulted and abandoned so many years ago, was about to reappear in his life in the guise of Teresa Foscari?

If not she had the advantage. Thank God she'd seen him before her entrance on stage. Had she spotted him in the audience then, all her experience might not have prevented her faltering. As it was, she had time to take several deep breaths and prepare her mind to think of nothing but the task in hand. She took a sip of water and turned her thoughts to music. But before thrusting Max Hawthorne firmly from her consciousness she permitted a fleeting—and doubtless vain—wish that he would be as agitated by her appearance as she.

LA FOSCARI KNEW what she was doing. There was little point challenging a fashionable audience with anything obscure. She sang several well-known Italian songs, staples of polite after-dinner entertainment, but delivered with a skill and intensity that no amateur could match.

Max hardly noticed. The moment she emerged from the screen his deepest hopes and most profound dread had been fulfilled. It was, without doubt, Tessa Birkett. Yet what did the reserved, innocent young girl he'd fallen in love with have to do with this haughty beauty in red velvet and diamonds? But of course the reserve—and quite probably the innocence—had been a pose. The girl he'd adored had never existed. The avaricious opera singer, mistress to emperors, had always been there behind the sweet façade. Unfortunately it was his duty to use his millions to tempt her once again. His lips curled derisively.

"Disappointed, Max?" Somerville murmured beneath the roar of applause that greeted the end of *Caro mio ben*.

"Not at all, Somerville. She's exactly what I expected."

REFUSING A THIRD encore, Tessa braced herself to greet the horde waiting to engulf her. The praise and fond embrace of her cousin might have eased the familiar tension engendered by crowds of strangers, but the presence of the one person she was determined to avoid roiled her stomach with dread.

"Do you need any refreshment?" Jacobin asked.

"A glass of champagne would be agreeable, cousin, but nothing to eat. I always sup late."

"Call me Jacobin," Lady Storrington replied. "May I call you Tessa?"

"Please do. No one does any more. It reminds me of my childhood."

And of Max. Max had always called her Tessa.

"And I hope I can tempt you to taste a little pastry," Jacobin went on. "I make them myself."

"How unusual. I wasn't aware that peeresses were in the habit of preparing food for their guests."

Jacobin laughed. "They're not. But I was a pastry cook before I became a countess and I like to keep my hand in. I'm very good, you know. I can assure you I won't poison you."

Tessa smiled, warming to her cousin and hostess. She was beginning to feel guilty about her fee. Sofie, displaying an unexpected flair for extortion, had demanded a princely sum for the evening, expecting to come down in price. Lady Storrington had agreed without a murmur.

"Just one, then," she said, "but only one. It wouldn't do for La Divina to become La Rotunda."

"You can afford at least two," the countess replied. "Your figure is much better than Catalani's."

"Angelica," said Tessa gravely, "doesn't watch her diet as carefully as she should."

"Is there anyone in particular you'd like to meet?"

Tessa tossed down her glass of champagne in a single gulp to give her courage. While she was here she might as well take care of some business.

"Pray present me to Lord Allerton," she requested. Anything to avoid Max Hawthorne, whom, out of the corner of her eye, she could see in conversation with the Marquess of Somerville and another gentleman.

Her hope that Allerton was on the other side of the room was dashed. Jacobin led her toward the paunchy older man who stood chatting with Hawthorne. Of course he had to be chatting with Hawthorne. Such was her luck.

Jacobin stopped behind Max and tapped on his black-clad shoulder.

"Excuse me for interrupting," she said. "Please allow me to present you to my cousin, Signora Foscari. Tessa, this is Lord Allerton. Also"—indicating the other two—"Lord Somerville and Sir Henry Waxfield."

Tessa wasn't sure how she managed to retain enough self-assurance to curtsey. Only years of experience in the public arena prevented her from gaping like an idiot at the discovery that the enormously wealthy impresario of London's new opera house was also her former love. Panic seized her throat and she doubted she was capable of uttering a single word.

Apparently he was not so affected. He looked down at her with maddening self-assurance.

"Mrs. Foscari and I have met," he said in a voice that would freeze morning chocolate.

"Really?" Jacobin asked. "You didn't say so, Tessa. Or maybe she doesn't remember you, Allerton." Her tone was teasing then her smile faded. Apparently she noticed the frigid atmosphere.

"It's been many years," Tessa said softly. It took all her courage to speak at all, let alone with any degree of calm. "He was Mr. Hawthorne then."

MAX KNEW HE'D have to meet her and he was ready. He'd decided not to acknowledge their previous acquaintance unless she did. He had not counted on the potency of Tessa's presence. La Foscari's presence, rather. The press of guests around them made the distance between them a mere yard or so. The room's chatter faded from his consciousness, as did every soul in it. When Lady Storrington introduced them he managed to utter a few words with little idea what he was saying.

"Of course you know Madame Foscari, Allerton." Sir Henry Waxfield was speaking now. "You've been abroad often since Waterloo and must have caught her in some opera house or other." Having settled the question to his satisfaction, the pompous baronet addressed his next question to the guest of honor. "Must have been awkward, madam, traveling around Europe during all the years when Bonaparte was always at war with some country."

"Sometimes it was troublesome," she replied coolly, obviously not a whit discomforted by Max's presence, while he was agitated by the discovery that her speaking voice, soft and sweet, hadn't changed. Suddenly she *was* Tessa.

"Were you ever in danger?" Lady Storrington asked.

"Fortunately not," Tessa replied, "though one time I was almost caught between the lines of the Austrian and French armies. The coachman had taken the wrong road and we didn't know where we were until he heard gunfire."

"By Jove," Waxman said. "How did you escape?"

"I came through safely due to the chivalry of soldiers. A troop of Austrians on reconnaissance stopped my carriage and the officer recognized me."

She laughed. She and Max had shared a great deal of laughter as they explored the old streets of Oporto together. Now there was a brittleness to her mirth, a false note that had probably always been there but he had been too naïve and besotted to detect.

"He offered to escort us under flag of truce," she continued. "The Austrian, a very handsome man of excellent family, was also acquainted with my companion Signora Montelli."

Two or three others crowded around them to hear the diva's tale, which she delivered with dramatic effect. As he listened Max took the opportunity to examine her unobserved. She was tall for a woman and as capable of commanding a drawing room as she did the stage. Trying to observe her dispassionately, he wondered if the kind of glamour she cast over her surroundings was due to her fame. Would she seem as fascinating if she were unknown? The latter, he fancied. God knew he'd been equally struck when he first met her. One look at Tessa Birkett and he'd been head-over-heels and painfully in love. Except there had been no pain, only blinding joy when he thought she returned his feelings. The pain had come later and his heart ached anew as he'd hoped it never would again.

"After several miles, we approached the French line and we were terrified," Foscari went on. "A small platoon came out to meet us, muskets raised. Would the truce hold or would we be met with a barrage of bullets?" She held the audience in the palm of her hand.

"What happened?" someone asked amid several gasps.

She shrugged. "Nothing. *Rien de tout.* My Austrian gallant explained to the French captain that I was Teresa Foscari and had been admired by the emperor. He kissed my hand and rode away, leaving us under the protection of the French. The *capitaine* took us to the French camp where he served us wine. We drank a toast to *l'empereur* and the art of music, then he sent us on our way to Paris."

"What a marvelous story," Lady Storrington said. "And was the French officer as handsome as the Austrian?"

"But of course, and just as charming."

"It's wonderful that appreciation of great art transcends the conflict of nations."

Great art, my eye! Max didn't believe a word of it. Teresa Foscari had surely been given safe conduct on the French side because she was known to be the emperor's mistress. Quite possibly she'd given herself to the Emperor of Austria too. Why stop at two emperors when she could have three? His chest tightened and his head threatened to burst. God damn her to hell.

MAX HADN'T SPOKEN a word during her recitation, for which Tessa was profoundly grateful. The story was one she'd told dozens of times. She knew it as well as any operatic role and could have delivered it in her sleep. It was always well received and she never spoiled it with ugly truths about war: the ruined farmland and wretched peasants, mostly women and children; the constant cannonades, out of sight but audible all the way; the bodies of soldiers along the roadside and the groans of the wounded in the French camp. Why ruin a pleasant evening?

Unfortunately someone else had the power to do just that.

Jacobin turned to Max. "Where did you and Madame Foscari meet?" she asked. "Didn't you go to Vienna last year?"

"We met in Portugal," Max said. Tessa couldn't read his mood but had no reason to think his clipped tones friendly. "Miss Birkett, as she was then known, performed at the opera house there. I don't recall which role."

"Despina in *Cosi fan tutte*," Tessa said.

"Madam, it appears that your memory is better than mine."

"Since it was my operatic debut, it isn't an occasion I'm likely to forget. I'm sorry it made so little impact on you." How could he have forgotten? At the time he had told her she had dazzled him with her talent and her beauty. Only two weeks later he had declared his eternal love, a love she had discovered later was nothing but lust. Now, as she stared at the cold black eyes of the older Max, she realized, to her humiliation, that she wanted him to admire her still, secretly hoped he regretted the past.

"Of course I knew little of opera then and cared less." True enough, at least the first part. He'd pelted her with questions about her roles and her craft, seemed endlessly fascinated by tales of life on and behind the stage. New to the theater herself, she'd done her best to satisfy his voracious curiosity.

"How fortunate," she rejoined with a touch of sarcasm, raising her chin and holding onto her poise by a slender thread, "that the insipidity of the occasion didn't spoil you forever for the art."

"Since those days," Max said, "I've learned to appreciate it."

Vaguely aware that others were avidly observing this byplay, she tried to silence the ominous buzz that wanted to take possession of her brain.

Waxfield, whose eyes had scarcely wavered from Tessa's bosom since the moment of introduction, laughed. "Yes, indeed," he said. "There's not a man in London knows more about opera than Allerton. Or opera singers." He gave Max a little nudge. "Doubt if he's ever seen a singer to equal you, though."

Max seemed to give the innuendo consideration. "You may be correct, Waxfield. It's rare to find beauty combined with vocal talent. A beautiful heroine adds to the veracity of the drama. But the voice of the singer is more important than her appearance. Where both are present opera achieves the perfect marriage of music and drama. That is what we hope to accomplish at the Regent. But the music comes first."

Tessa could hardly argue with an opinion in complete accord with her own. And surely Max wasn't implying her own talents were lacking in musicality. She decided to take his comment at face value and make polite conversation. Small talk she could manage.

"All London is talking about your new opera house," she said.

"No," he said, his face harsh, "all London is talking about La Divina, who sings at the Tavistock."

She was prepared to accept this compliment graciously and had begun to incline her head in recognition when, in a voice dropped low but still perfectly audible to his companions and his hostess, Allerton continued. "You are too high priced for our humble venture. Somerville, perhaps, is better able to afford you."

The Countess of Storrington drew in her breath in surprise. Tessa felt every inch of her skin flush, horrified by Max's attack. The implication that she earned her fees for more than singing was all too clear. She longed to offer a reply that would hurt him as deeply as he had wounded her. But then, he had no heart. She knew that from bitter experience. Before she could think of a clever retort, Allerton spoke again.

"I will leave you to enjoy your evening's triumph, Mrs. Foscari. No doubt this success will yield other lucrative engagements." He sketched a bow in a manner almost mocking—as if he did not feel she merited such nicety—and moved off directly. Beyond rational thought, Tessa sought relief from the fearful noise in her head before she had to scream. She groped for a porcelain bowl sitting on a side table.

"Cousin, I beg you won't," Jacobin said softly and removed the bowl from her grasp.

Convulsively clenching her hand, Tessa stared at Max's receding back, appalled at what she had nearly done.

"I fully understand your sentiments," her cousin murmured. "If you will but wait a moment I'll have a footman bring you something. Do you have a preference for Sèvres or Meissen? Or Chelsea, perhaps. It would be easier to replace. But I cannot allow you to destroy my husband's favorite Song dynasty bowl."

The tension inside Tessa abated. She took a deep breath and managed a rueful laugh. "I'm so sorry. I don't know what came over me."

"I do," Jacobin replied wryly. "I too occasionally have the urge to throw china."

Panic retreated further at her cousin's sympathy, replaced by gratitude that Jacobin's light-hearted intervention had prevented the kind of scene Tessa would rather avoid. In London she wished to avoid the notoriety she'd achieved in Europe, to find a degree of comfort and serenity in the land she regarded as her own, despite never before setting foot in England.

She owed Jacobin an explanation as well as an apology. "It's an unfortunate habit I've acquired to hide my discomfort in company, particularly when I'm faced with…awkward situations. My husband advised me to do it when my nerves become unsupportable." She didn't add that Domenico had originally suggested the famous tantrums to enhance his diffident wife's reputation as a temperamental goddess of the stage. Or that his own actions had triggered the genuine attacks of panic that now beset her.

"I'm sorry to have endangered your porcelain," she continued. "I should have better control of myself but I really wanted to smash something on Lord Allerton's head."

"And I don't blame you a bit. I can't imagine why he was so rude." Jacobin's face was avid with curiosity. "He's not usually like that."

"Is he not? Our acquaintance was slight."

"Beneath that forbidding exterior he's one of the kindest men in London. I always enjoy talking to him because he really listens, and appears interested. Not like many men I could mention."

Tessa murmured something noncommittal. She had no argument with her cousin's assessment of the charms of Max's companionship. All too well she recalled the joys of his conversation. In light of her experience, however, she'd have to dispute that he was "kind."

"And I've always thought him so attractive," Jacobin continued. "Especially since he's completely unaware of it. Those serious dark looks, like a knight of old ready to charge into battle on his lady's behalf. Except there never has been a lady, as far as I know. There's hardly a woman in London, married or unmarried, who wouldn't welcome his advances—and not just because he's so rich—but he's oblivious to them all. He seems only to be attracted to opera singers." She clapped a hand over her mouth. "Oh Lord! I shouldn't have said that."

"It doesn't matter. I'd say he'd made it quite clear he isn't attracted to me."

Jacobin's eyes kindled with curiosity. "I wouldn't say that."

THE MARQUESS OF Somerville caught Max's arm as he strode toward the door. "Hardly the best way to woo a singer, whatever your interest." Somerville spoke with his usual mockery but something in his face suggested that even he had been taken aback by Max's behavior.

"I'm no longer interested in that woman in any way. She's all yours, Somerville, and I wish you good fortune—or rather large fortune." He laughed harshly. "You'll need it."

He stamped away and struck out blindly for the exit. He needed to get out of here at once. He knew he'd behaved badly and didn't regret it a bit. Or rather he regretted making a public scene in Lady Storrington's house. He wished he could have spoken privately. Sweet Tessa, he reflected bitterly, deserved everything he'd said to her and more.

"Max!" Oh, good Lord Almighty. His mother again.

"Yes?" he barked.

Lady Clarissa had too much strength of mind to be deterred by her son's obvious ill temper. "It's her, isn't it? The one from Portugal."

He didn't deign to reply. He was as furious at her as he was at Tessa.

"Keep away from her, Max, I warn you. Don't forget what she is. I'll buy her off again if I have to."

"I assure you, Mama," he replied through clenched teeth, "that I'd rather be stretched on the rack than see that woman receive another farthing from either you or me."

"Make sure you hold to that resolution. And come and see me in the morning. I have something important to discuss with you."

Inwardly damning all parents, he took a last glance across the room to find Somerville bending intently over the singer's hand, then favoring Lady Storrington with a melting smile. The man never stopped flirting with anybody in petticoats.

Storrington had noticed too. The earl walked casually across the room to join the group, careful, Max noticed, to stand between his wife and Somerville.

Max couldn't resist waiting to see how the rascal would handle the confluence of a ravishing, if greedy, prima donna, a beautiful countess, and the beautiful countess's husband. Not a whit discomfited, Somerville kissed both ladies' hands—again—before heading in Max's direction, a look of satisfaction glittering in his blue eyes.

"Still here, Allerton?" he asked. "I thought you'd had enough. But never mind. I have discovered something very interesting."

Max raised his brows and the marquess continued. "I was already fairly certain, but a good look at that bracelet confirmed my suspicions."

"A gift of the Tsar, payment for services rendered," Max muttered with a sneer.

"Either the Tsar of all the Russias is a pinchpenny," Somerville said softly, "or La Divina's visited the pawnbroker. Those diamonds are made of paste."

CHAPTER FOUR

"Miss Johnston has too much appearance of self-enjoyment and good living, to accord with our ideas of a tragic heroine, who is generally doomed to endure all the vicissitudes of life, in a perpetual round of starvations, imprisonments, swoonings, and all the train of operatic miseries. This lady however makes no pretensions to acting, and being more skillful perhaps in wielding a knife and fork than a dagger, wisely avoids attempting what must appear ridiculous, and contents herself with walking on the stage or off, lifting occasionally an arm or an eye, and frowning or smiling as in duty bound."

The Examiner

WHEN HE PRESENTED himself in his mother's small drawing room, days later than promised, Max's mood was no better, though for a different reason. The first night of opera at the Regent had enjoyed a full house, but the debut performance in England of Beethoven's sublime *Fidelio* had been received with what Max could only describe as muted rapture. The opinion of the newspapers was equally tepid.

Lady Clarissa was alone, without any of the hangers-on who normally surrounded the heiress, or the elderly female relative who resided with her as a matter of propriety but was rarely seen. She reclined on a Sheraton sofa and waved one of these offensive journals at him as he entered the room that was small in name only, almost the size of one whole floor of Max's house.

"My poor Max," she said jovially, without further greeting. "I've just finished reading the *Examiner*'s account of your first night. It's very wicked but has Miss Johnston's appearance precisely right. Wielding a knife and fork! Yes indeed! She really shouldn't be permitted to appear in male attire. How came you to engage such a—large—female for a breeches part?"

"When I saw the lady last year there was rather less of her," Max admitted. "But," he continued bravely, "her voice is very fine."

His mother gave him a look that said he hadn't fooled her and turned back to the newspaper. "The only defect in Miss Johnston's voice," she read, "is a piercing shrillness in her upper notes, which produces rather an unpleasant sensation in the ear."

Damned with faint praise, and unfortunately the reviewer was absolutely correct.

"You know, dear boy, I would have enjoyed the evening more if there had been elephants."

"Elephants?"

"Yes. Or perhaps a bear or two."

"The Regent is an opera house, not Astley's Amphitheatre."

"Such a pity. What about a shipwreck? I always enjoy a good shipwreck."

"Since *Fidelio* takes place in a Spanish prison one is hardly likely to encounter elephants, bears, or a shipwreck."

"No wonder it was so boring!" she concluded triumphantly, waving her newspaper for emphasis. "No elephants. And it's in German."

Apparently having had enough—for the moment—of torturing him, his mother set aside the paper. "Delorme is quite another matter. The man is as handsome as sin!"

"Unfortunately he is only too well aware of the fact," Max replied. "Insisted on appearing in a spotless shirt and perfectly arranged hair though his character was supposed to have spent two years immured in a filthy dungeon."

"The shirt was torn," Lady Clarissa said with obvious appreciation, "and offered a quite delicious glimpse of his chest."

"Mama!" Max expostulated. "Such comments are unsuitable for a lady of your years—in fact for one of any age."

"Don't be stuffy, darling. Just because I'm over forty doesn't mean I've lost the use of my eyes or that I'm dead from the neck down."

Over forty indeed! His mother guarded her true age as jealously as her sapphires, but Max could count. He, her only son, was thirty-one years old.

"It really didn't matter why he was dressed like that," she continued. "I had no idea what was happening since I don't understand a word of German. Not that I wish to."

His mother had put her finger on a major problem. No one had understood the plot. London operagoers, if they weren't enjoying Henry Bishop's butchered English versions of Mozart, preferred their opera in Italian. Not that they understood that language either, but they were accustomed to it. Besides, most of the overwrought tragedies on classical themes were so absurd it was a positive blessing not to follow the story. With Beethoven's masterpiece it was different.

He set aside the concern for later discussion with Lindo. Meanwhile he'd rather not hear any more of his mother's hideously perceptive comments.

"You summoned me, Mama. What can I do for you?" Some tedious chore, he suspected, not unrelated to an appearance at Almack's and a dance with the daughter of one of her dearest friends. He steeled himself for resistance at all costs.

Lady Clarissa didn't trouble with subtlety. "It's time you married, Max. You're past thirty and I need grandchildren."

Max sighed. "We've had this conversation so many times I don't know why you still bother. The answer, as ever, is the same. I don't wish to wed and have no intention of doing so. Is that plain enough for you? If you're so enthralled with the state of matrimony why don't you marry again?"

"No thank you. As you know very well, once was enough for

me."

"I know my father was a wretched husband. Why should I inflict myself on some unfortunate female and treat her to the same joy?"

"You're nothing like Hawthorne. You take after me."

He walked over to the window and gazed out onto the rain-drenched grounds behind the Piccadilly mansion. He hated to think of his father, a penniless adventurer who'd cozened a seventeen-year-old heiress into marriage. The fact that he was heir to his uncle's viscountcy made him marginally acceptable, but the reprobate had made her miserable for ten years until meeting his end in a tavern brawl. With his gambling and women he had little time for his wife, and even less for his only child. Max barely remembered the man and that was the way he liked it.

A certain intensity in his mother's manner this morning told him she wasn't going to let the subject of marriage drop. The gloves were off and he needed more than evasive tactics to escape.

He turned to face the room. "Why did you marry him?" He'd never asked before.

"I was young, a fool, and spoiled," she said. "He was handsome and charming and I wanted him, however much I was warned against him."

"Why did my grandfather permit it?"

"As I said, I was spoiled. He never refused me anything. I made such a fuss that he gave in. Your father's birth, at least, was decent."

Max could imagine his seventeen-year-old mother throwing tantrums, holding her breath until she was blue, making life impossible so that her adoring father caved in from sheer exhaustion. Things hadn't changed.

"I wish he had stopped me." The words were spoken so softly Max wondered if he'd misheard. He moved into the room and stood next to her sofa, examining her face intently. He'd never seen his mother look so vulnerable.

"I wish he had stopped me and saved me from disaster. The way I saved you."

Memories of the occasion when her money had "saved" him came rushing back. How could they not when he'd thought of little else for days, almost spoiling his pleasure in the long-awaited opening of his opera house? He scowled. If he could find a way to blame Teresa Foscari for the poor reception of *Fidelio* he would.

Lady Clarissa misinterpreted his scowl. "But I shouldn't say that, darling, because then I wouldn't have you. Although," she added with a return to her characteristic acerbity, "we've already established that you take after me. Maybe you'd be yourself whoever happened to have sired you." Her moment of weakness had passed.

"And I take warning from your own experience. I'm not going to tie myself for life to a fortune hunter."

"You needn't be as unlucky as I was. Not every woman is after your money."

"How could I possibly tell?"

This aroused her from her languid pose—feigned, of course. Lady Clarissa Hawthorne had vigor enough for two women half her age. "I don't understand you." She pouted, pacing in a cloud of royal blue silk. "What's the matter with you? Men of your age should wish for a wife."

"I can't imagine why."

"Don't you want children? And what about…companionship?"

Max's lips twitched. "I do very well in that area, I assure you."

"Singers and actresses!" His mother snorted. "It's time you grew up and saw to your responsibilities."

Her stride lengthened and her arms swung in wider arcs as she roamed the vast room, working herself into a rage. She stopped suddenly and turned to face him, pinning him with a fierce stare in her dark eyes, so similar to his own. Even he could detect the remarkable resemblance between them. Perhaps it was why he was so close to his mother, maddening as he often found her.

Unlike her, however, he controlled his temper. *He* hadn't been spoiled to death as a child.

"I believe I run my portion of the estates competently," he said calmly, "and I have built an opera house that is going to be the finest Great Britain has ever seen."

"Only by throwing my money at it." His grandfather had left him a tidy fortune of his own, a fact that Lady Clarissa liked to forget since it annoyed her that he was independent.

"The Regent is operated on sound business principles and will eventually turn a profit." He hoped so, though it wasn't something he'd worried about when he and his architect designed the lavish theater.

"I challenge you, Max. Let's have a wager. If you can manage your enterprise for two seasons without putting in any more of your capital, I'll stop hounding you about marriage. If you cannot, you marry a girl of my choice."

"That's ridiculous."

"Because you know you can't do it."

Building the Regent Opera House was the only thing he'd achieved himself, not through inheritance. If he couldn't make a success of it he wasn't worth much.

"I don't need to prove anything," he said, but he lied and she knew it, evidenced by the quirk of her eyebrows. "And the Regent *will* be profitable. Soon."

"In that case there's no reason not to take my bet. Unless you are frightened."

She was goading him, pricking at his pride and he ought to resist. Though he suspected he'd regret the effort, he was determined to prove her wrong. And if he couldn't, he might as well settle down to the life of a dull aristocrat, tending to his estates and producing dull, well-behaved children with a dull, well-bred wife.

He reached out and shook her hand. "Done. Two seasons it is. I have until next summer."

"And then wedding bells."

"And then freedom from the importunities of an impossible, meddling, mother."

"I can't wait to see the babies," she said, restored to good humor.

WHY HAD HE behaved like that? What had she done to Max that he should treat her so, in public too. Tessa had turned over the question in her mind a dozen times since Cousin Jacobin's soirée and the drive to the City of London, alone in her hired carriage, gave her time to think about it more.

Since the conclusion of their affair hadn't been her choice, she could think of only one reason for Max's hostility: Her triumph at the Tavistock threatened the success of his new opera house. Such pettiness on his part seemed out of character for the younger man she'd known. But so did leaving Oporto without a word to her, and that was what he had done, proving that she hadn't known him at all.

He'd been trifling with her all along. She was too lowborn to be a suitable wife for the future Lord Allerton. Even the recollection of his rudeness brought on the panicked buzz in her head and something more. The pain she'd suffered in the churchyard of São Francisco and for weeks, nay months, afterward, pierced her anew.

Over the years, whenever her husband made her miserable, she would look back on her short-lived first love and indulge in the foolish fantasy that it had been a mistake and she would wake up from a bad dream and find herself married to Max instead of Domenico. Such fancies solved nothing, so she would return to work, submerging her sorrows in the music that never let her down.

Max Hawthorne, Lord Allerton, had never been worth a single tear. Her half-acknowledged hopes for their reunion had been sheer stupidity on her part, hardly a surprise given her history. When it came to men she was a terrible judge. Blinking hard, she made herself think about the business matters that brought her out this morning.

Something about the premises of the solicitor recommended by Lord Storrington inspired trust: the diligent clerks at work in the outer office; the shelves of law books within; the neat bundles of paper tied with pink ribbon. Mr. Butterworth himself was as solid as his wide oak desk. The knot in Tessa's chest loosened. This man would surely know what to do.

He perused Tessa's contract with Bartholomew Mortimer. "Although the terms of the contract are generous," he said finally, "I would not, had I been consulted, have advised you to sign it. On the face of it a share of the theatre's profits for the season, with a guarantee of at least two hundred guineas an appearance, should come to a goodly sum."

"That's what I thought," Tessa said. "If I sing thirty times—and Mortimer would like it to be more—I earn at least six thousand guineas by the end of the London season. And likely much more. The house," she said proudly, "has been full every night. And that doesn't even include my benefit."

"What concerns me," said the lawyer, "is the clause relating to the timing of payments. Are you aware that Mortimer need not pay you a single penny until the season is over?"

"Except for my benefit performance. The other singers and musicians perform without pay and I receive all the profits from the evening. In a theater of the Tavistock's size it could bring in as much as two thousand."

"That doesn't take place until late May. I hope you have sufficient funds to keep you until then."

The knot tightened again. After a morning spent with Sofie trying to make head or tail of her accounts, she was concerned about covering even the necessities for herself and her little entourage. Let alone putting aside enough money to ensure their futures when La Divina could no longer perform.

"I have earned a great deal over the past years, and I have several engagements for private recitals." She wasn't going to admit that her coffers were perilously close to empty. "I shall survive till the benefit and in late June Mortimer will pay the rest."

"And are you so certain he will be able to pay you then?"

Tessa blanched. "But he must! It's in the contract."

Mr. Butterworth looked troubled. "I hope you are correct, madam, but I would be prepared for difficulties. Firstly…"—he raised a finger to count out his points—"you have to trust that Mortimer is a sober and dependable individual and will have such a large sum on hand."

Sober? Dependable? Not the first adjectives the figure of Bartholomew Mortimer brought to mind.

"Secondly, the contract is worded imprecisely as to the manner of calculating profits. A clever accounting may ensure that there are none. You'd then be left with nothing more than your two hundred a night."

Mr. Butterworth's sturdy fingers blurred before her appalled eyes. Two sets of "difficulties" that could set her back years, perhaps even reduce her to penury. Butterworth dropped his hand to the contract.

"Whoever advised you in Paris, madam, was guilty of neglect."

Advice? She'd taken no advice. Domenico had never used a lawyer and foolishly she'd followed his example. This document, this creation of paper and ink that she'd signed so confidently, was the disastrous result of her own naiveté. Just as her husband had always said, she needed him to take care of her interests.

Not her interests, but his, she reminded herself, lest she find herself regretting Domenico's departure from her life. Domenico had dealt brilliantly on her behalf with theater managers and made them a fortune. He'd also spent one, on gaming, mistresses, and the Lord knew what else, as she discovered after his death. She looked down at the lap of her expensive Parisian walking dress, thought about the splendid carriage she'd hired for the season in London, and her lavish suite at the Pulteney hotel. Domenico had insisted that such luxuries were in fact necessities. "They come for your voice, yes," he would say, "but half of them don't know the difference between Monteverdi and Mozart. They adore you for your beauty and most of all because you are La Divina with your gowns and jewels, your wealth, and your rages with flying china."

Butterworth's office lacked breakable objects but she didn't need them. Far from threatening, the lawyer seemed anxious only to help. She would *not* be destroyed by Domenico, nor by Mortimer either. "This is outrageous!" she said, tilting her chin like a goddess and trying to sound like one. "Is there no redress? I will take Mortimer to court."

"I sincerely hope it won't come to that, madam. A Chancery suit is a time-consuming business that tends to leave the antagonists bloodied and no one the richer save us lawyers. As your adviser I would have to counsel it only as a last resort."

At least her cousin's husband had sent her to an honest man. She might have ended in the office of as great a rogue as Mortimer himself. She hoped she had enough money to pay Butterworth's bill.

"Is the contract binding?" she inquired. "Could I break it and engage myself to sing elsewhere?"

Except that *elsewhere* meant the Regent and throwing herself on the mercy of the deplorable Max Hawthorne. Never. She would starve, rather. Or flee the country.

"I think not, but if you leave the document with me I will consider the matter further and render my opinion. In the meantime I recommend you try and come to an accommodation with Mr. Mortimer. Make him see that it isn't in his interest to be at odds with you. You are, after all, responsible for bringing in much of his audience."

"Thank you, Mr. Butterworth. That is doubtless sound advice.

Please let me know if you have any further thoughts on the contract. Meanwhile, there is another matter." Tessa reached into her reticule and removed a folded sheet of cheap paper.

"My late husband took care of all my business arrangements which entailed correspondence with opera houses all over Europe. Though he was fluent in four languages he used a translator for those he never learned, among them English and Russian. He employed a scholar from the University of Bologna, near our home at Busetto, to read and write letters in those languages."

"I'm surprised he didn't have you write in English. Your command of the language is perfect."

"Thank you." She nodded her acceptance of the compliment. "English is my first language though I have always lived elsewhere. My father was a scholar and insisted I speak correctly." A better scholar than merchant, she reflected, since he'd left her almost penniless.

"Signor Foscari didn't like to trouble me with business," she continued. "After his death, the translator sent me a package of papers. It turns out he was most meticulous in keeping copies of everything he wrote. I found this."

She handed Butterworth the letter.

Busetto, 24th June, 1816
J. Smith, Bristol

Sir

I regret that I cannot assist you in regard to your inquiry addressed to my wife. Teresa Foscari is not the daughter of Jonathan Birkett and Suzanne de Chastelux.

Yours etc.
Domenico Foscari.

"Short and to the point," was the lawyer's comment.

"Yes," she replied. "And untrue."

"Do you know why your husband denied the relationship?

Was he perhaps protecting you from importunity."

"I have no idea. But I'd like to find out whether the inquiry came from my father's family. I know nothing of his relations, even if any exist."

"You grew up abroad, I believe," Butterworth probed delicately.

"I was born in Paris but my parents fled from the Revolutionary terror to Portugal when I was a young child. My father gained employment in the port wine exporting company of Waring and Sons in Oporto. My mother died soon afterwards and my father when I was thirteen. After that I was taken in by his employers, the Warings."

"Have you asked them if they know of Mr. Birkett's connections?"

Tessa looked down at her lap. "I'm not in contact with them. They disapproved of my marriage."

Mr. Butterworth cleared his throat tactfully. "So I take it, madam, you would like to find Mr. Smith."

"Is it possible?"

"Very likely, though it won't be easy. Who knows how many J. Smiths reside in Bristol? It could well be a lengthy and expensive inquiry."

And that, Tessa thought, was the rub. She was in no position to fund the search. Not for the first time since she'd discovered Domenico's perfidy, she cursed her husband. Not only had he rejected an overture that might come from her father's family, he'd made sure she was in no financial position to undo the damage.

CHAPTER FIVE

"The actual subscribers to the Regent Opera House are entreated to observe that their Subscriptions are to be paid at the Office, where they may at the same time receive the Tickets for their boxes."

Advertisement

"WE HAVE TO fill almost nine tenths of the seats at every performance to break even?" Max tried to keep his voice level, not wanting to communicate any hint of panic to Simon Lindo.

Apparently he succeeded. Simon's response reflected no deeper emotion than mild exasperation. "We discussed the economy of the Regent at great length before the plans were completed."

True enough, but Max hadn't been listening, not really listening. What had interested him was the design itself. The Regent was modeled after the European court theaters: elegant; intimate; a jewel box of an auditorium where every action and note performed on stage could be seen and heard from every seat in the house. The opposite of that aging barracks known as the Tavistock.

Right now every one of the nearly three thousand seats in that seedy barracks was sold out. Meanwhile the jewel box, with its modest capacity of sixteen hundred, was playing half full.

He listened intently as Simon went into detail about revenues to be expected from tickets sales in the pit at ten shillings and sixpence a piece and gallery admissions at five shillings.

"What do we need to do?" Max asked, now properly impressed with the urgent necessity to fill the Regent's boxes and benches, soon.

"For a start we need to collect payments from the subscribers." People of wealth and fashion paid in advance, at a reduced price, for the right to occupy private boxes for the entire season. Max himself bought subscriptions at every major theater.

"I thought we'd sold almost every box for the season," he said. "Ours have the best view and most comfortable seats in London."

The Regent's manager raised his hands above his grey-streaked head and cast dark eyes heavenward, as though beseeching a higher power to bring enlightenment to his less experienced partner. "Ordering a subscription is one thing," he said with patience, "paying for it another. That's why we've been placing advertisements in all the newspapers for the past week." He flipped open a box on the desk.

Max surveyed the contents of the wooden case. He considered the care, not to mention the money, he'd expended in the design of the permanent tickets that subscribers would carry to gain entry to their boxes. Where the older London theaters, including the Tavistock, issued well-worn squares of ivory, the Regent's tickets were silver, handsomely engraved with the name of the theater and the box number. He'd commissioned a special case for them, of mahogany lined with green felt, with numbered slots for each box. Nobody received their tickets until the subscription was paid for, a theater box being one of the few items in London that the upper classes couldn't purchase on tick. Unhappily the Regent's ticket case was far from empty.

"The boxes were full on opening night," he remarked.

"We had no trouble selling every seat for the first performance. Naturally we weren't going to let the boxes sit unoccupied. That's bad business, and it looks bad too. But we need the income from the subscriptions to cover expenses we must pay in advance."

"Let me look at the subscription book." Max ran his eyes

down the list of names of those who, in the months leading to the opera house's opening, had reserved boxes. It was a glittering list of the great, the fair, and the merely rich. In short, the cream of London society.

"These people can well afford to pay, most of them," he said in disgust. Max always paid his bills as soon as they arrived. Or rather his steward did.

"You can be sure they've all sent the monies to the Tavistock," Simon said pointedly. "La Divina is the rage right now. It's the fashion to be seen at her performances."

Max had tried to forget Teresa Foscari since their unpleasant meeting but apparently he wasn't allowed to. He had, after all, promised Simon he'd talk to her.

"I spoke to her at Lady Storrington's," he said. "There's no chance she'll break her contract with the Tavistock. We'll have to become the fashion by ourselves."

Simon looked skeptical. "Without Foscari?" He coughed delicately. "It would be easier to lure her over to our side..."

Max interrupted before his partner could come up with a new, unwelcome plan requiring conversation with the rapacious soprano. He never wanted to speak to her again, or see her. Even on stage.

"Without Foscari," he vowed. "We'll have these misers crawling to us, begging to be allowed to enter the Regent. I'm going to make *us* all the rage."

WITH THE GOAL of making the Regent Opera House the destination of choice for fashionable London, Max had sifted through the long-ignored litter of engraved pasteboard on his desk. Little as he cared for the distinction, the Hawthorne heir was on the guest list of every hostess who could summon up a claim of acquaintance. He wasn't happy at the prospect of appearing in salons and ballrooms to talk up his precious opera house like a common street corner shill. But it had to be done. The evening found him attending a rout party at the house of Mrs. Sackville, together with some five hundred of that lady's closest friends and her one determined rival, the Countess of Storrington.

"I wish, Lady Storrington, that you will seriously contemplate taking a box at the Regent for the season. You won't want to miss the opening of Signor Rossini's new opera next week. And we can promise you the best in music, sets and costumes."

"Your theater is beautiful. I was there on the opening night." The lady was polite but unenthusiastic.

"You'll enjoy *The Barber of Seville* even more than *Fidelio,*" Max pressed, the strain of being charming beginning to prey on his nerves. "You won't regret it. We have several excellent boxes still available, although they are going fast."

For the seventh time he repeated this particular lie, and each time it got harder. Describing the superior qualities of the Regent's accommodations and musical offerings was no problem. He believed every word, though he hadn't expected to have to convince the public one member at a time.

He'd always striven for the common touch in his dealings with people, uncomfortable with the notion that wealth made him inherently superior to others. Still, as a Hawthorne, he wasn't used to asking for favors, let alone begging for them.

The countess tilted her head to one side. "I would enjoy it I'm sure. But my husband isn't fond of opera. I'm already trying to persuade him to take a subscription to the Tavistock so I can attend whenever my cousin sings."

He hadn't thought the conversation could be any more distasteful. He was wrong.

"But," she continued, "he's being a little difficult about it. He's annoyed with my cousin because she overcharged for her recital." There was a baleful look in her brown eyes. "I think that is your fault, Lord Allerton. He wouldn't have known if you hadn't told him."

Max raised his hands, palms out, to disclaim responsibility for Lord Storrington's recalcitrance, much as it suited his own interests. "He asked a question, I answered."

"I detected some rancor between you and Tessa the other night."

"I have great respect for Mrs. Foscari as a singer but she does not sing at my theater." Max flattered himself that he sounded calm and reasonable.

"I think there's more than that. Antagonism from your previous encounter, perhaps?"

Max didn't know if Tessa had told her cousin some untruthful version of their past, or if Lady Storrington was on a fishing expedition. Either way he wasn't biting. "I'm sure you will bring Storrington around to your way of thinking and get your box at the Tavistock."

She grinned. "I expect I will. And perhaps we'll take a box at your theater too. At the very least I'll come to *The Barber of Seville*. Reports from Paris are that it's most entertaining."

Relieved to have the conversation back where he wanted it, Max grazed her knuckles with his lips. "Thank you. You set the fashion and London will follow."

"Don't let Lydia hear that or you can say goodbye to her taking a box."

"She already has."

Though she hasn't paid for it. He kept that thought to himself.

What had happened to his comfortable, well-ordered life? Instead of savoring the fulfillment of his plans for the Regent, he was at this damnable rout. Longing to go home and sit in his library with a glass of brandy and a book, he set his teeth and stretched his lips wide.

Ten more possible buyers, he promised himself, and then he'd leave. And most of them had better pay before the week was out.

"Where is Storrington?" He peered through the crush, unable to distinguish the earl. "May I escort you back to him?"

"Oh, he isn't here. Someone else accompanied me tonight." She looked toward the double doors separating the gilded saloon from a more chastely designed music room.

Alerted by a lilt of mischief in her tone, Max turned around, followed her glance, and saw the Marquess of Somerville proceeding through the crowd with effortless grace, making a path for the lady on his arm. A lady who raised a rustle of interest as she approached and left murmurs of excitement in her wake.

"Here comes my companion for the evening," Lady Storrington said with cheer and a drop of malice. "I believe you've met my cousin."

An already horrible evening got worse. The last person he needed to see was the author of his humiliation. Setting aside, for the moment, his mother's share in his predicament, Max fixed all his resentment on Teresa Foscari. Nothing had gone right since the night he set eyes on her again. No, since the moment she had, unknown to him, decided to invade England and destroy his peace. If the dratted woman hadn't chosen this season to appear in London, the crowds would be flocking to the Regent without any expenditure of effort on his part.

The fact that she looked magnificent fed his frustration. Why should he even care? He wanted to ignore her but he could not. An unadorned white gown in some clinging material revealed her voluptuous figure without drawing attention from the cascade of golden curls carelessly bound by a filet of woven gold. The singer's flawless complexion was enhanced with subtle daring by sufficient rouge to make her appear dramatically sensual while remaining on the right side of disreputable. The simplicity of her garb showcased, as doubtless was intended, a necklace of antique cameos in an exquisite setting of worked gold.

Max knew where she'd acquired that particular bauble. Fascinating as the papers found the Tsar's diamonds, those gems were nothing to the notoriety of La Divina's gift from the former Emperor of France. As he stared at them, a slender hand carelessly stroked the central gem, as though to draw attention to the spoils of her affair with England's longtime enemy.

Stiff with outrage, Max sought Tessa's eyes. Luxuriant eyelashes (discreetly darkened as he had reason to know) rimmed oval aquamarines that glanced around the room and, for just a second, met his stare. He expected the practiced gaze of the courtesan she had become. What he saw caught his breath: vulnerability and the gentle honesty of the seventeen-year-old girl he'd walked home from the opera house in Oporto. Then her attention flickered away and she appeared as haughtily serene as ever. Her hold on Somerville's arm was surely that of a lover.

He must have imagined what he'd seen in her gaze, conjured it from some pathetic desire to return to the past. Yet he had an unaccountable urge to find out if the glimpse of vulnerability existed. Probably a waste of time, but Simon would be pleased if he approached Foscari again.

TESSA CLUNG TO Lord Somerville's arm with a great deal more enthusiasm than she felt. She enjoyed the rakish marquess's company but, inured as she was to evading the advances of the most determined plutocratic suitors, keeping Somerville at a distance demanded considerable skill. She was a little weary and her defenses weak. The last thing she needed now was a confrontation with Max.

Lord Allerton. She must think of him as Allerton.

It hadn't escaped her notice that he was on friendly terms with her cousin. Jacobin greeted them with her usual animation but Tessa barely noticed. The chatter of five hundred upper-class voices faded into a low buzz and all she knew was a familiar dark head and a pair of broad, well-tailored shoulders. And impenetrable granite eyes.

"Somerville," he said with a curt nod. "Mrs. Foscari."

The very address seemed an insult. The press, and the public following its lead, referred to foreign-born performers by the appropriate courtesy title. She was properly addressed as Signora, or Madame should the speaker find the distinction between Italian and French beyond his comprehension.

"My lord?" she said, arching her brows toward the heavens.

"A word with you, if I may."

"I am listening," she said, just as stiffly. What could he have to say to her? If it was an apology for his rudeness at their last meeting she'd like others to hear it.

"Would you step aside for a minute?" He offered his arm. "I won't keep you from your friends for long."

His tone was civil rather than warm. Impelled by curiosity, she relinquished Somerville's arm, gingerly placed her hand on Max's proffered sleeve and let him lead her to a spot near a window. Privacy was impossible in a house filled to bursting, but they were a yard or two away from any eavesdroppers.

"Yes, my lord?" she said, letting go of his arm and putting her hands behind her, exerting every muscle to appear calm and relaxed, the opposite of the way she felt. She had to tilt her chin to see his face, still grave, still inscrutable. "Well?"

He said nothing. With only a foot or two of space between them she sensed his tension. Or perhaps only her own. His gaze evaded hers and headed down, over her mouth, her chin, to her neck and the exposed area of her upper chest. Was he ogling her? It seemed unlikely. He had yet to display a gleam of admiration and she could see nothing lascivious in his eyes. What did he want? His silence accelerated her mounting panic. She took a step backward.

"That necklace," he said finally, his voice almost hoarse. "I know where..."

Everyone knew where she acquired it, and doubtless everyone thought they knew what she'd done for it. No one but Max Hawthorne had the ill manners to say so. In another second he was going to accuse her of bedding Napoleon Bonaparte. She stepped back again and sensed the nearness of other guests. He was going to imply she was a whore again, and once again people would hear him.

Pressure grabbed her chest like a giant fist and the room and all its inhabitants dissolved into a blur of light and color. Heat flushed her bare shoulders and neck and her fingers tingled with fear. One hand clenched tight enough to feel her nails digging into her palms through her glove as the other snatched a glass from the grasp of an astonished bystander.

Her aim was never very good with her left hand. The crystal wine glass spun over his shoulder, hit a silk brocade drapery and slid to the floor, miraculously unbroken. But the gesture wasn't entirely in vain. A carmine stain spread over Lord Allerton's white linen neckcloth and gray embroidered waistcoat.

As usual, the violent motion drove back her panic. The world came back into focus and her ears regained their function, the noise of the rout intensified by exclamations of shock from the guests. Tessa pinched her lips tightly, ashamed of her behavior, and furious with Max for provoking a scene she'd meant to avoid. Then she noted the avid glee of the onlookers and her actress's pride came to the rescue.

No one ever accused La Divina of not giving the audience what they wanted. She lifted her chin to an arrogant angle, cast a dismissive glance around the circle of spectators, then turned to her cousin who had pushed through the crowd to reach her side.

"I trust I didn't hit you, Jacobin."

Jacobin looked thoroughly amused. "How could you have done that at Lydia Sackville's house, of all places? London will be talking of nothing else tomorrow. I should have sacrificed Anthony's Chinese bowl." She surveyed her green silk. "Not a drop on my gown, but I can't say the same for poor Allerton."

Eyes like coal bored into Tessa over the shoulders of a couple of people who were dabbing at Max's spoiled clothing with their handkerchiefs. He didn't say a word but if looks could singe she'd be burned to a crisp.

She wanted to run away and weep, but she never cried. It was bad for her voice. Just as she stood arrogant in the face of provocation to maintain the aura of the operatic goddess, she also had to guard the vocal cords that were the foundation of her fame and fortune.

She would not weep but she could strategically withdraw. She was about to suggest to her cousin that it was time to leave, when her hostess appeared, wearing a broad smirk.

"Dear Jacobin," Mrs. Sackville said. "How good of you to bring your cousin to my little rout." She turned to Tessa. "Signora Foscari. Please come and look at the rest of the house. We must determine the best room for your recital."

Reminding herself how much she needed the fee for the engagement, Tessa let herself be let off like a spoil of war. Mrs. Sackville, in a state of elation that such a sensational occurrence had enlivened her soiree, was determined to show off her famous guest.

Scarcely attending as Mrs. Sackville presented her to a group and reminded them that Madam Foscari would be singing here soon, Tessa glanced over her shoulder at Jacobin, who mimed retching motions. As for Lord Allerton, the last she saw of him was his tall figure sailing through the throng toward the staircase and freedom. She wished she could do the same, though not in his company.

CHAPTER SIX

"On Friday Signor Rossini's opera of THE BARBER OF SEVILLE was sung for the first time at the Regent Opera House. The French singer Monsieur Delorme was very fine in the role of Count Almaviva."

The Morning Post

"The Tavistock Opera House on Saturday had a complete overflow from all parts of the House. Long before the curtain was drawn up, great numbers were turned away that could not gain admittance. Madame Foscari sang divinely and received the greatest applause. It is with great pleasure that we recall her genius is the product of an English family."

The Morning Post

MAX HURLED THE newspaper onto the desk in the manager's office, scattering Simon Lindo's neat piles of paper. "She is not English. To my knowledge she'd never even set foot on these islands till a month ago. We're the ones with the English soprano."

A review of the receipts had painted a worsening picture at the Regent. Musicians, craftsmen, and attendants had to be paid, but the money wasn't coming in. If things didn't change soon there wouldn't be enough in their accounts to meet expenses. Accustomed to writing a bank draft for whatever he needed, Max found his financial restrictions strained a temper already severely frayed by another disastrous encounter with Teresa Foscari. He'd like to wring the soprano's lovely neck, and his mother's too.

"Goddamn it!" he exploded. "Why don't they come?"

"Patience, Max," Simon said. "The new opera was well-received by the audience."

Max dismissed the offered consolation. "Much good that is when the house is half empty." His lovely Regent, which he'd designed with such care and lavished with every amenity, had been rejected and he took it personally. He had intended to make London appreciate what opera could be when done to the highest standards, to share with them his pleasure in the most sublime of all theatrical arts.

London showed every sign of not giving a damn.

Max folded his arms and glared at the newspapers. *The Examiner* was even worse than *The Morning Post*. "I can't believe what that idiot Mount Edgcumbe wrote."

"But you must admit," Simon said, "that his reservations about our soprano are not without justification."

The influential reviewer had opined of Miss Lucinda Johnston's coloratura that "it were to be wished she was less lavish in the display of her powers, and sought to please more than to surprise." The fact that he was quite correct in his assessment of Miss Johnston's tendency toward excessive vocal ornamentation did nothing to make Max feel better.

Max couldn't tell Simon what really troubled him. He knew why Lindo was so serene in the face of the depressing box office receipts. Without precisely promising unlimited funds, Max had always given the impression that he would carry the Regent financially until the new house got onto its feet. Simon assumed that if there was a temporary problem meeting bills, Max would step in and advance the cash.

And he would have but for his wager with his blasted interfering mother.

"I shall continue my efforts to drum up interest," he said. "I see that Mrs. Sackville has paid for her box. And I fancy Lady Storrington will be persuaded to purchase one."

Simon leaned forward with an arrested look. "Lady Storrington attended *The Barber of Seville* with Madame Foscari. It was gracious of La Divina to patronize us."

Max almost growled. "I don't see why. She should be grateful for the opportunity to see a superior performance of a great work in a magnificent opera house."

The manager lowered his voice as he did when he had a particularly juicy piece of gossip. "I've heard that Mortimer might accept an offer for Foscari's contract. Gambling debts, so the rumor goes."

"Surely he's making a fortune, filling the house every time she sings."

"The expenses of running a house as large as the Tavistock are very high. He might not be able to resist the temptation of a large sum in ready money."

Max said nothing, refusing to take the bait. He couldn't explain why it was impossible for him to try and buy the contract, and Simon wouldn't ask him point blank.

After a brief pregnant silence the manager realized his partner wasn't going to offer his millions to the cause. "If we can't hire La Divina, let's at least try to get her onto our stage. If she'd agree to sing at the Chelsea Hospital Benefit we'd be assured a full house. It would give those people a chance to see how superior the Regent is. I'd like to see a little of her luster rub off on us. Would you ask her to lend her services for the night?"

Please God, no! "Why don't you ask her?"

"I know my strengths, and tact isn't one of them. You are already acquainted with the lady."

"The lady doesn't like me," Max said curtly.

"You mean the episode at Mrs. Sackville's house?" Of course Simon's gossip network wouldn't have missed that. "Nothing to worry about. Merely prima donna histrionics. I know all about them, and in the end a singer will always pursue her own best interest."

Yes, indeed! Max was sure Teresa Foscari would do that. He had his doubts that she would regard singing without payment as worth her while.

"We will ask her to set aside the rivalry between our houses for a good cause," Simon added. "As a man of importance, she'll be more receptive to you than a mere theater manager."

Despite a deep reluctance to ask Tessa for a favor, Max had to admit Simon's idea was a good one. They had to do *something* to save the Regent.

When he'd let Lady Clarissa goad him into that foolish bet, Max had had no idea how ignominiously he might lose, or how soon. He could find himself betrothed to a horse-faced duke's daughter by the end of *this* season.

The choice was easy though not painless. He would rather face a thousand former loves than give Lady Clarissa the satisfaction of seeing him surrender.

AFTER A FEW weeks in London, Tessa was a famous figure, her portrait available in the print shops, her every move detailed in the newspapers. Her carriage and hired footmen were needed because she had only to set foot out into the street to be mobbed by the curious, anxious to share the reflected glory of the London Season's most celebrated visitor. Even a quiet visit to Hatchards bookshop had attracted stares and rude inquisitiveness about the books she was buying. She ended up smiling graciously at her fellow shoppers and leaving the selection of reading matter to Sofie.

As a result, Tessa had learned to take her exercise early when she could go out without being recognized and accosted. In the morning, her fellow walkers in Hyde Park were, for the most part, nursemaids and their charges. None of them had any idea that she was La Divina and wouldn't have cared if they had. She and Angela might as well be alone.

"Signora Foscari."

Not quite alone. She walked on, refusing to turn because she recognized the voice. But, as she well remembered, Max Hawthorne had a long stride and no difficulty catching her. Though she continued at a brisk pace, he walked alongside her without effort.

"Good morning." At least he'd addressed her with respect and his tone was perfectly civil.

"Good morning, Lord Allerton," she responded cautiously.

"A warm day, is it not?"

Covertly she examined his face while maintaining her pace. Though inscrutable, his expression didn't seem hostile. "Are we going to discuss the weather?" Then, unable to prevent a ghost of a smile from crossing her lips, she said, "How very English."

"Since I read in the papers that you are the pride of our country, the greatest English singer since Mrs. Billington, I assume you have adopted tea-drinking, fox hunting, and the ability to discuss the daily minutiae of our climate for hours at a time."

Tessa turned the words over in her mind, considering if this light-hearted speech contained an insult. As far as she could see it did not, so she replied in kind. "Fox hunting I've never practiced. Tea and prognostications of rain? Why not? Despite the warmth the sky looks threatening. I fear it may pour later this morning. Luckily I always walk early when I haven't performed the night before."

"So my spies tell me."

Suspicion that the meeting wasn't coincidental hardened to certainty. She found she was...not displeased...that he'd troubled to discover her habits. Yet she couldn't imagine he'd have anything to say to her after their last encounter.

He offered his arm. "May I join you?"

She ignored the gesture. "It appears you already have. I warn you I'm not in the habit of strolling idly. When I exercise I mean business."

"I can keep up."

"You always could." During that brief time, so many years ago, they'd walked miles around the old town of Oporto and the surrounding countryside. At the time she'd been grateful for her guardian's casual attitude towards chaperonage. It had never occurred to her that Max would take advantage of the laxity. She'd believed him the perfect gentleman in every way, until she had discovered otherwise.

She thrust aside that thought and its attendant bitterness. It was pointless to remain angry about an eleven-year-old incident. Her own bad behavior was recent and needed to be addressed. She hated herself for throwing that glass at Max even more than she hated him for provoking her. Swallowing her pride and summoning her courage, she murmured a few rapid Italian phrases to Angela and the maid drew several paces back.

"The other night," Tessa began, "I owe you an apology—"

He cut her off. "There's no need. My own behavior has been far from perfect. May we put the incident behind us and agree to say no more about it?" She wasn't sure from his tone of voice that he was really so forgiving, but decided to give him the benefit of the doubt.

"Very well," she replied.

Why didn't you meet me at the churchyard? Why did you leave without a word? The questions were on the tip of her tongue but she held back. If she spoke to him about the misery he'd caused her she'd never be able to maintain a façade of indifference.

"I would like to make something clear," she said, trying to convince herself as much as him. "Whatever happened between us before was long ago. We were little more than children. It is foolish to go on resenting the sins of the very young."

His expression held no trace of regret. Had he ever even wondered how she'd felt, waiting for him on another cloudy day in a different country?

They strode on in silence, pausing only to avoid two little boys who ran across the path in pursuit of their ball. Keeping her eyes on the way ahead, she was keenly aware of his presence at her side, his relaxed but purposeful gait, the lithe figure towering over her. So reminiscent of the past, yet different. He was no longer Max Hawthorne, a charming youth with a deceptive air of diffidence. It was a grown man beside her, with a man's muscular body and the confidence of his years and status: Viscount Allerton, one of England's richest citizens.

"I always wondered about you, whether Tessa Birkett was, in fact, La Divina." There was a new timbre to his voice, less guarded than before. She looked up and met his eyes. The breeze had blown a lock of straight black hair across his forehead and his expression matched that informality.

It was humiliating to find herself pleased that he'd thought of her. "Why did it take you so long to discover it? I've learned you are one of the greatest connoisseurs of opera in England. Didn't you ever think of coming to hear me?" She didn't intend to sound conceited, let alone offended, but her head was at sixes and sevens.

"Once the war ended I visited some of the European houses. Unfortunately for me, I never happened to be where you were singing."

His polite response enabled her to reply with more civility. "Your opera house, the Regent, is very fine. It reminds me a little of La Fenice."

"I've never been to Venice but I studied plans of La Fenice as well as several others. I wanted to emulate the smaller size and superior acoustical qualities of the European court houses. And their artistic standards. In England orchestra, chorus, and staging are not always of the best. The Tavistock, for instance, is so very large that only the largest voices can be heard to advantage."

She turned her neck sharply. "Are you suggesting that my voice is too negligible to be heard properly there?" She was joking, but only half. He still made her skin and her attitude prickly.

"I'm suggesting nothing of the kind, as you must know." He paused, as though to consider his words, with an air of gravity that added weight to his opinion. "Even when I first heard you, your resonance was extraordinary, not that I understood what that meant. You were always good and I don't need to tell you how great you have become."

His praise, though no more effusive than she had heard a thousand times, soothed her and she lowered her defenses. Her heart warmed at the compliment from Max, of all people.

A wave of regret swept over her, not for the brief period she'd spent in his company so long ago. More a wistful recollection of her youth, when things had been uncomplicated, and all she'd cared about was her music. Before Domenico Foscari came into her life and brought her dazzling success and profound misery.

They drew to a halt in the tree-lined path and he regarded her, grave as ever. Max had never been flirtatious in his manner.

"Thank you," she said. "I am gratified. You always had excellent taste." And because she suddenly feared she might cry, which would never do, she smiled at him.

A FIST SLAMMED into Max's chest when, for the first time, she tilted her head and gave him a full view of her face, unobstructed by the brim of her headwear: a perfect oval with flawless skin, as yet unmarred by years of stage makeup; arched brows a few shades darker than her golden hair; a straight, firm nose whose prominence had always raised her countenance above conventional prettiness; the full, pink mouth designed for the emission of ravishing sounds. And those blue eyes.

For a long moment their gazes meshed and there lay a hint of melancholy behind the smile, as though shadows had darkened a life once filled only with sunlight and hope.

Not melancholy, he corrected himself. Cynicism. It was cynicism her eyes reflected. As well they might, given her character and history.

Not wanting to be fooled again by Teresa Foscari's deceptively angelic beauty, he examined her from head to toe. Her costume was designed to draw attention to her figure. The pale blue walking dress topped by a satin spencer in a darker azure was simple on the face of it, yet embellished with fiendishly intricate pleats that molded to her bosom. Its skirt was narrow enough to offer tantalizing hints of her legs as she walked. This ensemble, like every garment he'd seen the diva wear, spoke eloquently of Paris.

Paris. Where the woman had bedded the emperor and Lord knows how many other men, all with one thing in common: deep pockets.

Yet he couldn't repress a curiosity to know something about her advancement from merchant's daughter to operatic luminary. A curiosity perfectly consistent with his role as a patron of her art.

"Tell me how you came to leave Oporto?" he said.

Her cheeks flushed a little. "Soon after my debut, I was offered an engagement in Lisbon. That's where I met Domenico Foscari who said I would never make anything of myself in Portugal. He persuaded me to go to Italy with him."

"Reports say that you eloped."

"Yes. My guardian, Mr. Waring, didn't approve of our marriage."

The name brought to mind his own final interview with Josiah Waring. There was a kind of bitter satisfaction in learning that she had parted ways with the family. When thieves fall out…

"And then?" he prodded.

She described how she started in the Italian opera houses, winning bigger and better roles, and continuing with acclaim in Vienna, Paris, and St. Petersburg. She spoke of her preferred operas and the theaters where she'd performed them. Caught up in her obvious devotion to the art, her manner lost any remnant of constraint and she talked as though to an old friend. Max reciprocated, trading stories and opinions about his favorite topic.

"Did you sing with Edouard Delorme in Paris?" he asked.

"Many times. Early in his career, less early in mine. His is a remarkable voice." The words were approving but her tone reserved.

"We were lucky to secure his services. Aside from the voice, what do you think of him?"

"He likes to flaunt his good looks," she said, then flushed a little. "That's unfair. We all do that."

"All of you with the looks to flaunt. We've encountered some…recalcitrance from *monsieur* when it comes to the selection of costume."

He didn't add that to his and Simon's profound relief Delorme had at least agreed to perform his most recent role fully clothed, up to a point.

"He likes to display his attributes," Tessa said with a little laugh. "Holy Saint George, I thought he would burst out of his breeches last week. I'm sure he succeeded in impressing the ladies."

"You still say Holy Saint George," Max said, all thought of the French tenor and his breeches blown away.

"What? Oh yes, I do. It's a foolish oath." She dropped her eyes. They both fell silent, the atmosphere thick enough to slice.

It came back to him, vividly as though it had been yesterday. They'd been walking around Oporto's old quarter. Max, always interested in history, told her of a medieval treaty between England and Portugal that included a clause by which Portugal adopted England's patron saint as its own, as a symbol of friendship between the two nations. Tessa for some reason found the tale hugely amusing. Infected by her laughter, they'd both almost doubled up with mirth and had to slip into an alley to recover their breath. Where he'd rather desperately wanted to kiss her and hadn't been able to summon the courage. That came later.

For so long he had assumed he meant nothing to her, yet she still used their oath. He halted and grasped her elbow. "Tessa…" he began, hardly knowing what he wanted to ask.

She brushed him off, kept walking, and interrupted him in a bright voice. "Anyway, despite his tendency to preen, Edouard is a fine artist."

"You didn't ever sing Rosina, did you?" he asked, referring to the lead role in *The Barber of Seville*, the Rossini work just debuted at the Regent.

"Not on stage, though I studied it in Paris just before I came here. It's a little low for me but within my tessitura." She threw back her head and trilled a few measures from the opera's most beautiful and difficult aria. By God, she had a spectacular voice!

"I have no doubt of that," he said. "I hope one day to hear you sing it at the Regent." Personal recollections gave way to a vision of Foscari singing Rosina at his opera house, every corner of the house filled with her admirers. Excitement at the idea led him easily to what was, after all, the point of this meeting. "I think you'll find the Regent superior in every way to the Tavistock. Regardless of your contract with Mortimer, if you would agree to come and sing there for a single night, a benefit performance—"

"Oh Lord!"

The sky had darkened unnoticed and fat drops of rain stained the blue silk of Tessa's spencer.

"Holy Saint George," she cried in alarm. "I must get home. My throat!"

Max needed no explanation. Most people might regard a head cold as a trifling risk; to an opera singer it was a looming catastrophe.

"We're near the Grosvenor Gate," he said, seizing her arm. "I'll find you a hackney."

Foolish thought! Whoever finds a hackney in the rain? By the time they reached Park Lane, with no vacant vehicle in sight, her clothing was soaked, the Parisian silk clinging to her body. Resisting the distraction, Max shrugged out of his coat and threw it over her shoulders. She huddled into it, shivering and unhappy. Her maid arrived at a run and fussed around her mistress, emitting distressed Italian squawks.

"I live only a step away," he offered. "I know it wouldn't be quite proper…"

"Never mind about that. I must get dry immediately."

A few minutes brought them to Max's house on Upper Grosvenor Street where one of his footmen admitted them. Tessa said a few words to Angela, then to Max.

"Would you be good enough to have your footman find my maid a hackney? She'll return to the Pulteney and bring me dry clothing."

"I'll send her in my carriage. Joseph, send word to the mews. Where is Babson?

"He's out, my lord," the footman replied. "I'm the only one here."

"Hughes too? What about Antoine?"

Both valet and cook were out on errands, along with the butler and the second footman. Since he didn't entertain much, Max kept a small, all-male staff with cleaning women coming in by the day.

"Hurry to the mews first, and return at once." He turned to Tessa. "You've caught my household unawares. I'll show you to a room myself."

Tessa and Angela followed him upstairs to the second floor where the door of the spare bedchamber closed behind them. Irked that he could offer only such inadequate hospitality, he returned below and paced the hall feeling useless.

The carriage appeared at the door just as Angela descended the stairs, asking for something in Italian. Max had never studied the language, though he'd picked up a fair amount at the opera. It wasn't hard to grasp that Signora Foscari would like some tea, but the maid's other request was a mystery.

What the Devil was *asciugamani*? In response to his look of blank incomprehension the maid resorted to mime, vigorously rubbing her arms and torso.

"Soap? A sponge?" he guessed.

She shook her head. Trying to understand her he noticed,

irrelevantly, that her nose was crooked, perhaps broken at some time in the past.

"Towels?"

She nodded vigorously. "*Si*, tow-elles."

Not a word often featured in an operatic libretto.

"I will take care of your mistress," Max said as he saw her into the waiting carriage, with no idea if the Italian woman understood him. "I'll find the *asciuga*-things."

He sent the reluctant footman down to the kitchen to make tea. Joseph didn't seem to think it was his job; Max firmly insisted he was better qualified for the task than his master.

But where the hell were the towels?

Finding them took some ten minutes of rummaging in chests and closets, all the time picturing Tessa falling into an ague. There wouldn't even be a fire in the bedchamber, he fretted. Never once did it occur to him that La Divina sick meant good business for the Regent.

STRIPPED OF EVERY garment—she had been soaked to her shift—Tessa opened the wardrobe and found it empty. Really, it was foolish of her to dismiss Angela before she found something to wear. She wasn't sure whether to laugh or cry at the irony of her situation: stark naked, in Max Hawthorne's bedchamber. Not his bedchamber, she amended hastily. In *a* bedchamber. In Max Hawthorne's house.

A knock came at the door.

The sensible thing to do would be to get into bed, but that wasn't where she wanted to be discovered. She pulled the counterpane off the bed and wrapped it around her body from the breasts down. Her shoulders were bare, otherwise it wasn't much more revealing than an evening gown.

"Come in."

Max entered. And stopped. He stared at her, his eyes so dark they looked black, and she turned hot all over, despite the lingering damp on her skin.

"I brought you some towels," he said hoarsely.

"Thank you." She remained where she stood, hugging her arms to her sides to keep the makeshift gown in place. Of a stiff material, it didn't flow easily around her body and would likely slip off with any sudden movement. She extended an arm and he leaned forward, awkwardly laid the linen cloths over it, then hastily stepped backward.

But not very far. Nor did he take his eyes off her. She concentrated on the carpet, a red and blue pattern, thick and soft under her curling toes. Now she was almost naked, in a bedchamber, *with* Max Hawthorne.

"It's chilly in here. I'll light a fire," he said. His voice sounded strangled.

"There's no need, really. You've been too kind already. Perhaps one of your servants…No, they're all out. I'll manage. Angela will be back soon."

"She could take an hour or more in this traffic."

She fell silent since she'd lost the power of speech save for incoherent babbling, and perhaps he felt the same way. Risking a peek at his face, she found him as still as a statue, his rigidity contradicted by his burning gaze.

She lowered her eyes and raised a hand to her sodden hair. Half the elaborate braids had descended. She must look a mess. She reached for the remaining pins but the towels got in the way of her free hand.

She couldn't think properly when he stood so close to her. Hastily she stepped back and her heel caught the trailing bedspread. The fabric slipped to the floor in a stiff silent mound and she lost her balance, about to follow the makeshift costume. Instead she found herself, without a stitch of clothing, in Max's arms.

"Well, well," he said, making no move to release her. Quite

the contrary.

She was completely naked, in a bedchamber, in Max Hawthorne's arms.

Her face nestled into his disordered neckcloth and he smelt of starch and cool rain. His waistcoat and shirtsleeves were still damp despite the heat of his body. She was surprised they weren't steaming. His arms were like brands around her naked back. Drawn closer, her breasts rubbed against silk twill and her belly sensed a swelling through the rough fall of his breeches.

"Tessa," he whispered.

Her singer's throat couldn't even summon a word.

"You are so beautiful." No hostility, no suspicion. He was her Max again.

Instinct told her to sink deeper into his embrace, to explore the six feet of hot, hard, muscled—albeit clothed—masculinity pressed against her skin. She hadn't reacted thus to a man in years, but apparently she wasn't dead to this kind of sensation after all. Warmth streaked downward through her veins. Instead of panic, she felt the beginning of desire, and that was even more frightening.

"Let me go," she breathed, pushing at his chest.

"I wouldn't want you to fall," he said, low but with a teasing note.

"I won't," she said, louder this time. "Let me go, please, and turn your back."

As his arms slackened she almost changed her mind. But she knew it was the sure route to madness.

When he released her, she dived for the counterpane and swung it round her shoulders like a cloak, a shield against temptation. Disobedient to her command, his dark gaze never wavered from her face. She glared at him and took a—very careful—step away.

"I'll find you something to wear," he muttered and left the room.

A minute later he thrust a blue silk dressing gown through the door.

"Put that on," he said from the passage. "Then I'll see to the fire."

"I told you, there's no need."

"You must warm up. I'm coming back in."

In a trice she snatched up the robe. It smelled of Max. It had touched his skin. She held it closed at the waist with her crossed arms. He came through the door and his lips twitched. Clearly he found her discomfort amusing, the blackguard.

"You look better in my dressing gown than I do."

Trying to look unconcerned, she feared her acting skills had deserted her. She perched on the foot of the bed, intending to dry her hair, but she couldn't keep her eyes off Max.

Kneeling on the hearth, he placed coals in the grate and struck tinder to coax a flame; she found his concentration on the humble task touching. He was going to a lot of trouble to ensure her wellbeing. She gazed at his broad shoulders and the way the muscles of his back rippled beneath the linen rear panel of his waistcoat. His genuflecting position could have been designed to display his narrow waist and hips and well-defined buttocks. Tessa began to feel warm again, and not because of the fire, which was yet in a state of infancy. Her flesh tingled in recollection of his touch against her nakedness. A seedling of undefined emotion—perhaps hope or joy—sprouted in the confusion that possessed her brain.

"The footman will be up soon with tea," he said, still intent on the immature flame.

How could he be so cool? Had she imagined his response to their embrace? Perhaps it had been merely an instinctive male reaction, not because he was attracted to her. She only wished for the same state of indifference. If a man was going to make her feel again, why did it have to be Max, the very last one she needed?

Turning her attention to her damp hair, she plucked out the

remaining pins and shook it loose. To avoid further accidents, she clung to the edges of the robe and used her other hand—not very effectively—to towel her head. The temperature of the room rose as the flickering coals settled into a red glow. Surely he'd leave now. Pray God he'd leave now.

He rose to his feet and turned around. Whatever his expression reflected it wasn't indifference. Surveying her from the tips of her toes, curled with embarrassment in the soft plush of carpet, over her silk-covered body, up to her hair, now lank and wet on one side and, doubtless, rumpled and fuzzy on the other, his eyes widened. His austere features relaxed into creases that meant pure mischief. Oh God! She remembered that look.

"Let me help you with that, Tessa." Once again he called her by her familiar name. Husky and amused, the tone curdled her insides.

He moved towards her.

"No." The word emerged in a whisper. La Divina had lost her voice.

He removed the towel from her nerveless grasp, and, using both hands, leaned over and applied it to her head. Staring at her lap, she stayed passive on the bed, as he worked the long strands of hair on either side, then rubbed her scalp. He applied the towel gently, with much less vigor than Angela would have used, as though he was afraid to hurt her. Peering through her lashes she observed a look of intense concentration on his face. Enjoying the gentle massage, she allowed herself to sink into a warm pool of contentment as he cared for her. Yet her ease was tempered by the keen knowledge that this was Max—*Max*—touching her and her flesh hummed in response.

"I think you're dry enough now," he said, running his hand around her head.

"Thank you, Max," she whispered and raised her eyes to his. Oh no, not indifferent at all.

He dropped the towel onto the floor and took her hands in

both his and she nearly swooned. *Lying on the bed...not a good idea.* She stiffened her back, allowed him to draw her to her feet. And found herself in his arms.

It felt good. So good that the fleeting urge to be free slipped away like late morning mist, forgotten in the rush of heat that suffused her at the sensation of skin against silk against warm male. It had been a long time since she'd reveled in the embrace of a man's body.

Did he speak? Did he use a hand? Surely she would have felt the withdrawal of one of those encircling arms. However it was, he directed her to look up and she complied and raised her face for his kiss.

He'd learned a lot since he'd kissed her in the churchyard of São Francisco. At first his lips, cool and firm, seemed familiar, propelling her back to a magic moment in a Portuguese evening in 1807. Then he opened them to ravish her mouth with a heat and passion beyond the capacity of the younger man. But he tasted the same. He was still Max.

He was no innocent now, and neither was she; every thrust and nip she returned with interest. Weaving eager fingers into his hair she urged him on, drawing him closer as his mouth swept the line of her jaw with a hot caress and down the curve of her neck to the sweet spot where her pulse hammered.

She was incapable of coherent sound; the renowned throat of Europe's most celebrated soprano emitted only low moans.

Nor was he any more articulate. Between kisses he made hoarse rasps that might have been words, but conveyed no meaning but that of want. His large hands, stroking her back and kneading her behind, pulling her against the evidence of his desire, carried the same message.

Something bumped the back of her thighs. The bed.

No! This isn't wise.

Yes! Her body, every nerve molten, urged her otherwise. Hands cradled his skull like a gypsy holding a crystal ball while their tongues tangled in a wild fandango.

No. She was still angry at this man.

Yes, yes, yes. Forget doubts, forget fear, forget the past, forget everything save this moment, this room, and this man. He reached for the closure of her robe and she leaned in, silently begging for his hands on her bare breasts.

But his assault on the garment was interrupted by a knock, eliciting a brief but violent oath from him. She broke free, breathing hard, uncertain whether to be glad or sorry.

"I've brought tea for the lady," said the footman.

CHAPTER SEVEN

Hail, sweet enchantress! Music's Queen,
Whose matching tones in mingling measure,
Have raised my soul beyond the scene
Of worldly woes or common pleasures.

Flung on the stage as a tribute to Madame Foscari

CURLED UP ON the Pulteney's elegant chaise longue, a soft paisley shawl thrown over her knees, Tessa tried to concentrate on her novel. She'd been enjoying *Emma*, a tale of quiet English country life given her by Sofie, who'd pronounced the book boring. Sofie preferred tales of headless specters, evil noblemen, damp dungeons, and ravishment. Not Tessa. Her life had been exciting enough without turning to literature for thrills. A life of respectability with nothing to worry about save one's neighbors' marriages sounded wonderful. She even envied the heroine her invalid father, wished she had a parent, even a fussy and demanding one.

But today her mind was elsewhere and she couldn't keep a foolish grin off her face.

"You look cheerful." Sofie, still wearing her bonnet, walked into the sitting room. "Angela told me what happened this morning. How does your throat feel?"

"It seems to have survived the experience," Tessa replied. "Sempronio ran through some exercises with me. There's no reason I shouldn't sing tonight. I am very well."

Better than well, in fact. She felt marvelous, filled with a kind of excited anticipation. "But how about you, my dear? I trust you didn't get wet. I forgot that you were going out this morning?" She'd never forgive herself if Sofie, who was prone to chills, put her health in danger running an errand for her.

"I took the carriage and was quite warm and dry. Lucky Lord Allerton was there to save you from the rain."

"Assuredly," Tessa agreed. "Though if he hadn't kept me talking in the park I would never have been in danger of getting wet."

"From what Angela told me, Lord Allerton behaved like a true gentleman," Sofie said.

Angela didn't know everything. Tessa wasn't ready to confess to Sofie that Max had treated her with anything beyond common courtesy. And certainly not that she'd enjoyed it. Dwelling on just how good his kiss had felt made her muddled and stupid.

Angela had arrived with an armful of dry clothing soon after the appearance of the footman with tea. Max had left the room, but the look in his eyes later when he kissed her hand and helped her into the carriage had spoken volumes. He admired her, yes, but perhaps he'd only kissed her because that's what men did when they found themselves alone in a room with a half-clad lady of reasonably good looks.

Did he feel anything beyond casual lust? And what about her? Could she possibly be thinking about Max Hawthorne, whom she'd sworn never to forgive, as a potential lover? He'd been very young when he deserted her. He could have changed.

"We had an agreeable conversation in the park," she told Sofie calmly, while inwardly she hugged herself in secret glee. She couldn't discuss her complicated feelings for Max, but they could still talk about him. She *wanted* to talk about Max. "He knows opera and his taste is excellent. Perhaps I should consider singing at the Regent next season. What do you think?" Sofie liked him so that should be enough to get her started.

Instead of launching into enthusiastic agreement, Sofie frowned. "Perhaps. But you should hear what I learned this morning."

"Did you manage to find Nancy Sturridge's woman at the Tavistock?"

Wishing to improve relations with her fellow soprano, she'd sent Sofie to open diplomatic channels.

Sofie's face held the intent look that heralded a particularly succulent piece of gossip. "It seems," she said, her voice lowering confidentially, "that Miss Sturridge was upset because both Somerville and Allerton asked you to supper after your debut."

"Allerton?" The name came out more sharply than Tessa intended. "I know Nancy hopes to become Somerville's mistress. I had no idea she was interested in Allerton."

Sofie cast aside her bonnet and settled on the end of Tessa's sofa, obviously ready for a lengthy session. "For years, it seems, the two men have been rivals for different singers."

Pushing aside the shawl, Tessa swung her legs off the chaise and sat upright. "You mean both have had many singers under their protection?"

"Yes. Allerton prefers great voices and the marquess is more attracted to..." Sofie moved her hands in exaggerated curves. "Allerton had Isabella Cavatini as his mistress for two years. A good voice, that one, but no bosom. Also some others I hadn't heard of. English singers," she explained dismissively. "Often he and the marquess fought over the same woman. Both were after Nancy—flowers, gifts, supper parties, the usual." Tessa nodded. She was familiar with the negotiations of backstage liaisons, even if she'd never conducted them herself. "Nancy expected to gain excellent terms from whichever man she chose. Then—" Sofie paused for dramatic effect. "Then you came along. It's bad enough that you are winning all the best roles. Now she's afraid you're going to get all the best men too!"

"Really?" Tessa said, ice in her heart dripping into her voice. "And which does she favor? Who usually wins this contest for the favor of sopranos?"

"Both men are rich, among the richest in England, but more often it is Somerville who has come out ahead. You remember Maria Tosti? A beautiful girl, though her voice is no more than mediocre. She was in London three seasons ago and they were both mad for her. She chose Somerville." Sofie's thin shoulders shrugged. "It seems strange to me. For myself, I would prefer Allerton. Perhaps you agree with me after today."

"My dear Sofie, I am not remotely interested in entering a competition with Nancy Sturridge, or anyone else, for the privilege of being bedded by an idle nobleman engaged in a contest of masculine dominance with one of his peers. I know everyone believes my body is available to the highest bidder, but I assure you only my voice is."

"Don't look at me like that, Tessa. Of course I know that. You would never go to a man for money. But what of marriage? You are of good birth. Why shouldn't he wish to marry you? Allerton, I mean. Or Somerville. But Allerton looks more the marrying kind to me."

Yes he did. She'd thought Max the marrying kind before, and been proven wrong. How foolish she was to hope he'd changed. He'd only ever wanted to get into her bed and, to her shame, she'd given him reason today to believe he might succeed.

"Marriage?" She tried to keep her tone amused. "Do you think I'd ever fall into that trap again, after Domenico?"

"Not all husbands are like that. Think how happy I am with Sempronio! Wouldn't you like to have children?"

Domenico had never wanted children. Early in their marriage she'd concurred, and they had taken precautions to make sure she never conceived. Later such measures had been unnecessary. Only at the end had her longing for a child made her resume conjugal relations with her faithless husband, the worst mistake of her life.

Damn Domenico. The legacy of her marriage was one of endless problems. Even if her reputation and finances could recover, her soul was permanently damaged. With no chance of happiness for her, she had been a fool to even think about Max.

Disguising her pain, she raised the most obvious objection to Sofie's ridiculous hopes. "This discussion is fruitless. You of all people know that noblemen don't marry singers, especially ones with my reputation. Thanks to Domenico everyone thinks I've been bedded by half of Europe. A respectable man would never offer for me."

Sofie tried to console her, though she knew as well as Tessa how Domenico's machinations had fed the prima donna's notoriety. "As the owner of his own opera house, Lord Allerton must be more liberal in his views than others of his rank."

It was the wrong thing to say, or perhaps the right one. Contemplation of Max Hawthorne's sins—past, present, and future—aroused Tessa from self-pity to anger. "He would want me only as a new pearl on his string of operatic mistresses. No thank you, Sofie. He can keep his money and his opera house. I want nothing to do with either."

HE SHOULD HAVE waited till tomorrow, Max thought as he bounded up the stairs to the hotel's best suite. She would be resting for the evening's performance, assuming she hadn't taken a chill despite his best efforts. But he needed to assure himself. And he had a perfectly good excuse. To settle the matter of the hospital benefit. She hadn't given him an answer. He'd never even completed the request.

Other events had driven the matter from his mind.

Despite the civility of their conversation in the park, his resentment had yet lingered, mingling with his anxiety for her health. When he'd entered the spare bedchamber with the towels, any kind of amorous encounter with La Foscari had been the furthest thing from his mind. From the moment he saw her barely clad—and then just bare—it had been the only thing.

He grinned. The truth was he couldn't wait to see Tessa again.

Tessa. Two fervent embraces and a kiss, and he was as enthralled as he ever had been. She'd seemed to reciprocate, at least physically. Was it possible that, at long last, he would be able to have Tessa Birkett? Exactly what "having" her would entail he didn't know.

The maid with the crooked nose greeted him in the vestibule and took his card. Hearing voices within, he stiffened. There was someone with her already. A man? Perhaps Somerville or another admirer. Without waiting to be announced he followed Angela into the room.

Tessa rose from the sofa looking magnificent in a midnight-blue dressing robe. Hardly typical dress for receiving guests. The look on her face was far from welcoming. Beautiful as a goddess, she resembled neither the sensual creature who had melted in his arms a few hours earlier, nor the shy girl who'd thanked him for his kindness as he sent her home in his carriage. This goddess was displeased. Apparently he'd interrupted something. He scanned the room.

Not, thank God, a tryst. Signora Montelli was the other occupant.

"Tessa—" he began. She glared. Maybe not. "Madam," he started again, off balance at the contrast between his expected reception and her current frigid demeanor. "I called to assure myself of your good health."

"I am quite well, thank you, my lord."

"No ill effects from the rain?"

"None."

"Then you are well?"

She didn't even bother to answer and he couldn't think of a thing to say. Why did he have to be such a dullard? Usually when pursuing a woman he could converse adequately if not with brilliance. But then usually the women he approached were eager to be pleased, happy to encourage the advances of a wealthy man. Tessa might be as interested in money as the average singer of his acquaintance, but at the moment she clearly wasn't interested in his.

She was tapping her foot. What the devil had occurred since they parted earlier? He glanced at Mrs. Montelli for help. She'd appeared to favor him in the past but her expression was impassive if not hostile.

"Madam," he turned back to Tessa. "May I speak to you alone?" Without the Austrian woman's unblinking observation he could perhaps find the words to ask what was wrong, to rekindle the warmth of the morning.

"Anything you have to say, my lord, can be said in front of my companion. I cannot conceive that you have any offer to make me in private that I'd wish to consider."

Mrs. Montelli sat down, signaling a resolution to remain.

Since it was impossible to bring up their recent intimacies in front of her, to discuss what he really wanted, he fell back on business.

"The rain interrupted my request this morning. I was inviting you to sing at the Regent on the twenty-fifth of this month."

Tessa stared at him as though he'd sprung a second head. Her fingers reached for a vase of flowers on a nearby table and he prepared to duck. But she snatched back her hand. Her fists clenched repeatedly. What had happened? If he read the signs correctly, she was furious. Or insane.

"It isn't, of course, a lucrative engagement but..."

"Lord Allerton," she said, her voice brittle. "I wouldn't sing a single night, not so much as a single song, at your opera house. Not if you offered me a thousand pounds. Not even for two! I have too much pride ever to take anything from you for any reason."

CHAPTER EIGHT

"The new method of lighting the house answers perfectly. Every object, either on the stage or in the different parts of the theatre, is as distinct as in the clearest daylight, whilst at the same time, unless we look upwards, we are not conscious of from whence the light proceeds. The beautiful form of the interior of the new Regent Theatre is seen to the utmost advantage."

The Morning Chronicle

"SHE SAID WHAT?"

Max again repeated Tessa's words for Simon Lindo's benefit, eliciting a whistle of disbelief from the theater manager. On leaving the Pulteney, Max had wasted no time tracking down Simon at the Regent to report the failure of his mission.

"Two thousand pounds?" Simon said. "Surely she must have been joking."

"I believe she may have been exaggerating, but she otherwise appeared quite serious in her refusal to sing." Unlike Tessa, Max was understating the case.

Simon paced. "It's a pity," he said. "The article in today's *Morning Chronicle* was most favorable on the subject of the Regent's design and facilities. Following it with the announcement of La Divina's appearance would be timely. Are you quite sure she won't change her mind?"

"Quite sure." Neither would he ask. Ever.

Hardly knowing what he said, he'd excused himself from the hotel suite and staggered downstairs and out into the street. He had wanted to believe she was different now. Fool that he was, he had for a few hours wanted to love her again. He could make no sense of her behavior today—in the park, in his house, or in the Pulteney—but he knew that she would always disappoint him. The woman's dominant character trait was greed and it always had been, as he learned on his last day in Oporto. The walk along Piccadilly to the Regent had been spent revisiting that long ago morning.

Portugal, 1807

MAX'S TRAVELING COMPANION, the Reverend Jasper Eldon, always lay abed late, usually sleeping off the effects of enthusiastic sampling of the local wines. His mother had selected the clergyman as Max's bear-leader not because of the man's status with the church, but for his eligible birth and worldly knowledge. Lady Clarissa had never been very interested in religion, though she certainly expected Mr. Eldon to protect Max from the pernicious lure of Papists, a breed found in large numbers on the continent of Europe.

So Max spent the morning scouring the Oporto shops for a gift for his beloved. That provincial city offered little in the way of quality gems but though he would happily have showered his Tessa with diamonds, he wasn't concerned. Once they were wed a large portion of the Tamworth jewelry collection would be his to adorn his bride. His sweet Tessa would prefer something unusual.

In a small, dark shop in the old quarter he found it: a rectangular plaque of ivory, exquisitely carved, depicting a couple dancing in a field of flowers and birds. The shopkeeper told him it was very ancient, and Moorish, from the time of the caliphs in the Iberian Peninsula. The carefree movement of the lovers—somehow he knew they were lovers—seemed to express the joy he and Tessa found in each other's company. He could scarcely wait for their agreed meeting in the churchyard of São Francisco.

But first he had to face Mr. Eldon who had chuckled appreciatively when Max had confessed his infatuation. Young men of good family who'd only just begun to shave, Eldon explained in his jovial fashion, did not wed. And more particularly they did not wed opera singers. Miss Birkett, he said, would make a splendid mistress, a very suitable *petite amie* for a young man just starting his amorous career. She was a dashed pretty girl and a lovely songbird. She wouldn't be foolish enough to expect marriage.

Max, well aware of his lack of savoir faire in such matters, had accepted his preceptor's advice without demur. He burned for Tessa. God, he burned for her. Just as her voice thrilled his soul, her beauty inflamed him physically so that he could scarcely sleep. Sheltered by his protective mama and without a father to provide masculine guidance, his sexual experience to date consisted of two kisses from one of the dairymaids at Tamworth.

When he'd finally plucked up courage to kiss Tessa he'd nearly exploded on the spot. Silky and sweet, she'd tremulously opened to his inexpert demand and murmured in shock at the tentative exploration of his tongue. When he'd dared reach a hand to her breast she'd flinched, then relaxed and, to his enchanted surprise, moved a little closer.

Even now, he remembered every second, relived the ecstatic sensation of her soft form in his arms, the evanescent scent of Oporto's mimosa in his nostrils. Impatient for further intimacies than could be achieved in a public place, he'd wrenched himself from her lips and cradled her against him while he'd explained his plan: meetings in a discreet inn, then passage to London where he'd find her a house. Despite his innocence, he'd learned enough from his more worldly schoolmates to understand the basics of keeping a mistress.

The ashen pallor of shock had apprised him instantly of his mistake. Speechless for a moment, her expressive face had conveyed her distress and humiliation.

The words had come in a whisper as she'd pulled away and stared at the ground. "How could you think of me like that?"

He was ashamed. And distraught that he'd insulted the girl he adored. Silently he cursed the cynical assumptions of Mr. Eldon. He'd assured her he would make things right if she would meet him again later in the same place.

His shopping expedition completed, he dashed into the hotel, ready to confront the clergyman and insist he perform the marriage ceremony as soon as possible. Thankfully Tessa was a Protestant, but that meant they couldn't be wed in a Portuguese church. He was ready to muster his best arguments so that he could return to his darling and formally propose marriage that afternoon.

Mr. Eldon was not alone. Tessa's guardian and his son were in the hotel parlor and all three men looked grim. Surprised that she had spoken to Mr. Waring, Max was ready to assure the man of his honorable intentions. Protective toward her, he was grateful that she had someone to see to her interests.

Eldon broke an uneasy silence. "Max," he said. "It seems you have insulted a young lady. Mr. Waring and his son have called to register a complaint on her behalf. But I believe we have reached an accommodation to satisfy all parties."

SIMON LINDO CONTINUED to pace the room until Max's frayed nerves could no longer endure it. "Sit down and show me the receipts from last night."

Examining the figures from the second performance of *The Barber of Seville*—they had, for the moment, agreed not to repeat the unsuccessful *Fidelio*—distracted Max from unwelcome memories though the numbers hardly improved his mood. Once again, the opera had played to a half-empty house.

Despite the bad news, Max found the process fascinating. He was almost ready to thank his mother for making it necessary for him to take an active part in the financial management of the Regent. It was a good deal more interesting than his normal daily pursuits. With little taste for gambling or sports, he'd often found time hanging heavy on his hands. He mused that he might have been a happier man had he been born into the merchant class. He could have married Tessa... But he would never have met her and in any case he had had a lucky escape.

"You seem preoccupied," he remarked to Simon, who had been discussing the reports with less than his usually razor-like concentration.

"I've been thinking," Lindo said, "that La Divina has a veritable genius for arousing the interest of the press."

"What of it? Since neither of us looks like Aphrodite or have engaged in love affairs with emperors I don't see how we can hope to rival her in that respect."

Simon's lips twitched. "You could take up crockery smashing."

"Would anyone care?"

"Probably not. But it occurs to me that we could turn her notoriety against her. The denizens of Grub Street are ever fickle in their affections."

"Not where Teresa Foscari is concerned. There isn't a writer in London, from the music critics to the society reporters, who doesn't adore her."

"Supposing they discovered she'd done something despicable. It would certainly be noted in the press. And where the newspapers lead, the public will follow."

"What has she done? Are you going to inform the *Morning Post* that she cheats tradesmen and beats her servants?" A vision of Tessa's maid with her crooked nose flashed though Max's mind. Surely not. The pair of them seemed on affectionate terms and nothing he'd read suggested that La Divina was a danger to people as well as dishes.

"It's not like you to be so slow, Max. We have evidence of La Divina's callous disregard for poor wounded soldiers."

"The Chelsea Hospital benefit," Max breathed.

"Precisely." Simon paused significantly. "I think her admirers need to be informed that Teresa Foscari, whom the English people have welcomed to their collective bosom as though she were one of their own, refuses to sing a note to raise money for the gallant victims of our war with France."

"Surely that would be dishonorable?"

"You're thinking like a gentleman, Max. Businessmen can't afford such scruples. Besides, where's the dishonor in speaking the truth? The woman refused, in the most insulting way, to lend her services to a worthy cause."

Insulting indeed. Surely it was no accident that she'd named two thousand pounds, the very sum Mr. Eldon had paid for his so-called "insult" to her.

Max stared at the pile of papers on the desk, emblematic of his quandary. Lady Clarissa's ultimatum came to mind, of her triumph should he crawl back to her and admit failure. Then came the memory of the youthful Tessa, soft and yielding in his arms, and the more ardent response of the adult woman.

Two thousand pounds. The words rang in his head. Two thousand pounds that she'd taken from Eldon, who had been supplied with ample funds by Lady Clarissa to guard the naïve Max against the lures of adventuresses. Tessa hadn't known how wealthy he was or surely she'd have asked for more.

He understood the dilemma of Faust, faced with the blandishments of Mephistopheles. His soul, perhaps, was not at stake. He risked only the future of his opera house and his personal freedom. But if he agreed to Simon's plan, he could kiss goodbye his chances of ever possessing Teresa Foscari.

He was mad to still desire her, even the slightest bit.

"Let's do it," he said. "How do we spread the tale?"

TESSA SHUFFLED THROUGH the pile of bills. "I thought we paid the hotel with the money from the Storrington recital."

"There wasn't quite enough left," Sofie explained. "I had mistaken the amount." Sofie was making a valiant attempt to make sense of their finances but arithmetic was not her forte and the accounts presented by the best hotel in London contained all sorts of unforeseen extras.

"We can't move to less expensive accommodations without paying off the Pulteney," Tessa said. "But I suppose we could give up the carriage."

"La Divina cannot go to the theater in a hackney!" Sofie said, shocked. "Perhaps you should send back the walking dress you bought. That would be one bill less to pay."

Tessa dismissed the suggestion. "I won't serve the modiste so ill. It's a beautiful gown and it would be unfair to leave it on her hands." She extracted a receipt from the pile. "Twenty pounds. At least this one has been paid. What was it for?"

"Two ladies called one morning collecting money for the Chelsea Hospital," Sofie said. "I'm sorry, I wouldn't have given them anything if I'd known how low our funds are, but I know you like to give to charity."

"What is this hospital?"

"A home for wounded soldiers."

"Then I'm only sorry the amount was so small. I've seen enough of the horrible consequences of war to understand how much these brave men need care. As soon as Mortimer pays me we shall send them a more generous donation."

"By the end of the week we should receive Mrs. Sackville's..." A spate of coughing interrupted Sofie's words.

"My dear," Tessa said with concern, putting an arm around her companion's frail shoulders. "You have caught a cold! You must rest, and I will summon a physician."

"No," Sofie said once the hacking subsided. "It's nothing. Merely the climate. And doctors cost money."

Tessa bit her lip. For Sofie to take ill in the English damp would be the crowning misfortune of an adventure that was starting to look misbegotten indeed. How she wished she'd remained in Paris and never succumbed to Mortimer's persuasion.

"You must see a doctor," she said. "And you mustn't worry anymore. If the worst happens I can always sell the Tsar's diamonds."

CHAPTER NINE

"Here is a woman who stands to put TEN THOUSAND POUNDS of English money into her pocket this year. She is asked to exercise, for one evening, the same art by which she amasses this money, for the purpose of bringing money to the relief of a most useful charitable institution. She refuses to do so, but most liberally gives twenty pounds to the charity. Her appearance at the Regent Opera House last night might have added 300 or 400 pounds more to the receipts of the evening. How therefore could the paltry gift of twenty pounds be an equivalent to make up for this act of ingratitude to the English public? The people of England have a very simple course to pursue on this occasion: and that is, to dispense with Madame Foscari in future—to decline going to hear her. Have we not good English singers and sweet English music! Shall we throw away our substantial roast beef, and feed upon the vile kick-shaws of France and Italy."

The Times

"I CAME AS soon as I read this filth." Lady Storrington tore into Tessa's suite from the vestibule, indignation writ large in every movement of her expressive body. "Who is responsible for this canard?"

Tessa and her entourage had already seen it, and similar diatribes in other London papers.

"I believe," said Tessa, who was almost numb with shock, "that it was your friend Lord Allerton."

"I don't believe it!"

"He's the only person who knew I refused to sing at the benefit."

"So it's true! But why would you do such a thing."

"Because," Tessa replied grimly, "he failed to inform me that the occasion was a benefit for charity. Had I known, naturally I would have agreed."

The atmosphere in the room, which had resembled a council of war, rapidly degenerated into an impenetrable din since everyone present had an opinion and no one stopped to listen to anyone else's. Sofie, between bouts of coughing, bewailed the fact that her decision to make a small donation to the hospital had given credence to the tale of Tessa's indifference to the charity. Sempronio was certain that Tessa's genius would make it impossible for the world at large to believe ill of her. Jacobin was in favor of storming Lord Allerton's house and subjecting him to stabbing, torture on the rack and application of boiling oil. Since none of the participants was accustomed to speaking in English alone, oaths and imprecations in French, German, and Italian flew thick and fast, creating a cacophony that threatened to explode Tessa's head.

Used to nothing but adulation from the press, the ferocity of her critics left her reeling. Although she'd never enjoyed the public interest in her personal life, and she loathed the lies that her husband had perpetrated, at least the tone of reports had been generally admiring. To find herself the object of hatred hurt. That Max, through a deceptive repetition of her angry remark, had instigated the attacks cut her to the core. In her heart, whatever their differences and his past behavior, she would never have believed him capable of such spite.

The drone in her brain was equaled by the rush of heat that signified an onset of panic. She looked for a missile. With nothing suitable at hand she opened her mouth wide and emitted a pure, lengthy high D.

Instant silence. Four pairs of eyes fixed on her in astonishment.

Then a murmur from Sempronio. "Beautiful, *cara*."

Tessa gave her shoulders a little shake and blinked, twice. Amazingly, she felt almost serene. She'd never tried singing to calm her affliction and must remember it next time. It was, after all, rather more civilized than throwing china. She tried to visualize the scene at Mrs. Sackville's rout had she gone this route instead of hurling a glass of wine at Max. Just as shocking, but less harmful to the gentleman's tailoring and her hostess's curtains.

"I must make a generous gift to the Chelsea Hospital, along with my letter of explanation and apology," she said. "If Mortimer still refuses to pay me any of the thousands he owes, I can use the fee from Mrs. Sackville."

"You're very decisive today, Teresa," Sofie said. "What has come over you?"

"Perhaps, my dear, I have finally realized that I must learn to take care of my own affairs. For too long I've allowed others to call the tune."

"I know what I can do," Jacobin said. "I shall call on my acquaintance and apprise them of Max's iniquitous behavior. He isn't going to get away with this."

"Thank you. But please be careful. Let's try and make people see the incident as a misunderstanding. I shall find it hard to forgive Lord Allerton for this, but I must confess that my own attitude has contributed to the state of war between us."

She would be calm and reasonable and behave like a lady. The character of Teresa Foscari, the tempestuous china-throwing continental termagant would disappear and be replaced by Tessa, the gently raised English girl who had been lost in Domenico Foscari's creation of an operatic monster.

And once she'd weathered this crisis she'd never speak to Max Hawthorne again.

"Do you attend my concert at Mrs. Sackville's house tonight?" she asked.

Jacobin's eyes narrowed. "I wouldn't miss it for anything. If Lydia Sackville shows you so much as an ounce of disrespect she'll answer to me."

Angela came into the room bearing a letter.

Tessa opened the sheet of expensive paper with its violet wax seal and scanned the curt note. "I appreciate your support," she said. "But I'm afraid it won't be needed. Mrs. Sackville has cancelled the event."

BY SOME WHIM of the calendar, the next night was one of the rare occasions when both London's serious opera houses played simultaneously. Max wasn't entirely happy with the production at the Regent: Edouard Delorme had insisted on singing the title role in *Don Giovanni*, though it entailed transposing the part to the tenor voice. It offended Max's sensibilities not to have the opera presented as Mozart wrote it.

"The arrogance of the man!" he'd grumbled to Simon Lindo. "Who does he think he is?"

"He thinks he's a tenor," replied Simon, "and he knows he's a good one. Arrogance follows naturally. Don't worry about it. Mozart would have understood."

Mozart would also have appreciated the box office business. The theater was full to bursting. Every box was occupied by a full assemblage of the wealthy and fashionable, led by the Honorable Mrs. Thomas Sackville who had persuaded two dukes and an earl to join her party. The pretty redhead was seen to applaud rapturously each time Delorme took the stage. As usual the tenor revealed a good deal of chest while his character seduced half the female population of Spain. At least this time the shirt wasn't ripped.

Max should have been thrilled. Simon, sitting beside him in the house box, beamed with relief at the Regent's splendid ticket sales. But Max's conscience pricked him that his triumph came at the expense of another. He wasn't even sure it had been necessary to traduce Tessa. The benefit had been an enormous success, filling every box with enthusiastic members of the *beau monde*. The Royal Hospital at Chelsea was a popular institution, and the last minute announcement that the Prince Regent would attend the concert had helped swell attendance. Maybe Max needn't have employed gutter tactics.

The morning after the benefit he'd planned to undo the damage. Lydia Sackville's musicale would provide an opportunity to cast oil on stormy seas. Although nervous about possible consequences to his attire should he encounter Tessa with a glass in her hand, he thought some gracious—and public—compliments to the prima donna would do much to convince the *ton* that the whole incident was a storm in a teacup. Only when he read the papers did he realize the tempest he'd unleashed had developed the force of a hurricane.

The ugliness of the news reports and commentaries shocked him. He could only imagine how the denunciations must affect Tessa. Although he had reason to think her a woman motivated by a desire for lucre, that didn't mean she was without a single charitable impulse. When she'd trembled in his arms and returned his kiss she hadn't seemed heartless.

What is more, in a secret, well-defended cave in his heart guilt burned like a glowing coal. What happened between him and Tessa that day—in the park, in his house, and at the hotel—had caused such turmoil in his head that he couldn't remember the details of their conversation either in the park or at the Pulteney. He harbored a terrible suspicion that the words *charity* and *benefit* had never been spoken.

He'd arrived at the Sackvilles' house to be greeted by the news that La Divina would not be performing that night. Lydia's explanation was vague, but the underlying message was that Teresa Foscari was no longer welcome among her friends.

Max feared the Devil had been sitting on his shoulder when he'd told a few of the worst gossips at White's Club that Teresa Foscari was a heartless vixen.

~

APPLAUSE RANG THROUGH the drafty expanses of the old Tavistock Theatre. The house wasn't full but the audience was large enough for a good show of enthusiasm. Nancy Sturridge made several curtsies and kissed her hands to her audience, reveling in their approbation.

Tessa stood in the wings, awaiting her turn. The audience had been polite thus far, although her arias hadn't been greeted with the usual level of rapture. How would it respond to her curtain call?

She didn't want to go out there.

Almost never nervous on stage, tonight she'd had to steel herself for every entrance. The stage was her province, the only place she felt in control of her life. She worked hard, had faith in her talent, and accepted applause with pleasure, as recognition of a job well done, as thanks for pleasure she had given others. Sometimes it got a little silly. On more than one occasion a besotted admirer had managed to leap onto the stage and kiss her feet. Only a week ago an execrable poem in her honor had been tossed at her. It had landed in the orchestra and the oboe player who retrieved it had given it to one of the papers.

How long ago it seemed, a whole week, when the paper had printed the foolish verse as though it were a literary pearl. Now the same journal hadn't a good word to say for her.

She felt terror rising inside her. She'd never had one of her attacks on stage. Taking several deep breaths she tried to concentrate on the moment. This was not the occasion for a display of histrionics. Dignity, calm, perhaps a touch of disdain. Those were the qualities she wished to project.

Nancy Sturridge retreated to the wings and the stage manager beckoned Tessa forward. She was distantly aware of the curiosity of the other singers. They'd all read the papers too.

Forcing one foot after another, she advanced into the light, clutching her skirts. Approaching upstage center she scanned the boxes, half of them empty tonight, seeking a friendly face. Her cousin was leaning over the rail of her box, smiling and nodding. Jacobin's husband, Lord Storrington, rose from his seat beside her. He wasn't smiling but he raised his hands and began to clap. The sound set off an echo of smattered applause around the house, growing in a gradual crescendo to a respectable level.

It was going to be all right. Tessa curved her lips into what she hoped the audience wouldn't identify as a grimace and swept a deep curtsey.

A single boo from a man in the center of the pit started it. A catcall in the gallery followed, setting off an ugly dissonant chant that soon drowned out any expression of approval. Tessa, who had never felt anything but love from her audience, reeled from the force of hatred she sensed in the theater. For a terrible moment she thought she might swoon. Gathering strength she would never have guessed she possessed, she held her head high, curtseyed again, yet lower, and left the stage.

She thanked God that no one in the audience would be able to see her tears.

CHAPTER TEN

"Madame Foscari sent 20 pounds to the Chelsea Hospital, before the Operatical Performance for the benefit of that Charity, for which she refused to sing; but the Governors have ordered this boon of charity immediately to be returned."

The Times

TESSA WASN'T ACCORDED the luxury of sleeping late to recover from her ordeal. Sofie had passed a restless night and, at Tessa's insistence, the doctor was summoned early. He presented a prognosis of reasonable optimism and a bill. Shortly afterwards the account from the hotel was delivered, with a polite but firm intimation that immediate settlement was expected. Then the modiste called with her bill, followed by a representative of the livery stable that provided Tessa with her carriage, horses and driver. With a bill.

When the note arrived from the Governors of the Royal Hospital Chelsea, enclosing a draft for twenty pounds, Tessa almost laughed. At least that pittance could be used to pay off someone else.

Returning to her bedchamber she changed into the new gown, the one she couldn't pay for but she didn't want to return, not only for the reason she'd given Sofie—not wishing to cheat the dressmaker—but because its sobriety seemed appropriate for the coming task. She surveyed her reflection in the tall glass with ironic satisfaction. She'd ordered the severely cut morning dress and spencer in claret and gray on a whim, evoking a shriek from Sofie, so far was it from the kind of lavish, figure-hugging garb that

Domenico insisted she wear to personify the character of La Divina.

But as Tessa had always known, the alluring prima donna was the role she played off the stage as well as on. This outfit felt closer to Tessa—not Teresa Foscari—as she was inside. It suited her current mood and new determination to make her own decisions.

She opened her jewel box and removed the Tsar's diamonds. The cameos presented her by Napoleon weren't worth much. Besides she greatly preferred the delicate necklace to the gaudy magnificence of the Russian gift. Most of her other jewels had been sold to pay Domenico's debts. The diamonds were her insurance and it was time to claim it. She folded the necklace, bracelets, brooch and tiara in their black velvet wrappers, placed them in her largest reticule and summoned the carriage.

EXAMINING THE RECEIPTS the morning after a full house was a new experience.

"Look at these numbers, Max." Simon didn't bother to conceal his glee. "And the boxes. Almost all the subscribers have paid. We must discuss expanding the repertoire."

While relieved about the financial picture, Max couldn't share his high spirits. He had heard about La Divina being booed off the stage. The newspapers had been unseemly in their elation at her downfall and not one had pointed out that La Divina, even on a bad day, was a greater artist than any singer in London. To hear genius was a privilege and she didn't deserve such a reception. He could guess how she must have suffered, listening to the jeers and heckles of the fickle audience.

The Regent's success had other drawbacks. A week earlier Edouard Delorme had been complaining about meager audiences. Now the tenor had fresh demands: new costumes (containing even less fabric Max guessed), his name in larger type on the playbills, champagne in his dressing room, a higher fee for each performance, and an extra benefit.

Since depressing the demands of a conceited artist was a task better suited to Simon's unyielding personality, Max took himself off.

As he turned into Piccadilly, he caught the spring fever that infected Londoners on a fine spring day. Tipping his hat to several acquaintances on the busy street, his conscience eased. The furor over the Chelsea Hospital benefit would soon abate and La Divina would regain her popularity. But now the new opera house was established as an alternative to the tawdry offerings of the Tavistock.

Picking his way through the throng, he noticed a carriage draw up at the Pulteney Hotel. He registered with interest, and an increasing heartbeat, a woman emerge from the door. But it wasn't her. This figure of restrained elegance appeared to be an English gentlewoman, no doubt up from the country on a visit to the capital.

A shrill cry from a passerby alerted him—and others—to his mistake. "It's her! Foscari!"

"The foreign woman!"

"Taking bread out of English mouths!"

"Won't help our English soldiers!"

"Shame!"

Max watched, stunned, as the scene degenerated and the happy spring-celebrating crowd turned into a rabble, parroting the denunciations of the newspapers. It took but a second, but seemed to his appalled eyes to happen slowly, for a roughly dressed workman to snatch a pear from a street vendor's cart and hurl it. It must have been overripe, for the fruit curved in a smooth arc and landed on its target's bosom, where it exploded in a splat, a pale patch against dark red cloth.

Jerked out of immobility, Max thrust his way through the mob and a shower of missiles, taking a stinging blow on his back from something round and hard. Reaching Tessa, he placed himself between her and her attackers, swung her around and, keeping a protective arm about her shoulders, hurried her back into the hotel.

"My reticule!" she cried, her voice panicked. "I dropped it."

"Leave it!" Her safety was more important than any small sum and minor feminine frivolities she might carry.

"No!" She pulled away from him. "I must have it."

"I'll get it." He wasn't going to let her go out and face a fresh assault of fruit. "Stay here."

On the street he couldn't hold back his expression of disgust. "You should be ashamed of yourselves, attacking a lady," he said loudly, raising his fists in a belligerent attitude and daring anyone to defy him. For a moment he thought the hail of missiles would come his way, but the crowd, balked of their prey, settled down. The noise diminished and the threatening mob became ordinary people again, going about their business.

Max searched the ground where Tessa had suffered her ordeal. A sack of gray-beaded silk lay on the pavement. The strings had come loose and a piece of black velvet protruded. He scooped it up, finding it surprisingly heavy, and stuffed the contents back in as he returned to the hotel reception hall. But not before he glimpsed a glint of diamonds. Very large diamonds.

TESSA SNATCHED THE reticule from Max's hands. It didn't occur to her to thank him for his intervention. She was shaken, yes, but also furious. He was responsible for the whole ugly incident.

"Is my carriage still there?" she demanded of one of the hotel footmen who hovered uncertainly in her vicinity. Much help he'd been. As soon as she paid the hotel bill she would give the Pulteney management a piece of her mind and never patronize the place again. "I must go to Ludgate Hill immediately."

"No, you will not," Max interrupted. "You're mad to go out into the rabble. Besides, your costume is ruined."

Looking down at her lovely, new, unpaid-for gown that a few minutes earlier had seemed emblematic of a fresh start and was now stained with shreds of fruit, Tessa wanted to burst into tears. Disdaining to show such weakness in public, especially in front of Max, she turned without a word and headed for the staircase.

"I'm coming up with you." He was right behind her.

She restrained the urge to slap him. Very well, let him come. She had a few choice words for Max Hawthorne, Viscount Allerton and the hotel lobby was not the place to say them.

Brushing aside Angela's anguished squawks at the ruined gown, she marched into her sitting room, Max still at her heels.

"I'm sorry, Tessa," he began.

The man had a nerve! As though an apology could begin to make up for what he'd done, for what she'd endured through his lies.

"Why? Why?" she asked. "What did I ever do to you? What have I ever done to anyone to earn such treatment?" Her voice broke on a sob but she was determined to speak her piece. "Since you left me I've lived only for my art. I've tried to use my God-given talents only for good—to give pleasure to others. I'll have you know that when I was able I've given huge sums to charity, not to be thanked but to alleviate the suffering of others who were not born with my good fortune. And never once have I refused to lend my voice to a worthy cause. What you did was despicable when you know I had no idea what I was refusing."

Through her tears she could see him poker-backed and frowning. If that was guilt written on his features, good. But guilt wasn't enough. She wanted him to grovel. She wanted him to crawl to her on hands and knees with sorrow for what he had done. For the indignities he'd inflicted on her in London and for the misery he'd caused her in Portugal.

"What did I ever do to you?" Her voice rose. "All I did was love you." There. She'd admitted it. She could no longer pretend she didn't care.

His face twisted into a sneer. "Love, madam? You speak of love? You have conveniently forgotten the two thousand pounds you received to forget that love. You never understood the meaning of the word."

"Two thousand pounds? I told you I'd never take two thousand pounds from you, or so much as a single penny." She was screaming now and she seized a vase from the mantelpiece.

He stepped back, color staining his cheekbones. "Wait, Tessa." He held out a hand but she was beyond reason. "What do you mean…?"

"Out! Out!" She launched the vase and it missed him, shattering against the wall. "I never want to see you again."

THE JEWELER SET down the last earring, removed his eyeglass, and surveyed the diamonds spread over the desk in a discreet back room of the shop. Raising his eyes he examined Tessa with a penetrating look, then returned them to the gems. She fought the urge to squirm. The new walking dress she'd wanted to wear to project an air of respectable prosperity was ruined. Its replacement, the soberest garment in her wardrobe, screamed with theatrical flair and overt sensuality. The man probably thought her a tart trying to cash in the wages of her trade.

But why should she care? It was what everyone thought.

"Am I to believe, madam," the jeweler asked, "that you are unaware that these gems are false?"

She inhaled sharply and spoke in a whisper. "False?"

"Paste. Every one of them."

For a moment she considered laughing it off, salvaging her pride by pretending she'd merely been testing the man's expertise. But it wouldn't do. She'd clearly stated she wanted to sell the diamonds. Bad enough he thought her a whore, without believing her a fraud into the bargain.

"No," she admitted, fighting tears. "I had no idea."

Tessa knew the occasion of Domenico's final betrayal. It was in Paris and they'd quarreled. The emperor had commanded a private interview to congratulate La Divina. So went the public statement, though everyone knew better. She'd turned him down, of course. To preserve his pride Napoleon presented her with the cameo necklace, a token of his deep admiration for her talent. The tacit understanding was that his court would believe he'd succeeded in his object.

Domenico had been furious. The cameos were trumpery compared to the jewels and other emoluments she'd have received as the emperor's mistress. As usual she'd heard his rant in resigned silence. But he never gave up. He had another candidate in mind for her bed, a parvenu Bonapartist duke with a fortune derived from military supplies. When she'd continued to resist he grabbed her shoulders and shook her, and the clasp of the Tsar's necklace broke.

Even then she'd been surprised. Domenico had never been overtly violent; he had too much respect for the health of his most valuable asset, herself. He'd also been careful of valuables. With a muttered apology he'd taken the entire Russian parure to be cleaned and mended.

And that, she concluded, was the last time she'd seen the genuine article.

"The quality of the reproduction is excellent." The jeweler broke into her thoughts. "And the setting is fine Russian work. When worn, only an expert, or a very observant eye, would detect that the gems aren't what they appear. The best French paste."

The sympathy in his voice summoned her pride. "I take it their value is negligible?"

He didn't bother to reply, merely nodded his agreement and continued to regard her with pity. A claw of fear in the pit of her stomach threatened to overcome any remnant of self-possession. Her eyes darted around the room, seeking a weapon. *No*! It was hardly the jeweler's fault that her husband had been a scoundrel.

Instead she experimented with some light breathing exercises and the panic subsided a little. Should she try singing again? With a flash of dark humor she envisioned the effect of a high note. It would be heard throughout the shop and even on the street and broadcast news of her presence to the world. She might count on the merchant's discretion—London's premier jeweler wouldn't retain its reputation by tattling about its clients' secrets.

"Be so good as to pack them up for me," she managed with a semblance of calm. "I am sorry for wasting your time."

On her return to the Pulteney, she found Monsieur Escudier, the French-born proprietor of the hotel, his manner conspicuously devoid of the caressing flattery he'd lavished on his famous guest at every opportunity.

"Madam," Escudier said, "I must request that you depart from this establishment at your earliest convenience, whether you are able to settle your account or not. Your behavior is upsetting the sensibilities of our English patrons."

The worst was not over. The manager's departure coincided with the sound of another arrival in the vestibule, Angela's protestations overborn by masculine rumbles in a voice she recognized only too well.

"I must see Madame Foscari."

She rushed to slam the doors through which Escudier had just passed but she was too late. Eyes ablaze, Max stood on the threshold, while Angela tugged fruitlessly at his arm.

Tessa wasn't in the mood for another "apology."

"Kindly refrain from bullying my maid and leave at once," she said, arms stretched wide and ready to drive him from the suite if necessary. "I have nothing to say to you."

"I have something to say to you." He shook off Angela's restraining hand without effort.

"Ange—"

"If you think your maid can throw me out of here you are much mistaken."

"You don't know what my maid can do. She'll do anything to protect me."

"I can assure you, madam, that you're not in any danger," he said. His voice softened as he removed his hat and bowed. "I beg only that you hear me out. And answer a question."

She pursed her lips and gave the shadow of a nod. She didn't want Angela hurt again. "I will give you five minutes."

Max glanced at the maid. "What I have to say is of a private nature."

"Angela understands little English. And I would prefer not to be alone with you." She murmured a few words in Italian and Angela perched on a chair in the corner of the room.

"Well?" She refused to offer the unwelcome visitor a seat, or even a chance to shed his outer garments. Instead she stood with hands on hips, cocking her head with a derisive air, and tapped her foot. "What is this question?"

He met her gaze, looked away, bit his lip, then returned his eyes to her face. "Tessa," he said finally, "ever since I left you in the hotel this morning I've been wondering if I made a terrible mistake."

"Of course you did. You ruined my reputation and livelihood in London."

"Not that. I must know. Did you or did you not accept two thousand pounds?"

"That sum again! I don't understand you."

"Mr. Eldon—do you remember Mr. Eldon?"

She wrenched her mind from the disastrous present and recalled the name. "Your clergyman companion in Portugal."

"Mr. Eldon paid your guardian, Mr. Waring, two thousand pounds. In exchange you agreed to relinquish any claim to my hand in marriage, to release me from any promise."

"Impossible. I never heard such a thing. You never even mentioned marriage. You asked me to be your mistress." Despite all the indecent proposals she had received since, the memory of the proposition from the young man she had adored so madly still had the power to pierce her with shame. So innocent had she been, it had never occurred to her then that a man would offer anything but marriage.

"Mr. Waring said you had agreed to the settlement and the money was to be used for your future dowry."

"This is the first I ever heard of it. You're lying." He had to be. Yet his voice rang with the candor she'd once admired in him.

"No. Waring accepted the payment on your behalf." He stepped forward to stand only a couple of feet from her and met her eye to eye, the intensity of his stare demanding the truth. "How can you not have known? Didn't you receive the money?"

Tessa's mind reeled and she could barely remain on her feet. She couldn't believe it. She didn't want to believe it. "Why would I accept a paltry amount?" she asked, gathering her indignation and coating it with sarcasm. "You're one of the wealthiest men in England, in Europe for all I know. Surely the adventuress you believe me to be would have demanded more to renounce such a prize."

"I didn't think you knew how wealthy I was."

His simple words deflated her. "No. I had no idea. I knew you weren't poor, I suppose, but I never thought of money." She blinked hard. "Only of how much I loved you."

"Good God, Tessa." He extended a hand as though to come to her, but she shook her head. "Apparently your guardian knew who I was. The typical English tourist couldn't raise such a sum on short notice and Eldon said Waring negotiated hard on your behalf. He said you complained that I had insulted you and would accept no less."

"I never said a word to Mr. Waring about your proposition."

The truth flickered into her mind. "Joshua," she said, hardly aware she spoke aloud. She sank down, just catching the edge of a sofa.

"Joshua?"

Staring at the floor she reached back into the past. "Mr. Waring's son. I told him."

She'd come home starry-eyed that night and told Joshua, who was the same age and her closest friend, that she and Max were in love and she expected him to offer her marriage at their next meeting. But Joshua's indiscretion hardly mattered now. The elder Waring, her guardian who was supposed to care for her interests, had deliberately ruined her chance to make an advantageous marriage.

Max crouched down and reached for her hand, cold in his warm, firm grasp.

"Why wouldn't Mr. Waring have wanted us to marry?" The question was more to herself than to Max. She feared she knew the answer. She had been aware that Waring's port wine export business had been in difficulties, but soon afterward the company had prospered due to a new influx of capital. An "investment," she had no doubt, from the deep coffers of the Hawthorne family.

"I can't answer that." He looked down and ran a forefinger over the back of her nerveless hand. "I wasn't of age. It would have been difficult to find a Protestant clergyman in Portugal who would wed us without my mother's permission." He spoke with hesitation, as though examining the question in his own mind. "I was too naïve to realize it, but I'm sure Mr. Waring was not. He must have thought it a safer bet to take the money Eldon offered."

Was their parting, then, the result of a misunderstanding brought about by her guardian's greed? Waring had later proven eager to exploit her talent for his own profit, and thereby driven her to elope with Domenico. Yes, she could credit his duplicity.

"So I concluded that you must have been aware of the difficulties." Max leaned forward and his eyes were dark and warm, as she remembered them. One part of her wanted nothing better than to sink into his embrace and forget everything that had kept them apart for so many years. "I believed you preferred to get what you could from our acquaintance."

She snatched away her hand and snapped to her feet, almost knocking him to the floor. "A fine opinion you had of the girl you claimed to love."

"I didn't want to believe it, but how could I deny the evidence?"

His excuse dispelled any urge to throw herself into his arms as he stood upright. "By meeting me as we had arranged and asking."

"You came to the churchyard? It never even occurred to me that you would."

"Of course I did. I thought I loved you." She folded her arms to fend off his attempt to take her hand again. "But don't concern yourself. I didn't pine for long. How could I regret the loss of one who treated me so?"

"I was a stupid young fool. I'm sorry, Tessa."

"You may address me as Madame Foscari," she said, raising her chin and curling her upper lip.

"Please forgive me."

"Forgive you? Forgive you? What good is forgiveness now?"

"I can't bear to think how I misjudged you. I need your forgiveness."

His plea plucked at her heart but she resisted. It wasn't as though they could turn back the clock to that time of perfect joy. Summoning her powers as an actress, she immersed herself in the role of wronged woman. "The past perhaps, I might ignore," she said with ice in her tone. "By now what happened in Oporto is a matter of supreme indifference to me. But I can never forgive what you have done now, in London."

"I am not proud of myself, but can't you see? That's why I did it. Because I believed you to be heartless and mercenary."

She curtsied. "Thank you so much. I can't tell you how much better that makes me feel."

She thought of everything that had happened since the day Max had left her: her own quarrel with Mr. Waring, her marriage and its series of betrayals, the fact that the world regarded her as an immoral adventuress, and now as a selfish, cold-hearted monster.

"I feel responsible for what you have become," he said, uncannily echoing her thoughts. "If you were entirely innocent then, I share the blame for the course of your life."

She knew exactly what he meant. He had the unbelievable gall to refer to her supposed amorous history and the condescension to imply that said history was somehow his business. Any part of her rage that was an act became real. She wanted to hurl every vase and ornament in the room at him.

She wouldn't do that and confirm his low opinion. Closing her eyes, she took several deep breaths. When she looked at him again, he stood before her, tall, stiff, unyielding. Whatever had happened in the past, he was no longer the boy she had loved but a grown man and her enemy. In the present.

"We have nothing more to say to each other," she said, with all the dignity she could muster. "There is only one thing you can offer me, and that is the restoration of my reputation which you have destroyed by your lies."

Arranging her skirts with a flourish, she spun on her heels and stalked out of the room, slamming the door behind her.

DEFIANT OF CONTRACTING Sofie's infection, Tessa visited her friend's room.

"Teresa," Sofie croaked. "Is everything well? Have you been able to stop the lies?"

Lovingly Tessa bathed Sofie's brow with lavender water. "All is well, my dearest. In a day or two we shall be back to normal. You mustn't worry about anything but getting well."

She didn't even have the satisfaction of paying off the Pulteney's proprietor with the last of her funds and seeking other lodgings that very afternoon. Sofie was too ill to be moved and Tessa had to suffer the humiliation of begging the manager to let them stay. Besides, she had no idea how to find inexpensive but respectable rooms in London, especially with almost no money. Did one have to pay rent in advance? So sheltered had she been from practical considerations, she had no idea.

Her sleep that night in the Pulteney's luxurious bed was restless, visited by nightmares she'd hoped never to repeat. "Angela, help me!" she screamed in her dream, feeling the weight on her chest, struggling against her bonds.

She awoke to find herself in Angela's arms. *"Va bene, signora,"* crooned the maid. *"Qui che sono, Angela."*

CHAPTER ELEVEN

"Madame Foscari, who lately refused to sing for the benefit of the Royal Hospital, now would have us believe that she was unaware of the nature of the occasion, that she would otherwise have accepted the invitation. Her donation of twenty pounds, this from a woman who earns thousands a year, tells us how much to credit the singer's claim of liberality."

The Times

MAX LEFT THE hotel with a flea in his ear and confusion in his soul. Irked that his heartfelt expression of regret had won such a frosty reception, he reviewed the exchange with Tessa and came to the unwelcome conclusion that he'd invited her scorn. It was hardly the action of a gentleman to throw her amorous past in her face, even by implication. But the thought of the other men she'd bedded was a dagger to his spirit. His sweet, lovely Tessa, mauled by half the men in Europe.

The very sight of her sent him into an agony of longing and repulsion. He wanted her, yes, but he wanted her as she had been, not as she was now.

Though not a rake by Somerville's standards, Max had enjoyed his share of women and none of them had been models of purity. He neither expected not desired his mistresses to be virgins. He didn't understand why he cared so much about Tessa's experience. Not that she was his mistress, nor ever likely to be so. She hated him.

Max was close to hating himself too. Or what had happened to him since the day she had returned to London. A man of honor and good sense, a trifle reserved perhaps, but affable and friendly to his fellow humans, had turned into an irrational imbecile who went around ruining inconvenient women for reasons that weren't only specious but downright unacceptable.

Approaching St. James's Church, he saw a bill advertising Delorme's next performance as Don Giovanni at the Regent gracing a wall, along with a number of other playbills, including one for the Tavistock. Across the name Teresa Foscari, rendered in large letters, someone had scrawled an unprintable word. Max ripped it from the wall, crumpled it into a ball and stamped it into the gutter, but he couldn't stamp the ugliness of the obscenity out of his head.

He must repair the damage he'd wrought. Before he turned his footsteps towards St. James's Street and White's Club, he tore down the advertisement for his own opera house. It was only fair.

Starting the rumor that had led, with such spectacular results, to the demise of La Divina's popularity, had been easy. Reversing the impression proved harder. A few words in his clubs to his least discreet acquaintance was all it had taken for Max's tale to reach the greater public. Polite indifference greeted explanations of his "mistake." In desperation Max called on the editor of one of the newspapers most vociferous in its condemnation of Tessa.

"The man had the impudence to suggest she was my mistress," he complained afterwards to Simon Lindo.

Lindo raised a dark brow. "Was he right?"

"No, damn it. Of course not. Why would you suggest such a thing?"

"I know something's been bothering you and I've heard tales of a confrontation between you and La Divina. In my experience you don't see that much smoke generated without fire."

"I've been concerned about the Regent," Max replied stiffly. "As have you."

Simon shook his head. "It's been more than that. In my case it's the money. But that's not your first concern."

"I am only sorry we had to purchase our success at the expense of another." The depth of his remorse couldn't be revealed without confiding more than he wished to Simon.

"If we served Madame Foscari an injustice, I'm sorry for it too," Simon said. "I have nothing against the lady. But I can't regret the result."

"I didn't mean things to go this far, only to tarnish the sheen a little."

"Foscari has always cultivated the newspapers. You don't think she attracted so much attention by accident do you? Someone spread the stories about the lovers, the jewels, the dramatic fits. Fed the beast you might say. And now the beast has discovered a flaw and enjoys tearing her down." Simon smiled cynically. "This little affair of the hospital sells newspapers. They won't give it up in a hurry."

"You say someone spread the stories. Did she do it herself?"

"Perhaps. But I'd guess it was her late husband, with or without her connivance."

"What makes you think that? Why would a husband expose his wife's infidelities?"

"When I worked for Mortimer, he tried more than once to engage La Divina for the Tavistock. Domenico Foscari had total control over his wife's business and he was the most ruthless negotiator I've ever encountered. Mortimer never got close to a reasonable agreement until Foscari died. I saw those letters. You think Mortimer is a bastard? My impression is Foscari was his match, and more." Simon frowned. "I also had the impression that Foscari was toying with Mortimer. He never intended to come to terms with him. For some reason, he didn't want to bring his wife to London. Strange, since she could have made a great deal of money."

Max latched onto one part of Simon's recitation. If Foscari had been responsible for disseminating stories about Tessa, had he also invented them? The hope subsided almost as soon as it had kindled. A man might use his wife's infidelities to his own advantage, but surely he wouldn't make them up from whole cloth.

He returned to the immediate problem. "How can I correct my error if no one will listen?" He looked at Simon, hoping his partner's greater experience in the theatrical world would produce a solution.

Simon rested his chin on his fist, deep in thought. "I believe her reputation would be restored," he said, "if she could win the approval and sponsorship of someone of impeccable standing in society. Someone whose opinion no one dares ignore."

Max knew just such a person. Little as he might relish it, he must ask his mother for a favor.

CLIMBING THE STAIRS at Tamworth House, Max met one of his mother's lawyers escaping like a beaten cur. His chances of finding Lady Clarissa in one of her rare cooperative moods looked poor.

"You know I'm not overly fond of singing," she said to his carefully couched suggestion that she host a musicale. "And why would I wish to patronize Teresa Foscari?"

"I doubt you would," he replied with all the patience he could muster. "You'll do it because I am asking you as a favor to me."

"You're not thinking of marrying the woman again? I won't have it."

"No, Mama. As I just explained to you, at sufficient length that I'm quite sure you understand, it's a question of honor. My honor."

"Just give her some more money. It satisfied her before." She was being provocative. He'd already told her not a penny of her money had ever reached Tessa.

"Money isn't enough." He'd give almost anything to walk out of the room. Instead he gritted his teeth and hoped he wouldn't be reduced to begging. "To be sure, I expect you to pay Madame

Foscari a handsome fee for her appearance at your musical evening, but receiving her is more important. I must and shall repair the damage I've done to her reputation."

"And if I agree to hold the largest gathering at Tamworth House in years, in *honor* of this opera singer, what will you do for me in return?"

"I'm not getting married. Not to Teresa Foscari, nor to anyone else."

"You will when I win our bet."

"Restoring Madame Foscari's popularity will increase your chances of winning. Business at the Regent has improved since her disgrace." It was an argument he'd far sooner not have to make. He was well aware of what he risked.

Lady Clarissa's eyes grew beady as she considered the implications. Still, she had to wring another advantage out of him.

"I shall invite a number of suitable young ladies to the event." She warmed to the idea. "And you shall meet them. You shall treat them civilly, give them a chance. You might very well take a fancy to one of them."

"Hah!"

"You'll have to marry one of them in little more than a year, so you may as well start thinking about whom you prefer." She smiled gleefully. "I am quite prepared to take your choice into consideration, as long as she is suitable."

"How very good of you."

"Never say I don't play fair."

"I accept your terms," he said, shaking his head in surrender. It couldn't hurt to greet his mother's guests, regardless of age or sex, with courtesy. Not even his mother could force him to propose to one of them.

"And..." There had to be an "and."

"And you will ignore Madame Foscari."

"Ignore your honored guest when the object of the evening is to show her favor? I don't think so."

"Very well. You will accord her no more than the barest politesse. I won't have you using my house to pursue that woman. Make her your mistress if you insist, but not on these premises. In fact it would be better if she left after her performance. I'm not in the habit of entertaining those hired to entertain."

"You know why that isn't good enough. It's essential that she be seen to gain your approval. It's not as though she isn't of good birth. Lady Storrington is her cousin."

Lady Clarissa sniffed. "It's all very well for a flibbertigibbet like Jacobin Storrington to receive an opera singer. I have standards to maintain."

"I can't think of any standards you've ever maintained except your own. And you always enjoy making others accept them."

Lady Clarissa gave up the argument. It was some time since she'd given a large entertainment and he could almost see the invitation list running through head. Especially, alas, the names of young unmarried ladies. She didn't even bother to quibble over the huge figure he suggested for Teresa Foscari's fee.

If Somerville had been correct that the Tsar's diamonds were false, then Tessa might well be in financial difficulties, though he couldn't imagine why. But she'd been on her way to Ludgate Hill with the diamonds in her reticule. Ludgate Hill, where London's most fashionable jeweler was situated.

"One more thing," his mother said. "Since this soirée is to include some rather dubious characters…" He closed his eyes and fought for calm. "…I insist you invite that deliciously handsome tenor of yours, Monsieur Delorme. I might as well have something interesting to look at while *that woman* is singing."

"BUT HE APOLOGIZED?" Jacobin prompted. Tessa had poured her tale into her cousin's sympathetic ears over tea and pastries in the countess's private sitting room.

"Some apology!" Tessa replied, burning with renewed indignation. "He said he felt responsible for what I had become."

Jacobin gave her characteristic Gallic shrug. "Typical man. He bungled it. They hate to apologize and when they do they expect you to be grateful and make a big fuss of them."

"Grateful! He wasn't the one who had to wait for three hours in a freezing churchyard. *He* isn't the one who was accused of being a greedy foreigner by every newspaper in London. *He* isn't the one who was jeered off the stage after a remarkably fine performance, though I say it myself."

Jacobin replenished their teacups, adding a slice of lemon to Tessa's and milk and sugar to her own. "I agree. It's not good enough. He needs to grovel."

"Holy Saint George! I hate men."

"They are impossible, yes, but they can be taught."

"Does Lord Storrington apologize?" Tessa asked, curious. Domenico certainly never had. Their marriage, after the initial honeymoon, had been an endless battle in which her husband usually emerged the victor. He would demand and she would acquiesce, until he asked for something she would not, could not accede to.

"Oh yes! And I'm always very nice to him afterwards."

Being "nice" to Domenico had achieved nothing. The last time she'd tried she ended up with the nightmares that had returned and plagued her every night so she scarcely dared sleep.

"How are you, Tessa?" Jacobin asked. "You don't look well. Has it been very bad at the theater?" Obviously her troubles were affecting her appearance.

"A little better. The audience is still thin but I haven't been booed again." As far as Jacobin knew her public reputation was Tessa's only problem. She'd confided nothing about her financial straits.

Tessa reached for her reticule. "I did receive this letter today."

Jacobin perused the bold handwriting on heavy cream paper, nodding vigorously and emitting hums of approval as she turned over the page and read to the end. "But this is excellent! Lady Clarissa is a powerful force. Not a single member of the *ton* will refuse her invitation, or dare cut you in her house."

"I'd rather throw it back in her face."

Handing back the note, Jacobin shook her head. "Much as I appreciate the urge, you'd be a fool to do so. A recital at Tamworth House will be quite an occasion. It's an amazing place."

"What kind of woman is she?"

"Most people are terrified of her but I like her. She's very entertaining and not at all stuffy. And as I said, where she leads there isn't a soul who will dare not follow."

Tessa knew she couldn't refuse Lady Clarissa's offer, if only because the eye-opening fee for a single evening's work was almost enough to clear her outstanding bills.

"Very well. I shall accept," she said. She didn't have to do so happily.

"This is Lord Allerton's doing, you realize, don't you? Lady Clarissa would never have thought of holding a musical evening by herself. Max is trying to make amends."

Tessa would have none of that. She read from the letter. "*It will be a pleasure and a privilege to hear you sing and to receive you at Tamworth House*. Why shouldn't this grand lady wish to have Europe's greatest soprano perform for her guests?"

Jacobin chuckled. "By all means, believe that if it makes you feel better. I'm glad to hear your spirits revive. I was worried about you." She waved a plate of golden-edged, aromatic delicacies in Tessa's face. "And for God's sake eat something. I shall feel mortally insulted if you won't even taste my fruit tartlets."

Tessa only hesitated for a moment before accepting a delicious morsel of pastry filled with wild strawberries under a rose-tinted glaze. She thought of Domenico's constant admonitions against gaining weight and losing her allure. She bit into the tartlet and relished every morsel.

Jacobin observed her enjoyment with an air of satisfaction. "I have an interesting item of gossip," she said in a casual tone. "Somerville has come to terms with Nancy Sturridge."

"Jacobin! I didn't think proper ladies were supposed to know of such things."

"They're not, but of course we all do. According to my maid she accepted his carte blanche yesterday. Do you mind?"

"No. It's just that Miss Sturridge and I have a different dispute. Some of the newssheets have reported stories about my attitude to the other singers in the company and I believe it is Nancy who spread them. She's jealous of me."

"Perhaps she'll stop now that she has landed Somerville as a lover. He should keep her busy."

During a visit to Jacobin's adorable twins in the nursery, Tessa reflected on the novelty of a friendship outside the world of opera. How lovely it would be not to think about her voice. Not to worry about the dangers of the changing temperature or a passing shower. Not to consider every sip or bite and its effects on her vocal cords. She never touched cream or cheese. How many years had it been since she'd enjoyed a cup of milky tea or coffee?

Burying her nose in young Lord Storrs's neck, she inhaled his baby scent, wholesome yet to her more exotic than the perfumes of Provence. She listened to Jacobin soothing the fussing of little Lady Felicity and relished the vital importance of such a commonplace action.

When, she vowed, Mortimer released the funds she'd earned, she'd take a long holiday, far from the theater and, above all, far from men. Too bad the wretched creatures were necessary for the conception of children. She would like an infant of her own, but not enough to consider another husband. Perhaps she should get a cat.

Max, Somerville, Waring, Domenico, Mortimer. She'd had enough of them.

Somerville's defection didn't trouble her. There had been a

moment, when she learned the diamonds were false, that she'd feared taking a rich lover was her only choice. Then she remembered all the times that Domenico had enumerated the assets of this Milanese *conte* or that Austrian Archduke and what they'd pay to take La Divina to bed. Sometimes he'd turn nasty when she resisted. "Lucky he doesn't know what a cold bitch you are, or he'd never offer so much to own you for a night. Since you can't please your husband you might as well make yourself useful elsewhere."

The baby in her arms squirmed as her arms involuntarily tightened. *"Desculpe, meu querido,"* she whispered, as her Portuguese nurse had to the infant Tessa.

Never. She would never sell herself.

Pride had saved her, and the other reason. The reason it was impossible for her to take a lover.

Absently rocking the baby in her arms, she blocked the memory of Domenico's worst legacy. But the other result of the evening that had led to her nightmares had to be faced.

Desperate and distraught, she'd determined to take revenge on her husband by bedding another man, but in a way that wouldn't yield Domenico a sou. She shuddered as she recalled the plush chaise against her back, Edouard Delorme's flashing blue eyes and bare chest looming over her, the scent of mint, his soft, pampered tenor's hands tugging at her bodice.

Taking another man to her bed wasn't an option. For any reason.

CHAPTER TWELVE

"A certain singer of Continental habits will entertain tonight at the house in Piccadilly. Does the Beau Monde, then, so easily forget the insult lately dealt our brave wounded by Madame F?"

The Morning Post

TESSA WAS FAMILIAR, both as entertainer and guest, with some of the grandest residences in Europe. Since coming to London she had learned that, compared to the palaces of Vienna and Paris, the houses of the English aristocracy were often modest affairs. Her cousin's husband, Lord Storrington, was as wealthy as an archduke, yet his London house, though commodious and well-appointed, was part of an unassuming Brook Street terrace. With a few notable exceptions, Englishmen preferred to display their wealth and power at their country estates.

Lady Clarissa Hawthorne was one of those exceptions. While the Piccadilly front of Tamworth House was unprepossessing, forbidding even, massive double doors led into a courtyard revealing an imposing classical front flanked by well-proportioned wings. Marvels awaited the visitor admitted to the marbled and gilded two-story hall, lit by giant chandeliers and attended by an army of footmen.

Tessa found herself trembling as she and Sempronio made their way up one side of the double-curved staircase to the main floor. Though accustomed on stage to moving with confidence in the most unwieldy costumes, she held the long train of her gown as insurance against an embarrassing accident. This house was the equal of any she'd seen, aside from royal residences.

This was where Max had grown up. She now understood why Lady Clarissa had been ready to pay handsomely to save her only son from a nobody like Tessa Birkett.

More magnificence greeted her in a saloon worthy of a king, a richly furnished double cube hung with a series of historical paintings by Rubens. She could hardly take in the décor, receiving only a fleeting impression of lots of marble pillars and the lavish application of gold. Tessa found the room sparsely peopled this early in the evening, and at once saw Max in a far corner, conversing with two young women.

She had no trouble identifying the tall woman in blue who came forward to meet her, the very image of Max with the same dark coloring and severely handsome features. Despite her age, which must be close to fifty, Lady Clarissa Hawthorne's curls, intricately arranged under a stylish turban of silver tissue, sported not a hint of grey. Experienced in theatrical artifice, Tessa saw that Lady Clarissa hadn't abandoned her coiffure to the vagaries of nature but had confided it to the care of a master. Tessa wouldn't mind knowing the name of her hairdresser.

"Madame Foscari," Lady Clarissa said, in tones that brought to mind the haughtiest grand duchess at the Tsar's court, "I have heard a great deal about you."

Tessa swept a low curtsey and resisted the urge to kiss the huge sapphire ring on the proffered hand. Then she raised her head and stopped short at the sight of Lady Clarissa's necklace. Those sapphires couldn't really be the size of hen's eggs could they? Not quite. Maybe bantam's eggs.

The other woman examined Tessa's neck in return. While not exactly welcoming, when she spoke again her voice was curious rather than hostile. "I see you're not wearing your diamonds this evening. I had been looking forward to seeing the famous Russian jewels."

Thank God! Tessa had found herself unable to even look at the damned things once she knew they were false. Neither had she worn the French cameos. Displaying Napoleon's gift was unlikely to assist her return to English social respectability. Instead she'd chosen her most elaborate evening gown, a low cut affair of ivory satin, heavily encrusted with pearls, embroidery, and gold lace. Even without jewelry she'd felt overdressed. Until she saw Lady Clarissa. No one could feel overdressed in the presence of those sapphires.

"With this ensemble I felt diamonds would be gilding the lily," she said. "My compliments on your own necklace. I have rarely seen such brilliant stones."

Lady Clarissa's eyes narrowed at the blithe response. Good! Tessa was determined not to let this woman intimidate her. She might be monarch of her own realm—the London *ton*—but within her own sphere Tessa was her superior. She tilted her head proudly. And almost lost her composure when Max approached with a cautious smile on his face.

Cool civility was the attitude she was determined to maintain with him. She wouldn't let herself be again provoked into discourteous behavior. However offensive he became she would remain calm. Unfortunately Max had the ability to ruffle her feathers like no one else.

"My dear Signora Foscari." At least he'd dropped the obnoxious "Mrs." He raised her gloved hand to his lips. "How beautiful you look! Welcome to my mother's house. I am, as always, looking forward to hearing you sing."

"Thank you, Lord Allerton. I trust I will do justice to such a setting."

"I have no doubt of it." His dark eyes caressed her with what looked like admiration and placed her serenity at risk.

"Max! Miss Bellamy has arrived with Lady Caroline. I know you will wish to greet her. *I* shall see to Madame Foscari." Lady Clarissa's interruption was delivered with a stern look that Max apparently comprehended, though not without a mulish cast to his countenance.

He took his leave of Tessa with a murmur that he'd see her later and strolled off to join a lady and her rather pretty daughter. The lady's dragonish expression made Lady Clarissa look like a pussycat.

"Dear Max," Lady Clarissa said. "He has gladdened my maternal heart by agreeing, at last, to find a suitable wife." She placed the smallest emphasis on the word "suitable." Since this kind of confidence to a stranger, and one hired for the evening, seemed hardly typical of a woman of Lady Clarissa Hawthorne's eminence, Tessa took it as a warning. A most unnecessary one.

"Let me introduce to you some of my guests. Are you acquainted with Sir Henry Waxfield?" Her ladyship was anxious to fob her off on another man.

"I don't usually mingle with my audience before I perform. I need to prepare myself."

Lady Clarissa waved aside the objection. "Surely not just for a song or two? I wouldn't want to take advantage of you with excessive demands."

Tessa tried not to laugh. A song or two was hardly an excessive demand given her handsome fee for the evening. The suspicion that Lady Clarissa had exaggerated her passion for music hardened into certainty.

"I had planned a program with several long arias, including two in German," she said with a straight face and was rewarded with a barely disguised look of horror.

"I won't hear of it," Lady Clarissa said. "One short song is all I require. Maybe two. Did you say you knew Sir Henry?"

Reassured that the engagement wouldn't overtax her vocal powers, Tessa turned her mind to the other object of the evening—that of restoring her acceptability in London society. She curtsied to the baronet, whom she remembered meeting at her cousin's house, and prepared to make herself agreeable. He eyed her with a lascivious gleam and took his time about kissing her hand.

"And here is Mr. Lindo," Lady Clarissa added, summoning a passing gentleman with an imperious nod. "You must meet Mr. Lindo, the manager of my son's opera house."

Lindo was in his mid-forties, Tessa guessed, a good-looking man with a serious, intelligent cast to his features.

"I'm happy to meet you," she said. "I very much admired your company when I heard *Il Barbiere di Siviglia*."

"And I," Lindo responded, "have been rendered speechless with admiration each time I've had the honor of hearing you, *madame*."

Sir Henry interrupted their exchange of compliments. "May I help you to procure a glass of wine, madam?" he asked. Then he lowered his head and his voice. "You must be anxious to escape the present company. It's bad enough for Allerton to consort with a Jew, without allowing him into his mother's drawing room."

The words were perhaps meant for her ears alone, but they were perfectly audible to the object of Waxfield's malice. Tessa pulled away from him and placed her hand on Lindo's arm, dismissing all thought of impressing Sir Henry.

"I was not aware," she said, "of Mr. Lindo's race or religion, but knowing his exquisite taste in music I am not surprised. You must know, Sir Henry, that many great musicians and artists are Jewish. It is always a privilege to find oneself in the presence of talent." She wrapped her arm around Lindo's. "Would you be good enough, sir, to escort me to the piano? I must prepare for my performance."

"YOU DIDN'T NEED to do that," Simon murmured, as Teresa Foscari dismissed Sir Henry with the briefest of nods and dragged Simon towards a door. "I'm grateful, of course, but I'm quite accustomed to such treatment. It's why I tend to avoid social occasions."

"I have no patience with such bad manners. Nor such prejudice. Why, then, are you here tonight?" She quivered with indignation.

Simon eyed her in surprise. La Divina at close quarters was a stunning beauty who made the most of nature's considerable gifts by the clever use of cosmetics and the dressmaker's art. But she seemed younger than he expected and, beneath the glossy veneer, simpler and more sincere than any operatic diva he'd ever met. Her willingness to snub a wealthy baronet in defense of him—and his race—intrigued him.

"I came to see you, of course. To hear you sing is always an honor. To meet a woman of such exquisite beauty was an additional incentive."

La Foscari examined his face. "You don't seem the kind, Mr. Lindo, to engage in fulsome flattery."

"You are correct. That was no flattery."

While she attended to his words, Simon noticed her eyes flicker around the room and narrow as they rested on Max, deep in conversation with a pretty young brunette. How interesting.

"I am here because Max requested it," he said. "He is distressed about what he did to you."

Foscari's face hardened. "I hear the Regent has been playing to full houses lately."

"I can't deny that we have benefited from your misfortune. Max wishes to see you restored in the public estimation. This evening is his attempt to help, as I'm sure you have guessed."

She tilted her head in consideration. Then her lips twitched. "If I hadn't, it became clear to me once I deduced Lady Clarissa's astonishing lack of enthusiasm for hearing me sing.

"I too owe you an apology, for it was my idea to spread the word of your refusal to sing at our benefit. I hope you will forgive us both and accept my assurance that we are doing all we can to set matters right."

She shrugged her shoulders. "I bear you no animosity, Mr. Lindo. I accept that there was nothing personal in *your* actions. I'd like you to meet my répétiteur, Sempronio Montelli."

FROM THE BEGINNING of the evening, Lady Clarissa kept Max supplied with marriageable girls to entertain. It could have been worse. He'd expected to loathe every moment he spent fulfilling his side of the agreement with his mother but he was surprised to find the youthful beauties—every one of them well-born and well-endowed—quite tolerable. Learning that Tessa truly had loved him had adjusted his view of all women. No longer certain that he saw the reflection of gold in avaricious eyes, he found that suitable young ladies could be perfectly agreeable. They even appeared to like him.

Perhaps he should look for a wife after all. But not, he swore, until the Regent was turning a profit. He wouldn't allow his mother to think she'd won their battle.

Besides, his interest in any one of the ladies was negligible. From the moment Tessa made her entrance, stunning in ivory and gold, he'd been constantly aware of her location in the saloon. Rushing over to greet her arrival, he'd been driven off by Lady Clarissa and forced to converse with Miss Bellamy, a complete widgeon, and her ghastly mother. Miss Bellamy he might acquit of mercenary intentions; Lady Caroline Bellamy was most assuredly guilty.

With only half his mind on the conversation, he noted Tessa leaving the room with Simon Lindo. Simon? Surely not. As far as he knew, Simon, a widower, had nothing to do with women. On the other hand, he was still a handsome man and they seemed to have become friendly rather quickly. By the time his mother moved into an adjoining room, he was ready to eat the carpet.

Finally he could make his escape.

It took a while to extract himself from Lady Caroline's talons, but at last he made it to the door through which Tessa and Simon had disappeared, and followed the sound of mirth into the smaller of the mansion's two music rooms. Tessa's laugh, which his ears singled out from a group of merrymakers, fed his sense of urgency.

"And then," Simon Lindo was saying, "his foot hit the horse dropping and his voice hit the rafters. I swear the fellow had never achieved a higher C."

"One should never perform with animals," Tessa asserted through a chuckle. "One time in Bologna they put hens on the stage for *La Finta Giardinera*. One of them laid an egg, which wouldn't have mattered except I trod on it and the bird nipped my ankle."

"Did you stay on key?' The question came from Lady Storrington.

"Of course," said Tessa with a careless wave. "I always stay on key. I did not, however, stay on my feet. I delivered the rest of the aria from a sitting position."

A shout of laughter arose from her audience of Simon, Sempronio Montelli, Lord and Lady Storrington, a couple of the latter's friends and—damnation—his mother! It was infuriating that he'd been obeying her wishes and being bored to death by respectable young ladies while she was swilling champagne and trading stories with the theatrical set—which was supposed to be his milieu. A set of people she professed to despise. She was leaning on the piano, at which Montelli was seated. The Italian lent occasional punctuation to a dramatic point with a fanfare on the keys. A footman had been commandeered to keep their glasses full and the whole party was obviously having a fine old time. Not one of them even noticed his entrance.

"Tell me, *madame*," asked Lady Clarissa. "Have you ever appeared in an opera featuring a shipwreck?"

His thoughts softened at the sight of his mother's face, alive with amusement and without a trace of the discontent that often dressed her features. Was it possible that she had spent the past decade as bored as he had been?

But he hadn't come here to see his mother, and his eyes were drawn irresistibly to Tessa and something shifted into focus. For the first time he perceived neither the seventeen-year-old girl nor the avaricious prima donna. In the curve of the piano stood a woman, a great beauty, yes, but also a woman of maturity and intelligence. A woman who held an audience in her grasp, not because she was playing a part on stage but through the allure of her own personality and wit. A woman of character. Yet the delineation of that character was a mystery to him. He wanted to know the adult Tessa.

He walked up behind Simon, standing on the periphery of the gathering, and tugged on his arm. "Distract my mother," he said quietly.

Simon turned and threw him a quizzical look. "And how am I to do that?"

"I'm sure you can think of something to say. You're not afraid of her, are you?"

"I am not afraid of her. Though I can see why some people might be."

"Damn you, Simon. Don't look at me like that. Just do as I ask."

SIMON SHRUGGED. HE couldn't identify the undercurrent between Max and his mother but it had something to do with La Divina. Max hadn't confided in him, but perhaps her ladyship would respond to subtle questioning.

She was an extremely handsome woman. And she looked like the sort who gave short shrift to subtlety. "My lady," he said, raising his glass to her. Her attention was drawn away from Teresa Foscari who had moved on to reminiscences of Paris. "My compliments on your magnificent hospitality."

"Are you speaking ironically, Mr. Lindo? If I'm not mistaken, one of my guests insulted you earlier." He was right. This was a woman who didn't beat about the bush.

"I don't see it as a slur to call me a Jew. It is what I am. The insult was in Sir Henry's mind." Keeping his tone mild he added. "Perhaps you are in agreement with him."

She regarded him with interest. Not used to getting an argument, he guessed. "I'm not sure I've ever met a Jew," she said in accents that reeked of self-confident entitlement. "How can I know if I agree with him?"

He bowed. "I am pleased to be able to enlarge your ladyship's experience."

"Now I've met you, that makes one. Not enough, I think, to form a favorable opinion of the entire race. Or an unfavorable one either."

He laughed. "An ambiguous statement."

"Precisely," she replied with a gleam in her eye. She moved away from the piano and came close enough to rest a hand on his arm. A little tremor of awareness ran through him. It must be the shock of finding himself in such close proximity to sapphires the size of the Bank of England.

"Walk with me a little," she said, her voice commanding but with a hint of enticement. "How did you make Max's acquaintance?"

"We fell into conversation outside Covent Garden one night and ended up supping together. At that time I was assistant manager at the Tavistock and he had conceived his plan for a new opera house."

"You must tell me all about the theatrical business."

"And why would you want to know that, my lady?"

"Why, Mr. Lindo, it's my son's greatest passion. Everything that concerns him concerns me."

MAX HAD RID himself, at least temporarily, of his mother's interfering presence and maneuvered Tessa away from the rest of the company. Now he found he couldn't think of a thing to say. An intimation of gardenia tickled his senses and his eyes focused on the intricacies of braids and curls entwined around a double-gold filet, gleaming through the rich gilt of Tessa's hair. He felt as shy as the youth who'd plucked up courage to present himself at the stage door of the Oporto Opera House.

"Unusual for a singer to drink wine before a performance, isn't it?" he managed after a few moments' charged silence.

She raised her glass. "Water."

He was behaving like an ass.

"But don't worry, my lord," she continued. "My voice should be able to meet the demands of my hostess."

Acquaintance with his mother's tolerance for music restored his balance. "Excessive are they?" he inquired with a faint smile that elicited a relaxation of Tessa's defensive posture.

"I believe Lady Clarissa would be happy if I confined my performance to a single nursery rhyme. And happier still if I remained silent." She met his gaze in amused accord.

"What are you going to sing?"

"I was considering *Abscheulicher.*"

He gave a crack of laughter. The opening section of Beethoven's aria addressed the villainous Don Pizzaro as "Monster."

"In honor of the success of *Fidelio* at your opera house," she added, lowering her eyes demurely.

"Are you calling my mother a monster?"

"I wouldn't be so bold." Her laugh found an answering warmth in his breast. Sharing a joke felt as intimate and precious as a kiss. "But seriously, it's a noble piece, one of the most beautiful I know."

"I would love to hear you sing it," he said, wondering if her choice had any significance beyond the artistic. The aria developed into an anthem to the power of marital love and fidelity. Not what she was known for.

A footman appeared, bearing tea and slices of lemon on a

salver. "You see," she said. "I do know how to take care of my voice. A warm drink to loosen the vocal cords, even for a nursery rhyme."

While the business of pouring tea was accomplished, Max thought about their last meeting and came to a decision.

"Tessa—"

"Max—"

They spoke simultaneously. He gestured her to continue.

"No, you go first," she said.

He paused, formulating a speech that had run through his head for a day or two. "When we last spoke I tried to apologize."

"Yes." Her face turned stony.

"I don't think I did a very good job."

Her expression was an eloquent assent. "You said you were sorry for what I had become," she said with awful calm. "I believe I can live without such condescension. Not to mention your unmitigated arrogance in believing you played such a significant role in my life."

"Let me try again. I apologize for spreading a lie about you." He lowered his voice though no one else was near enough to hear. "And for leaving you to wait for me in the churchyard in Oporto."

"Did you know it rained? That I spent three hours getting wet when I had a performance that night?" The tremor in her voice contradicted the indifference she had claimed at their last confrontation. He found the fact perversely pleasing. Not only had she cared for him then, but the memory had the power to upset her.

"I must confess the weather wasn't uppermost in my thoughts as I climbed into the carriage to leave Oporto." Her expression told him his feeble attempt at humor was not appreciated. He sought the words to tell her what he'd thought without insulting her again. "I wished then that what I believed was untrue. And I wish now I'd never believed it."

MAX SPOKE WITH hesitation and his words were awkward. Yet examining his face, his once dear face, Tessa accepted their sincerity. Unspoken of course was what he believed of her now. She had long pretended to herself that Domenico's creation of La Divina the amorous adventurer was no great matter, merely a necessary part of her success in the world. She realized she resented it, and never more so than now, when the only man whose love she'd ever craved had heard and believed every tale spread by her husband. The sculptural planes of his severe features were immobile; Max had never been a man whose emotions were written on his face. Yet the dark eyes expressed genuine contrition and regarded her with an anxiety she felt compelled to assuage.

As he looked down at her, awaiting her response, he raised a fist and rested his chin on the knuckles, close to his wide, well-formed lips. She recalled his firm, sensitive hands on her bare skin, caressing her through the silk of his dressing robe, and that mouth claiming hers. Such a short time ago, yet it seemed an age during which the affair of the hospital benefit had interrupted a rapprochement of sorts. Then their ardor had been tempered by their mutual anger about the past. Now that issue had been put to rest for both of them. Neither could be blamed for anything save the mistakes of extreme youth.

She fought an impulse to touch his cheek. Too much had intervened to make it possible to reclaim the past. The moment she'd stepped into this house she'd known in the back of her mind that she and Max were worlds apart. Even could her reputation be repaired, an inconceivable outcome, the heir to all this magnificence would never stoop to wed an opera singer. The very idea had been nothing but the impractical dream of an inexperienced boy. Besides, even if a fairy godmother could banish all other differences with the wave of her wand, Tessa was irreparably damaged inside. After Domenico she could never make a satisfactory wife. Barring Max at the entrance to her heart was essential to her sanity.

Moving backwards a step, as though physical distance could induce mental detachment, she noticed a hint of distress replace the anxiety in his eyes. She remembered Jacobin's remarks about men needing approval when they troubled to apologize. And truly she felt no further need to punish Max.

"That's very handsome of you. I accept your apology for Oporto."

He smiled tentatively.

"As for the rest, I understand that this evening's event is your effort to set things right. I'm not unappreciative."

His entire body relaxed and the smile became wholehearted. "Thank you, it was the least I could do to make up for my unconscionable behavior," he said, and kissed her hand with a warmth and grace that soothed her battered heart.

"You seemed to be enjoying yourself just now." For once there was no trace of edge in his tone.

She smiled back at him. "I was, and I hadn't expected to. Lady Clarissa knows how to give a good party. This is a beautiful house. Did you grow up here?"

"Here, and on my grandfather's estate. Tamworth is the place I regard as home. As for this house?" He rolled his eyes north to the gilt coffered plasterwork lavished on even a minor reception room. "I've always found it too large and too ornate for comfort. I prefer to live on a modest scale."

Sternly refusing to dwell on any details of her visit to Max's house save those relating to interior decoration, she ventured a tease.

"Modest compared to this, perhaps. But I couldn't help noticing a flair for drama in the furnishing of your home."

"Really? Are you referring to the tapestries in the hall, or the bed hangings? You didn't see enough of the house to admire the dark red and orange library."

"Red and orange? How very brave of you."

"I seem to have a taste for drama. No doubt why I am drawn

to opera." His eyes raked her body, lingering almost imperceptibly at her low bodice, and falling to the floor where gold slippers peeped out beneath the gold-encrusted hem of her satin gown. "Your gown is superb. Is it the work of a theatrical costumier?"

Tessa told herself his question was innocent, merely the natural curiosity of a man who was involved in the business of theater. But she wanted to squirm with embarrassment. How she wished she were garbed in the kind of understated attire she'd noticed on the backs of those proper young ladies Max had mingled with earlier. She hated—hated—this garment. It was one of the last Domenico had picked out before his death. Paying for it had taken a substantial portion from the sale of her jewelry.

HE'D UPSET HER again, though why a simple compliment on her dress should cause that look of discomfort Max couldn't imagine.

"Is there a place you call home, Tessa?" he asked, to change the subject.

"I had a small house at Busetto where we stayed during the times when I had no engagement. Quite an ordinary little town but peaceful." She emitted a ghost of a sigh. "Most of the time there's an opera season somewhere so I was never there as much as I would have liked. Sometimes it seems most of my life has been spent in carriages and hotels. Domenico liked to keep me busy."

Curiosity about the motives of Domenico Foscari aside, Max wondered what had happened to all the money Tessa earned. And tried not to regret that he hadn't spent the past decade traipsing around Europe with her, a life that sounded much more interesting than his own.

"Yet you never came to London before?" he asked, recalling Simon's impression that Foscari had deliberately avoided England.

"Domenico always refused offers from the theaters here. I suppose they weren't rich enough."

"What changed your mind, once you were widowed?" He had a moment's mad hope that she'd come to find him.

"Mr. Mortimer offered me a good contract."

"More than you could have made in Paris or Vienna? I find that hard to believe."

"I had another reason."

"Yes?" He leaned forward.

She delayed answering and the flicker of hope became a physical presence in his chest.

Finally she nodded, as though making a decision. "I want to find my father's family," she said.

He rocked back on his heels. "I see," he said. He looked around the familiar room a little wildly, composing his disappointed thoughts. "Don't you know where they are?"

Tessa seemed blissfully unaware of his discomfiture. "I don't even know *who* they are. My father never spoke of them. When I asked once, he told me his father had disowned him and the whole family remained estranged."

"Your father was a wine merchant, I believe."

"Yes, but only from necessity." She smiled wryly. "And not a successful one. His interests were scholarly and I know he attended Cambridge, but not much else."

"Then how do you propose to find your relations?'

"I have one possible line of inquiry."

"Tell me about it." He almost held his breath waiting for her response. It seemed terribly important she should confide in him.

She described the discovery of a letter, just a copy, from her husband, rebuffing the efforts of someone in Bristol to find her. Her narrative was delivered simply, without commentary on Domenico Foscari's denial of her identity. The omission spoke volumes. Neither did he refer to her husband, though a number of questions sprang to mind. Instead he listened, asking for occasional clarification and committing the details to memory.

"I have no idea," she concluded, and she sounded despondent, "how to trace Mr. Smith without an expensive investigation."

He wondered if she realized how revealing this statement was. Had he not good reason to believe her in financial difficulties, his obvious response would be to recommend the engagement of a Bow Street Runner. But he wouldn't embarrass her. She had suffered, he thought with slow-burning anger, far too much embarrassment at the hands of her husband.

"I am glad you told me about it," he said instead. "Let me think about it and I will let you know if a solution occurs to me."

She murmured her thanks and they stood in silence for some time while he relapsed into reflection, his thoughts straying from the subject of her lost family to the state of his own tangled emotions.

He was, he very much feared, still infatuated with Tessa, a state of mind that promised no possibility of a happy ending. So much time and so much history had intervened since they'd been innocent children. Marriage was out of the question. Even if he set aside what she had become, he couldn't ignore what he owed to his family and name to wed a notorious singer.

He could pursue her as a mistress. In a sense that's what he'd been doing ever since they parted: seeking her replacement from the ranks of opera singers. But would she have him? She claimed to have loved him once, and he believed her, but that was long ago. The girl he'd known and loved no longer existed, any more than he was still an eager boy. Although it hadn't been his fault, he'd killed her love when he left her.

She broke into his gloom. "I must go to Sempronio. It is time to warm up my voice for the recital, short though it may be."

"Of course. Let me escort you."

He raised his arm and prepared to return her to her accompanist, to the world where she belonged and where he couldn't join her. The room around him came back into focus and he became aware of its other inhabitants. Montelli was at the piano, playing a Mozart sonata with extraordinary lucidity and haunting emotion to an enraptured audience gathered around the instrument. Lady Clarissa and Simon Lindo were deep in conversation in another corner. Simon had done his job well. Yet he couldn't help a twinge of uneasiness. God only knew what his mother was up to, what information she was extracting from Simon, and what she planned to do with it.

A footman entered the room followed by another guest, one quite familiar to Max. Clad in the continental fashion, the man's close-fitting, high-cut trousers and skin-tight coat and *gilet* were designed to stress his height and muscular physique. Dark hair, expertly cut, framed well-chiseled features and set off gleaming blue eyes and very white teeth. From the corner of his eye Max saw his mother come forward to greet the newcomer but his concentration was on Tessa's expression. One of surprise, pleased or not he couldn't tell, then carefully assumed neutrality. Whatever she felt for this vision of masculine splendor it wasn't indifference.

"Monsieur Edouard Delorme," the footman announced.

CHAPTER THIRTEEN

"With little astonishment we learn that Madame Foscari's lack of generosity extends to the good English singers of the Tavistock company. Cruel disparagement and displays of temper are the lot of those forced to share the stage with Madame F."

The Morning Post

"MA CHÈRE THÉRÈSE!" Having greeted his hostess with a sweeping obeisance to the hand and a few lavish compliments in broken English, Edouard Delorme took Tessa by the shoulders and saluted her on each cheek. *"Quelle joie de te voir."*

Tessa suffered his touch, though she'd sooner embrace a scorpion. "Edouard," she murmured. "I didn't expect to see you here."

The tenor rattled on in rapid French. "You should have let me know where you are living in London. I would have called."

"My residence has, of course, been a big secret."

"You are upset with me, *chérie*. We have meant so much to each other. But now I shall call. Do not worry."

As though his absence would disturb her for a single second!

"Ne te dérange pas," she said, unclenching her teeth. "But we must speak English, Edouard. It is not polite to our fellow guests." She guessed that most of those observing the meeting were capable of following a conversation in French, but knowing the tenor's work habits she doubted he'd troubled to prepare for his London engagement by thoroughly studying the local language. Her superior knowledge gave her a much-needed advantage.

He flashed a smile at the gathered observers and seemed not a whit discomposed. "I do not speak the English so good. Not like you. *Mais je fais l'effort.*"

Lady Clarissa cut into the exchange. "You know each other, I see. Have you sung together?"

"Many times…" he began.

"We appeared together in Paris…"

"When I was *très jeune*. Thérèse was already the prima donna." He implied was that she by far his elder, and Tessa resented it. They were, in fact, the same age, but her career had blossomed earlier than Delorme's. She had been an established luminary when she'd noticed his talent in a small role and asked the Paris management to engage him to sing opposite her.

He took her gloved hand in his and gazed soulfully at her. "It 'as been too long, Thérèse, since we sing together. I 'ave missed you. *Quelle tragédie* that we sing now for different 'ouses." He leaned in and she smelled the mint lozenges he sucked to keep his breath sweet. "I am *désolé* to 'ear of your *difficultés* in London."

Like hell he was. An embryo of panic formed in her chest but she fought it. Even the thought of her breathing exercises was enough to arrest it stillborn. Buoyed by her success, she smiled tolerantly.

"I have been generally received in London with great éclat. This little contretemps will pass soon." Dear Lord, she hoped so. "Doubtless we will appear together again someday. Perhaps in Vienna or St. Petersburg."

Maybe China. If she had her choice it would be when they performed opera on the moon, and not a day sooner.

"Why not tonight?" Simon Lindo's voice broke in. "It would place the cap on our hostess's superb hospitality to have the two most admired singers in London appear together."

Lady Clarissa's eyes lit up. "A brilliant idea, Mr. Lindo! Madame Foscari, Monsieur Delorme, please honor us by performing a duet."

Like Lindo, veteran showman that he was, Tessa instantly

perceived the benefit to herself in an event that would cause so much fascinated comment. Could she get through an hour in Delorme's company?

"I think we presume too much." This came from Max. "It is hardly fair to Monsieur Delorme to sing unprepared."

Why was Max against the idea? Her suspicions of his motives resurfaced. Despite his handsome apology they were still rivals for the attention of the London audience. If Max was against it, she should say yes. She ought not to have a problem with Edouard as a *singing* partner. Well, not much.

She nodded graciously to Lady Clarissa. "I will be delighted to sing with Edouard. *If* he feels that his voice is ready."

"I am always ready." Delorme struck a pose, a hand to his well-developed chest.

Tessa watched as the room emptied. Lady Clarissa had Max's arm in a firm grip and appeared to be addressing him with some vigor. His departure left her a little forlorn. She had warmed to his company, even found herself confiding in him. Now he was returning to his own world, that of marriageable aristocratic virgins whom no breath of scandal had ever touched. And she must return to hers, that of the professional performer. She and Delorme had half an hour to prepare and Sempronio remained at the piano to assist them.

Tessa needed to take control of the situation immediately.

"We shall sing the duet from *Cosí fan tutte* since we've done it before."

Delorme nodded. She knew he'd be pleased, since the scene involved him seducing her.

"And beforehand, I shall sing 'Per pietá.'"

He pouted, also as expected. The beautiful and exceedingly difficult aria would overshadow his relatively simple task.

"This is my recital," she continued, before he could argue. "If you have any objection I shall sing alone, as originally planned. But if you wish, you may deliver a short address at the beginning.

Since we shall be singing in Italian and not everyone in the audience will be familiar with the opera, both scenes should be explained."

"You know my English is not good enough," he said sulkily.

"Oh dear! I shall have to do it myself if you don't feel equal to the task. But do not worry, Edouard. You will be on stage at the end."

Predictably he was satisfied. The man had the inflated self-esteem of…well, of a tenor.

MAX LOATHED EDOUARD Delorme. Before, he'd merely found the tenor's posturing and overweening vanity annoying. But when those disgustingly handsome features had slobbered over Tessa he'd discovered an unsuspected bent for violence.

"Don't think I didn't notice you with Madame Foscari," his mother said with a hiss, clasping his arm in a steely grip. "You promised."

"And I promised to be polite."

"You've been quite polite enough. You will come with me to find Lady Mary Greville and escort both of us to the ballroom for the recital."

He took a last reluctant look back at Tessa, who had joined Delorme and Montelli at the piano. The tenor had arranged himself in a graceful pose, designed, like everything else he did, to show off his figure. His mother would like that, Max thought dourly and half expected to find her ogling the Frenchman. Her attention was elsewhere.

"Tell me about Mr. Lindo. He's a most interesting man."

"You spoke with him for some time. What was the subject?"

"He told me the most fascinating things about the opera and theater business."

"I'd prefer it, Mama, if you would keep out of my affairs." God only knew what she'd managed to winkle out of Simon. He didn't trust her expression, which was one she wore when she had mischief in mind. And since he strongly suspected that mischief concerned him he was not amused.

"Whatever can you mean, darling? I merely spent an enjoyable quarter hour or so while you, I should mention, were entertaining *that woman.* Is Mr. Lindo married?"

"He's a widower, with two sons."

"Quite a good-looking man. I wonder he hasn't remarried."

Could his mother be looking around for a husband for Tessa, as insurance? Max didn't like the idea one little bit.

"By the way, I've decided I shall introduce Madame Foscari and Monsieur Delorme myself," she added. Now he was certain she was up to something.

Half an hour later Lady Clarissa stood between the two famous singers on a raised platform at one end of the ballroom. The trio was framed by a pair of Corinthian columns arising from marble palm trees, in keeping with a palm motif in the whole room, one of the mansion's most insane in Max's opinion. The vast room was packed and few of society's influential members were absent. If all went well, Tessa would regain her standing as an artist among the London cognoscenti and even enhance it.

If all went well and his mother didn't have a little surprise up her sleeve.

"My friends," Lady Clarissa began. "I promised you the pleasure of hearing a performance from one of the most admired operatic sopranos in Europe, Madame Teresa Foscari." She nodded graciously at Tessa who responded with a curtsey and a smile.

"But Madame Foscari is not the only great singer honoring us in London this season. Monsieur Edouard Delorme has been delighting us at the Regent Opera House." Delorme made an extravagant bow accompanied by a sweeping arm gesture. As though he were Sir Walter Raleigh at the court of Queen Elizabeth and not a guest in a private house in the year 1818.

"I have persuaded these two great singers to appear together in London for the first time—perhaps the only time—for the diversion of my guests."

An intrigued rustle passed through the crowd. Lady Clarissa had her own flair for drama and the audience well in hand.

"And," she raised her voice and paused until the whispered comments subsided. "And in honor of this notable occasion, and to show my appreciation to Madame Foscari for consenting to share the stage, I shall donate one thousand pounds to the Royal Hospital, Chelsea."

The room erupted into applause as Lady Clarissa stepped forward, nodding her head to the adoring multitude. A pity she was an aristocrat without a musical bone in her body. She'd have made a superb prima donna.

"That was brilliant, Mama, quite brilliant," Max whispered when she returned to his side, relinquishing the attention to Tessa.

"I know," she said modestly.

"Why did you do it?"

Lady Clarissa's eyes widened with a look of innocence completely foreign to her character. "For you, Max. Why else? You asked me to save Madame Foscari from the consequences of your indiscretion. I believe I have succeeded tolerably well."

Max couldn't argue with that.

"The audiences will flock back to the Tavistock Theatre whenever she appears."

How true. Now Max thought he guessed his mother's motivation. The renewed popularity of La Divina threatened the success of the Regent and his own independence. He couldn't but admire her while simultaneously wanting to strangle her. The fiend!

"Lady Mary." Lady Clarissa turned to the young woman at Max's side. "Are you fond of opera? If not, my son will explain it to you."

"Hush, Mama," Max hastily interpolated. "Madame Foscari is speaking."

"For those unfamiliar with the plot of Mozart's opera, *Cosí fan tutte*," Tessa was saying, projecting through the crowded ballroom so that every word could be heard without her appearing to raise her voice, "I do not propose to explain it in every dctail. Sufficc it to say that my character, Fiordiligi, is betrothed to a soldier who is away at war. In his absence she has been wooed by another man. The attraction is great and she fears for the fidelity of her heart. In the aria 'Per pietá' which I shall sing first, she prays for the strength to resist her seducer. Later she decides to run away, disguising herself as a soldier, and join her promised husband. But her other suitor—" She indicated Delorme who stood at her side with a smirk on his face. "—interrupts her flight and threatens to kill himself if she will not stay. It will be clear even to those who do not understand Italian whether he persuades her to yield."

While Delorme retreated behind the piano, Montelli played a few chords and La Divina's voice, pure and strong, began the stark prayer for resistance, then glided into the swoops that made the piece a vocal challenge. Every precise note, every articulated syllable, conveyed her anguish. *"My courage and constancy will sever my wicked desire,"* she sang.

Did she also resist when first tempted to betray her husband?

"I will forget these thoughts that fill me with shame and horror."

Shame and horror? Were those her feelings about her many infidelities?

Montelli's playing brilliantly evoked the horns of the full orchestral accompaniment, a device Mozart used to comment on faithlessness—the cuckold's horns.

The conclusion to the aria found Tessa—no, Fiordiligi—strong, determined and rewarded with a storm of applause. A decent shower of floral tributes made their way onto the platform, torn from gentlemen's buttonholes or their ladies' corsages. La Foscari was back in the esteem of London's most influential audience.

But the clamor subsided in obedience to the soprano's gesture for silence. The gathered *ton* was eager for novelty, the pairing of Foscari and Delorme.

She began the duet the picture of determination. That didn't last. As soon as Delorme stepped forward her resistance crumbled. "*With these looks and words I begin to weaken.*" Her looks and words expressed an overwhelming yearning.

"*She begins to weaken,*" sang Delorme.

Although he knew the outcome, Max found himself urging her on. *Don't believe him*, he thought, as the tenor, his voice like creamy honey, mimed the drawing of his sword and bade her stab him. *Don't believe him.* Delorme's gaze was hot enough to melt the stoniest female heart.

"*Surrender, beloved.*"

"*Gods, help me!*"

"*Delay no more, my adored one!*"

He's using you. Run! And though in his head Max spoke to the character of Fiordiligi, on some deeper level he addressed Tessa herself.

The soprano and tenor voices, surely the most beautiful sounds in the world, entwined in both harmony and opposition until…

"*You have won, cruel man. Do with me what you will.*"

Tessa crumpled into Delorme's arms and the music was all harmony, an expression of love and urgent passion. The duet reached its triumphant climax, the piano accompaniment faded away and Delorme, instead of releasing his leading lady to take his bow, tightened his embrace and kissed her on the lips, fully, ardently, and at length.

Max wanted to rush forward and rip her out of Delorme's arms. Instead he made himself a promise. If she could kiss that preening snake then she could damn well kiss him too!

"YOUR GOWN IS torn. Would you like to slip away and repair it?"

Max's whisper tickled her ear from behind. Given the jostling of enthusiastic guests offering her compliments Tessa was unsurprised to look down and find a piece of the gold lace on her bodice hanging loose from her left shoulder.

She was worn out. Exhausted from two hours of smiling and chatting until her teeth ached. Two hours of ignoring the too-frequent presence of Edouard Delorme who kept suggesting she slip away with *him*, for purposes only too obvious. Two hours of somehow knowing, despite the throng, exactly where Max was and with whom. And that whom was always a woman—a young, comely, and no doubt eligible woman. Going apart with him was probably a stupid idea, but she needed to escape.

With relief she sank into the cushions of a comfortable sofa in a room that was, by the standards of the Piccadilly mansion, small. The arrangement of quite ordinary furniture was graced with evidence of a cheerful untidiness: a mahogany sewing table had a couple of pieces of cloth and several ribbons protruding from the lid; the corner escritoire was scattered with letters; next to the fire a ragged basket appeared to be the sleeping quarters of an absent, and sharp-toothed, dog. A room that was lived in but not, Tessa guessed, by her formidable hostess.

"This is my cousin Sarah's sitting room," Max said. "She lives with my mother but she won't mind us using it. No one will look for us here."

Tessa raised her eyebrows.

"I thought you'd like to be alone for a while. Can I find you some refreshment? Knowing Sarah, she has a bottle of Madeira tucked away somewhere. Or I could ring for tea." This last suggestion was spoken with very little enthusiasm.

"Nothing, thank you. But I would like to sit for a few minutes."

"Put your feet up." He reached for a footstool and positioned it in front of her. Gratefully she raised her feet and relaxed, enjoying the sensation of being cared for. Not that Sofie and

Angela didn't pamper her, but it was, after all, their job to do so. Domenico's concern for her comfort had been strictly the protection of a valuable investment. She might as well have been a gold bar in need of regular polishing.

"Are you tired from your performance?" he asked, taking the seat next to her. When he'd said she wanted to be alone, he apparently meant alone with him.

"Hardly," she replied, staring at her golden slippers and trying to ignore the fact that eighteen inches of air separated her bare arm from his dark evening coat. "Not as I would be after a full opera. But making conversation is weary work. I don't enjoy it, at least not in large crowds. In fact I don't much enjoy assemblies of any kind."

"Your reputation says otherwise."

"My reputation says many things," she replied.

"I hope now it has been restored, at least as far the guests in this house are concerned. The newspapers and the rest of the public should follow."

She managed a wan smile. "Thank you. Perhaps now the other stories will cease too. I should do something about this lace."

"You can use Cousin Sarah's sewing things."

"Unless I remove the dress," she said with a reproving look at his interested expression, "I can't do it myself. Perhaps you should find Cousin Sarah."

"Cousin Sarah is much too busy running around doing whatever a lady's companion does when a lady is giving an entertainment. I couldn't possibly tear her away from her duties."

"Someone else then. A housekeeper? Your mother's dresser?"

"I could help you." He edged a little closer.

She looked at him askance.

"I can sew," he assured her.

"What an unusual accomplishment for a gentleman."

"My nurse taught me. I was a careless little boy and tore my clothes a lot. She used to complain about the piles of mending and one day I offered to help. In this instance I'm glad I had no brothers to laugh at me, nor sisters either."

"Didn't your parents object?" she asked, intrigued by this peep-show view into Max's childhood.

"I don't imagine they ever knew. My father had nothing to say in my upbringing." His relaxed features stiffened for an instant. "As for my mother, what she might or might not approve of remains unpredictable to this day."

"And are you a skilled seamstress?"

"I believe I can manage to stitch up that lace as a temporary measure. If you don't find my skills adequate you can get your maid to do it again later."

"Very well. I place myself—or rather my lace—in your hands."

"Let's see if we can find a needle, and thread of the right color."

He rummaged through Cousin Sarah's workbox, examining and discarding several spools and a rat's nest of embroidery silks. "What about this?"

"Close enough."

Max reclaimed his seat next to her, uncoiled and snapped off a length of dull yellow silk with an air of competence, then licked the end. Holding a needle at about half an arm's length, he aimed the thread at the eye with exaggerated concentration. The awkward way he attempted to jab the strand through the tiny slit dispelled any illusion of proficiency. The intent eagerness on his harsh features made her see not the grown man but a small boy, determined to succeed in an unfamiliar task.

"Uh, Max," she said, suppressing a grin without much success. "When did you last sew anything?"

"I think I was about seven," he replied, "but I'm sure it's not something you forget. There!" He held up the threaded needle with a triumphant flourish.

"You seriously expect me to let you come near me with that?"

"It's hardly a lethal weapon."

"Easy for you to say."

"I won't prick you." His voice and the atmosphere grew thick.

"Do your worst then," she murmured.

He surveyed the damage with an eye that held a glint of something not commonly seen in the assessing look of a modiste or ladies' maid. A wide expanse of bare skin offered itself to his examination and she was nervously aware that the tiny bodice of the dress barely covered her nipples.

He stood up. "I think I should sit on the other side."

"But the tear is on this side." The protest came out in an unmelodious squeak.

"You'll see."

She was rather afraid she would. And that he would. See too much.

He reseated himself on her left and, since there wasn't much room on that side, his thigh, rock hard yet palpably alive, jammed against hers. Heat emanated from him like the Italian midday sun and a flush infused her from her scalp down to the tips of her gold-enclosed toes. Bending his long torso across her, he inserted his left hand into the edge of the bodice where the lace was damaged. Trying to escape the arm that rested across her chest, she shifted around and leaned back into the cushions, giving him better access.

"Good," he said, and lowered his head. His face was inches from her bosom and sultry breath warmed her skin. "Now keep still or I *will* prick you."

An earthquake couldn't have budged her. Exposed and embarrassed, half reclining on a sofa completely at his mercy, she closed her eyes and reveled in her prostration. The soft cloth of his sleeve, closely fitted so she could feel the quivering muscles within, caressed her. She imagined Max's bare skin against her own and ventured to peek at his face. The hard planes were set in concentration as he applied himself to the task of placing the rent lace against the satin. Yet she caught his gaze flickering downwards to the breasts pushed up by her specially constructed singer's corset. When their eyes connected she hastily lowered hers. To his mouth. Had she ever noticed how beautiful his lips were? Not full, but well-shaped, they softened his harsh features with creases along the cheeks when they broadened into a smile or, as now, into a grimace of concentration. For some reason her nipples hardened. No, she knew the reason.

Having arranged the tear to his satisfaction Max held it in place with his left thumb while the back of his hand lay flat on her shoulder under the gown. Tessa's whole world narrowed to that spot. She fought to breathe.

Carefully he inserted the needle through the fragile lace and the heavy satin beneath, drew it through and extended his arm. The look on his face turned comical when the thread followed all the way and swung useless and free.

"You're supposed to tie a knot at the end," she whispered.

"I forgot that bit." He frowned. "We'll have to start again."

"We?" Her nervous tension had slipped away like the thread, leaving her relaxed, amused.

"I will have to start again. Don't move."

She had no intention of moving when she was enjoying herself so much. Watching him make heavy weather of his simple task, that internal warmth blossomed into tenderness. He looked so young, so much like the old Max.

When the strand was knotted to his satisfaction, he repeated his arrangement of the gown. Tessa watched his long fingers, more adroit this time, and drifted into a state she scarcely identified. Happiness, perhaps. A clock ticked but otherwise there wasn't a sound in the room except Max's breath. His dark hair brushed her cheek and prickles of excitement arose at his slightest touch on her skin. A tremor emanated from somewhere inside her, centered on the left side of her chest.

The knot held. With infinite care and without a single prick he affixed the lace back to the satin with long inexpert stitches that made her ache with tenderness.

Too soon he straightened to survey his handiwork. "What do you think?" he asked, raising a smile at the eager pride in his voice.

"The Parisian dressmaker who made the gown couldn't have done better," she said with a hitch in her voice, and meant it. She rather thought the dress she'd earlier donned with such revulsion might become her favorite.

"Now how do I detach the thread?" he mused.

Before she could suggest scissors he bobbed his head close to the shoulder, bit through the silk filament and tossed the needle aside. His lips had to move less than an inch to find the sensitive skin over her collarbone where they lingered a long moment before progressing up her neck. It was a smooth move, and the thought glimmered that he'd been planning it. She really didn't care. She heard a little moan of pleasure—hers? his?—as he nipped her lobe then sent warm breath into the hollow of her ear, followed by a gently probing tongue.

"Oh God, Tessa!" he whispered, drawing her close. "You're so beautiful."

Then he kissed her. Gently at first he nibbled her lips, then harder. Her mouth opened to his on a sigh and he ravished the sensitive flesh with his tongue. Heat spread through her body, unfurled by his kiss. And she responded, pulling him closer with both hands. As a quiet, barely attended corner of her mind acknowledged, this was what she'd craved since the footman had interrupted them in the spare bedchamber of his house.

She made no protest when a hand found her breast, rather strained to meet it, urgently presenting herself to his caress. His fingers penetrated beneath satin and the silk-covered buckram of her stays to find a nipple that crested to a harder peak at his touch. Never breaking their kiss, he tugged at her clothing. While the miniscule bodice of the gown yielded without argument, the corset was made of sterner stuff and a growl of frustration expressed his failure. His body pressed hers back until she lay semi-reclined, half swooning when the heat of his mouth moved to the tender cleft of her breasts. Fine hair tickled her chin and his scent filled her nostrils while a yearning ache centered itself deep in her *fica*. Then he pulled at her skirts, struggling to gain a purchase on the stiff satin. The air of the room cooled an ankle, then a silk-clad calf, and his hand reached her knee and the bare skin above her garter.

"Max!"

He grunted incoherently and continued the upward progress of his hand. Faint alarm clashed with desire.

"Max, we should stop," she whispered.

He raised his head. "Don't make me stop. Please." Brown eyes glowed with a passion she feared and a tenderness she wanted more than anything in the world.

Could she do this? Could she give in to the importunities of Max's desire and her own longing without disaster? Should she? Conflicting urges shook her as she met his hot, pleading gaze.

"Tessa?"

She couldn't speak and could answer only with the movement of her head. A shake or a nod? Denial or surrender? Retreat to safety or a step forward into an unknown future that could offer happiness, or agonies worse than any she'd yet suffered.

"Ahem." Someone had entered the room.

"Damnation," Max muttered, struggling to his feet and standing in front of her to shield her from the newcomer. "Bedeviled by footmen."

"My lord. Her ladyship sent me to find you and request your immediate presence in the drawing room." The liveried servant showed commendable lack of emotion or curiosity and bowed his way out of the room.

"Next time, my love," Max said as he helped Tessa adjust her gown—thank God for that intractable corset or things might have been far more embarrassing. "Next time I kiss you I'm going to make damn sure there isn't a footman within half a mile."

CHAPTER FOURTEEN

"Mrs. STURRIDGE respectfully informs the Nobility, Gentry, Subscribers of the Tavistock Theatre and the public that her Benefit is fixed for this Tuesday when will be performed Le Nozze di Figaro with Mrs. Sturridge in the role of Countess Almaviva. Madame Foscari will appear at the entr'acte to sing THE SOLDIER TIR'D."

Advertisement

AN URGENT MATTER at his estate called Max out of town and he told himself it was a good thing. He needed to put some distance between himself and Tessa. A few days at Tamworth reminded him how much he loved the place: the rolling Staffordshire acres, the mellow brick of the Tudor mansion and its multistyled accretions, appended over the decades as the Earls of Tamworth augmented their wealth and consequence. Despite its grandeur the house still remained a manor house at its core and there was no place in the world Max felt more comfortable than in his boyhood home.

As he rode and inspected the fertile farmland, he almost convinced himself that there was nothing between him and Tessa but healthy lust and a wistful regret for the past. Once he'd dreamed of bringing her here, of living with her and their children in this enchanted place. Now he couldn't imagine it. Tessa had grown into a different person. She was a creature of cities, a glorious empress of silks and jewels, ballrooms and theaters, a queen of the night. The idea of her sharing his rural peregrinations, plain cloth riding habit splashed with mud and hair disordered by the wind, was absurd. He didn't even know if she could ride.

At times like this a suitable match arranged by Lady Clarissa didn't seem so bad. Until recollection of an interrupted embrace left him aching and eager to summon his carriage and return to London as fast as a coach-and-six could make it.

Could he persuade Tessa to be his mistress? Why not? He was at least as rich as most of her lovers. Not quite up to emperor standards, but he could outspend the average duke. Of any country.

He didn't want to be that kind of lover. He only wanted Tessa if she wanted him back. For himself, not for money. She claimed to have forgiven him. She'd let him kiss and caress her. They'd have made love on Cousin Sarah's sofa if that footman hadn't been sent by his damned interfering mother.

Tessa *did* want him, surely. He hadn't forced himself on her and she had returned his kisses. Hadn't she?

The truth was, he wasn't certain. She hadn't rejected them. She hadn't struggled in his arms or pushed away his fevered caresses. But neither had she been an active participant. Some women weren't of course. He'd had bedmates who preferred to lie still and let him do all the work. Not the most satisfactory arrangement, and he couldn't believe a woman as warm and passionate as Teresa Foscari would be that kind of mistress. She had kissed him back and they'd hardly got started on other things.

And yet.

Just before the interruption she'd asked him to stop. It hadn't seemed like the "I don't want to do this" kind of objection. *We should stop*. Those were her words. They could have meant anything from "we're at an assembly in your mother's house and this isn't the time and place" (a fair argument) to "the state of our relations has not yet reached the bedding stage." He'd been trying to persuade her to continue—with every confidence of success—when the footman arrived. But he could be wrong.

His horse snorted, demanding his attention. The compulsion

to storm the Pulteney Hotel and sweep her into his arms subsided, leaving him unsure and frustrated.

On his return to the house he found a letter from Simon Lindo informing him that while the receipts at the Regent continued respectable, there was a distinct leakage of audience back to the Tavistock, especially among the members of the *ton*. Max read the notice of Nancy Sturridge's benefit and learned that Tessa was to sing in it. If Sturridge, as shrewd a woman as he'd ever met, thought it advantageous to advertise Foscari's participation in her evening, then La Divina's popularity was on the rise again. His debt to her was paid. They were back to where they'd been a month ago, their interests in direct opposition.

Except everything had changed. He no longer resented the past or wished her ill. He'd be perfectly content if both Teresa Foscari and the Regent Opera House could prosper. More that that, he wanted success for her. She deserved every plaudit because she was a great artist and a woman of character.

Damn it, why was he trying to fool himself? He wanted Tessa but he wasn't sure he could or should have her.

TESSA SNATCHED THE card that accompanied the white roses. Were they from Max? Had he remembered the very first flowers he'd ever given her?

It was just a card. "The Viscount Allerton" engraved in copperplate on a rectangle of pasteboard. Eagerly she turned it over. "Best wishes" in a plain, upright hand. That was all. Not even a signature. With slumped shoulders she gave it a last look, as though those two words might transform into something warmer, more substantial.

That was it then. A few kisses, a threat—or promise—of a repetition then nothing for days. Seven days to be precise. How shaming to have counted.

The gossip around the theater was all about the conclusion of

Nancy Sturridge's long negotiation with Somerville. With the marquess no longer in competition, Tessa's appeal to Max must have diminished. It was nothing but a game to him and, without an opponent, no longer worth the playing.

But he had been interested. Tessa hadn't been so long without masculine company that she couldn't recognize arousal when she felt it. She rather feared things would have reached an unstoppable conclusion if the footman hadn't interrupted them. She wouldn't have long resisted Max; at least she didn't think so. She'd been enjoying herself as much as she had with Domenico, in the days when she'd thought she loved him. Before the incident. A tiny seed of hope that she might once again be capable of love kindled and was resolutely extinguished.

"Angela," she called, tossing the card aside along with such futile reflections. "Do you have the jewels?"

One thing hadn't changed. Tessa had no desire to be a mistress, a kept woman, Max's or anyone else's. Never again would she place herself and her future under the control of another. Now that she had another chance to repair her fortune, she'd make certain she did not squander the takings.

"I can't believe you're wearing the Tsar's diamonds for that *Weibsstück*." That Sofie, recovered from her cold, had used a somewhat impolite term for Nancy Sturridge bespoke the force of her indignation. "Watch out for her. Instead of being grateful to you for singing at her benefit she'll do her best to undermine you."

"And how, precisely?" asked Tessa with exasperated affection. "It's not as though we shall be on stage together."

"No. She's out there now singing your role," Sofie said with a sniff.

"She's always wanted to sing the Countess and I suppose it's her right at her own benefit."

"She's not doing herself any favors," Sempronio broke in. "We've just come from the front of the house and her performance suffers by comparison with yours."

Tessa tried to not to feel satisfaction. Usually happy to lend her services for the benefit of her fellow artists, helping Nancy Sturridge stuck in her gorge. Her fellow singer—she disdained to call her a rival—had been all too obvious in her delight at Tessa's troubles. But not to have appeared on this occasion would have informed the world that La Divina refused to support the other soprano and confirmed every lie about Tessa's prima donna histrionics. Nancy, equally aware of her power, had exercised it with glee, relegating her adversary to the minor, albeit prominent, role of entr'acte performer.

Tessa had no choice but to agree for another reason. She couldn't risk the Tavistock company refusing to perform at her own benefit, scheduled for two weeks hence. Artists performed without pay at benefits and all the receipts went to the honoree. Mortimer had to pay her the proceeds of the benefit immediately, and she was counting on it. Lady Clarissa's handsome fee would just about keep her solvent until then.

Angela fastened the necklace around Tessa's neck and arranged the tiara in her curls. The bracelets went over her gloves and the double-headed eagle brooch was pinned to her red velvet bodice. On stage not even a jeweler would be able to spot that they were fakes. Tessa surveyed herself in the dusty mirror and knew she looked magnificent. A major role or a single aria, it didn't matter. La Divina's ten minutes on stage would be noticed.

SOMERVILLE GREETED MAX in the entrance lobby of the Tavistock Theatre with his usual mocking smile. "Still in pursuit of La Foscari?"

"I'm here because I want to see what Miss Sturridge makes of the Countess's role."

"Really, Max? You're a poor liar. Did you know that I installed Nancy in a very comfortable house this week?"

Max hadn't heard and didn't care. About Sturridge.

"Congratulations. Why did you give up on La Divina?" His curiosity on this subject wasn't to be repressed.

"I decided the pursuit would be too fatiguing," Somerville said.

"You aren't usually so easily deterred."

The marquess shrugged. "In this case I deduced that the lady wasn't to be had—"

"Indeed?" That Tessa had rebuffed the incorrigible marquess gave Max intense pleasure.

"Wasn't to be had," Somerville continued, "by me or likely by anyone else. There was perhaps a moment when I thought otherwise, but I soon saw that this soprano reserves her passions for the stage. It's a wonder she has such a reputation as an *horizontale*. Perhaps our continental brethren prefer their women cold."

"Are you sure?" Every instinct told him Somerville was wrong, despite his own doubts about Tessa's response to him.

"Quite sure. You see, Max, I understand women. It's the secret of my success."

"I thought it was good looks, charm, and deep pockets."

"Many men have those. Yourself, for example." Somerville stroked the tip of his nose thoughtfully. "Indeed, you are much richer than me. But more often than not I win the woman. Think about it."

As far as Max was concerned, it meant he had a chance with Tessa. According to every report, Somerville was the kind of man upon whom she'd bestowed her favors in the past. Yet she had repulsed a worldly and generous lover whom she could have had by raising a finger.

But she hadn't repulsed Max.

He wondered if she remembered the significance of the white roses he had sent her this evening.

MAX ENJOYED HIS view from the center of the pit, toward the front, despite the discomfort of his perch on a cushionless bench. Since box holders had to pay for benefit tickets, just like less favored patrons, he'd decided to let his box go for the evening and purchase a single ticket where he could see better. Pity the performance wasn't better. The absence of Foscari displayed the Tavistock company in all its mediocrity and couldn't help but please the co-owner of its rival house. Sturridge sang well but she'd have been wiser to stick with the role of Susanna.

The house was full, partly because Nancy Sturridge was a popular singer, but also because the audience was curious to see La Divina in an unaccustomed role. As the second act drew to a close there was a distinct restlessness among the patrons, a sense of anticipation. How intriguing it was to be in the belly of the beast, to feel the emotions of the crowd packed into the floor of the old house. What he couldn't sense was whether the beast was friendly. He suspected the audience wasn't sure itself. The individual members were waiting for the consensus reaction to decide whether the foreign prima donna would be accepted back and granted her former adulation.

The denizens of the beau monde in their boxes, softened by Lady Clarissa's imprimatur, would receive Tessa politely. The pit, open to anyone who could afford a five-shilling ticket—or cajole or bribe a check taker into a free pass—was a different matter. It was hard to predict the reaction of a miscellany of merchants, professional men, ladies of the night, and gentlemen unencumbered by their female counterparts.

Tessa had taken a risk in her choice of music. "The Soldier Tir'd of War's Alarms" was perhaps the most famous single piece of English operatic music, a bravura aria from Dr. Arne's *Artaxerxes*. Though the opera itself was less popular than it had been in the last century, the aria was often performed alone, most notably by Mrs. Billington who lived in the affectionate memory of London's theater-goers as the most beloved and most English of sopranos. Max felt a twinge of alarm at Tessa's audacity. The crowd might accept it as a compliment. But if they saw it as a foreign insult to a national heroine, her reception would be terrible.

Once the curtain fell, the usual exodus in search of relief and refreshments failed to materialize. For once no one wanted to miss the entr'acte performance.

Nerves taut, Max strained his ears for comments from his immediate neighbors and caught disjointed words and whispered phrases. Foreign. Chelsea Hospital. Tsar's jewels. Bonaparte. Better than Catalani. Sturridge is the English soprano. Foreign. Insult. Foreign.

His immediate neighbors—a citizen of respectable appearance and his wife—sat in companionable silence. A couple of rows forward an obvious demimondaine was intent on flirtation with a stout middle-aged worthy whom Max guessed might be a banker. Not far away, he glimpsed a pair of bucks, aspirants to dandyhood rather than arrivals at that blessed state, judging by a pair of loud waistcoats in clashing stripes and overblown neckcloths. The young men did little to disguise their hilarity, likely fueled by an abundance of wine at dinner, or their possession of a knobbly parcel. It wasn't unheard of for solid citizens to being their own refreshments to help them survive a long evening of entertainment, but these two didn't seem the type. Max vowed to keep half an eye on them and if they had anything to throw he swore he'd jam it down their throats till they choked on their own Adam's apples.

An expectant hush fell as the curtain opened again, revealing a painted flat of vaguely classical design, depicting some pastoral ruins. Then Teresa Foscari, resplendent in red velvet and gemstones, glided to the center of the stage.

Not a cough or rustle disturbed the silence of the vast auditorium. Every eye was fixed on the most glorious sight to ever grace a London theater. In the glow of the footlights she stood proud and tall, gazing haughtily at her observers as though daring them to do their worst. Then, as the orchestra broke into the introductory measures, she swept them a curtsey and bestowed upon them a dazzling smile.

It occurred to Max that La Divina on the stage was very different from Tessa off it. Her personality in the drawing room was unaffected and even reserved—always excepting that one glass-throwing incident, which Max acknowledged to have been provoked. In artistic matters she was consistently bold. Now she held some three thousand souls in her grasp as she embarked on the well-loved air. Almost every individual in the place knew it, but Max defied the memory of the oldest music lover to have heard it sung better. As she ran with ludicrous ease through the virtuoso trills of the first finale, Max knew it was going to be all right and relaxed into pure enjoyment. Even the Tavistock orchestra seemed to rise to the occasion, with a splendid trumpet voluntary signaling the soprano's final ascent to unimaginable vocal heights. Max was ready to burst into applause. Surely everyone would feel the same way.

Then she stopped in mid-trill and was shaken by a paroxysm of coughing.

Max half-leapt from his seat.

A thin but steady cloud of smoke emerged from under the painted flat, and the theater erupted into panic.

THE SMOKE HIT Tessa's lungs with her intake of breath for the soaring culmination of Arne's masterpiece.

My God, I am going to die, was her first thought as searing pain filled her chest. Even as she coughed in desperation she realized what was happening. She'd been present in the wings when a theater in Prague caught fire and she had never suffered such terror. Pivoting on her heels, her first instinct was to flee off stage, but smoke now curled under the backdrop in several places. For all she knew the entire back of the theater was in flames.

Oh my God! Sofie, Angela, and Sempronio were all there, but to reach them she would have to thread her way through the scenery stored in the backstage area. She recalled the cries of agony of a Bohemian stagehand who'd been struck by a blazing beam falling from the flies. It was too dangerous to go that way and she could only pray that those in the dressing rooms got out safely.

Screams and shouts from the front of the theater penetrated her consciousness. Since the old Tavistock didn't run to modern gas lighting, the auditorium was brightly illuminated by oil lamps and candles.

Panicked patrons shoved their way to the exits. In Prague over one hundred people had died, as many of them trampled during their escape as had been caught by the flames and smoke. But that had been a small house. There were almost three thousand people out there in the galleries, boxes, and pit of the Tavistock.

Including Max. For a moment she looked frantically into the milling crowd until a fragment of sense told her there was nothing she could do to help him. Unless…

Retaining just enough wit not to take a deep breath, she edged to the very front of the stage, standing between two oil-fueled footlights. Should she extinguish them? No, she decided, a desperate plan forming in her frightened brain. It would be better if people could see her. Just below her feet, members of the orchestra fought for the exit, some through the under-stage door, others abandoning their instruments and scrambling over the barrier into the auditorium to join the teeming crowd. Countless men and women were on the move, shoving along the rows to the aisles or leaping over the benches, but with the same end: to reach the door in the center back of the pit. A door that looked very small and very far away. Unless the retreat was made in some kind of order, hundreds would be injured and trapped.

Taking a quick, shallow breath she found that the air downstage was still clean and inhaled deeper. *Not too high*, she thought. *It might be mistaken for a scream.* With as much concentration as she'd ever brought to a single note, she pitched an octave above middle C.

"Sto-o-o-o-op!"

To her surprise the terrified cries subsided and a thousand eyes turned back to the stage.

"My lords, ladies, and gentlemen," she said, summoning her training to project her voice as though she were singing. "Please be calm. Let me guide you to safety."

While far from silent, a good portion of the crowd gave her its attention. But she sensed the backward surge had only abated and would continue in force at the least provocation. Somehow she needed to control the crowd.

"The fire has not yet reached the front of the theater," she went on, enunciating slowly and trying to ignore the smoke behind her. "Those at the back should leave first, everyone else stand still. There is ample time for all of you to find the way out."

Holy Saint George, she hoped that was true. She had no idea of the state of things behind the backdrop, of how far the fire had spread. If it took hold and reached the cellar area below the pit, how much time was there before it broke through the floor of the auditorium? Pray God her friends managed to escape.

She continued to speak calmly, repeating the call for order. A number of men appeared to be taking charge of the evacuation of the pit. Those at the rear had already exited and the crowd moved slowly, disturbed only by the occasional panicked scuffle. Heart in her mouth, she scanned the tiers of boxes, trying to recall exactly which one was Max's. She could find no sign of him but was encouraged by what appeared to be an orderly migration from those levels. At least the broad corridors outside the boxes were manned by members of the theater staff to assist the departing *ton*. As for the galleries, she sensed movement and noise above her and could only hope her calls for calm were having their effect.

Her own mind settled into eerie tranquility. "Be quiet, walk slowly, wait for those in front of you," she said over and over again.

While keeping up her soothing litany, she considered her own escape. Directly in front of her the descent to the orchestra was about three feet and there was a further decline to the audience level. She'd be hampered by the heavy skirts and long train of her velvet gown and there was the danger of injuring herself among the instruments. She could imagine spearing herself on the floor spike of a cello. At either end of the stage the floor was clear of orchestral accoutrements but the drop was deeper. In some theaters there would be stairs but they had been removed at the Tavistock to prevent patrons invading the stage. Quickly she decided she'd take that path, but not until the way ahead was almost clear of people, or until the fire reached her.

Smoke now billowed onto the stage and caught her throat. She tried to cover her mouth and still speak loud enough to be heard. If she got out alive would her vocal cords survive?

AT THE FIRST puff of smoke, Max's only instinct was to charge forward and grab Tessa. But a dozen rows of panicked citizenry surged in the opposite direction, cutting him off from the red-clad figure alone on the stage. He shouted her name and raised his arms helplessly as she approached the edge of the orchestra.

A single word on a single note from that matchless voice pierced the shrieks of terror surrounding him and he realized what Tessa was trying to do. What incredible courage! And what could he do to assist her? His own seat was close to the center aisle and once he reached it he stood firm, blocking the way of those who would push their way along the already clogged corridor.

"Stay back," he shouted. "Let others go first."

His erstwhile neighbor, an arm around his hysterical wife, tried to press through.

"You'll be crushed if you go forward now," Max warned.

The man nodded. "I'll help you with the crowd," he said, "but let my wife go ahead." He whispered something to the woman who gulped back her tears and quietly joined the queue in the aisle.

"Let the ladies through," Max commanded. One of the drunken bucks jumped onto his bench and started to bound from row to row, knocking several others back onto their seats and scattering rotten fruit in his wake. As soon as he was within reach Max snatched the fellow by his neckcloth and thrust him down.

"Let others go first, especially the ladies," he ordered.

"Ladies!" The man sneered at a couple of members of the world's oldest profession coming up behind.

In Max's opinion the whores were showing a great deal more refinement than this young idiot. "You can behave like a man," he said firmly. "But if you'd rather not I'll be happy to put you under until it's your turn to leave."

The sight of Max's brandished fist sobered the youth and he took his place quietly in the aisle, even standing aside to let the prostitutes pass.

His area of the house now reduced to order, Max scanned the rest of the place. Several others were organizing their own corners and above he could see most of the boxes empty. Then, on the opposite side of the house, a figure swung down from a second tier box, landed gracefully on his feet and offered a hand to a woman who'd stumbled and fallen in the side aisle.

Somerville. Max had to give the marquess credit for courage. It would have been easy for him to make his exit via the broad corridors and staircases of the upper level.

And all this time, Max had no idea how long, Tessa stood on the stage, keeping up a stream of soothing directives. "Not long now," she assured the crowd. "More than half the pit is empty. The fire remains backstage. You have time."

But did they? Max knew a good deal about theatrical fire hazards. The Regent was designed with every modern safety precaution, but the Tavistock was old. He could almost imagine he felt the heat under the floor and flames bursting through at any moment. And every time he looked back at Tessa, terror clutched his chest. More and more smoke billowed under the scenery. She didn't have much longer until the fire reached her.

Glimpsing a passage to the stage over the seats, mostly empty now, he leaped up, bounding from bench to bench towards the stage where Tessa stood, an incongruous vision in red and diamonds, lit by a pair of footlights amid growing darkness. Her beautiful voice continued to roll out words of calm and encouragement into the emptying chamber.

Then the golden tones faded into a fit of coughing as the backdrop burst into flames.

TESSA DOUBLED OVER, hands pressed to her mouth, and found a swirling haze of black smoke masking her feet. A blast of heat struck her back and terror seized her, her escape plan vaporized from her mind.

I'm going to die, she thought. *I'm going to burn like Joan of Arc.* A sob racked her grated throat. Stiff as a gouty old man, she straightened her back and looked upward. The flies were on fire. A burning beam swung loose from its ropes and descended, slow as the stateliest largo.

Paralyzed, unable to move an inch, she didn't want to see the instrument of her demise. Saying a silent last prayer, she peered into the auditorium. If only everyone had escaped … Then a figure appeared through the smoke, a dark angel come to take her to death.

A FIERY BEAM was falling right over Tessa as Max crashed through the instruments of the orchestra.

"Jump, Tessa!" he cried. But she didn't hear, or move.

Kicking aside everything in his path, he stepped onto the tight vellum membrane of a timpanum and seized her around the legs. She slumped over his shoulder and he staggered backward until he lost his balance, landing with a mouthful of velvet and his back against something sharp.

An incoherent croak emerged from her throat and somehow she managed to get her arms about his neck.

The stage had turned into an inferno as burning beams and rolled backcloths rained from the flies. The main curtains and the old wooden proscenium arch were fully engaged by flames.

"Come, we need to move," he urged, trying to loosen Tessa's death grip. "Come on, love, it's time to go."

Terrified beyond reason or movement, she refused to be dislodged, clinging and moaning through bouts of coughing. Murmuring words of reassurance, he pushed away her weight, struggled to his feet and helped her up.

"Up you go," he coaxed, lifting her over the low orchestra wall and scooping up the train of her gown as he followed. "Can you run?" He snatched her hand, dragged her to the aisle and back towards the exit. If any lights remained, they did nothing to pierce the black smoke that filled the chamber. He ran blind, on instinct alone, knowing only that he had to keep hold of Tessa or lose her in the impenetrable darkness. His lungs burned but he dared not stop. He closed his mouth tight and clenched his nostrils against the invading fumes. Time enough to breathe when they reached clear air.

Her hand slipped from his grasp and he sensed her fall. Heedless of her weight, he hefted her onto his shoulder and staggered on. Mercifully he found the single door out of the auditorium and burst into the lobby.

Still clutching Tessa, he fell to his knees and sucked in welcome gulps of air.

"Is she alive?" Somerville pulled Tessa's limp body off his back.

Max labored to stand up and pulled her back into his own arms.

"Tessa," he croaked. "Tessa. Wake up, love, wake up." He feared his heart would stop.

Her head lolled on his shoulder but she opened her eyes, glazed with fear, and managed a nod. Max had never felt such exquisite relief in his life.

"Did everyone get out?" he asked.

"Yes, thanks to her," replied the marquess. "Without her the theater would never have been safely cleared. We're the last. I came back to find you. Now let's go."

Frightened people thronged the street. Several fire engines had arrived on the scene, but none of the water pumps were yet working and there seemed to be an argument going on among the firemen.

"Why aren't they doing anything?" Max asked.

Somerville looked grim. "It seems the theater management failed to make payments to the fire insurance company. They are only agreeing to work at the insistence of owners of the neighboring buildings."

A loud bang drowned his words and a column of fire erupted from the roof of the theater, reaching high into the sky and lighting the street as though it were noon.

"I don't think it matters," Max said. "Nothing can save it now."

TESSA STOOD WITHIN the circle of Max's arm, her head against his chest, the steady beat of his heart assuring her that she was, miraculously, alive. Beyond rational thought or independent movement, she'd been half-carried out of the lobby. Aroused from her state of shock by the noise and glare, she tried to speak.

"S..." Not a sound emerged. She followed Max's gaze to the conflagration in the sky. No one left in the theater could possibly survive.

She tugged on his shoulder with her free hand.

At once he looked down, his eyes and voice gentle and concerned. "What is it? How do you feel?"

"So-fie," she managed to articulate in a husk. "Sem... Sem..."

"Sempronio? You want to know what happened to Mr. and Mrs. Montelli."

She nodded. "An-ge-la."

"And your maid?" She nodded again.

"Somerville. Do you know what happened to those backstage?"

"I'll find out," Somerville said. "Stay here with Madame Foscari, Max. She doesn't look in any condition to move."

"We'll wait across the street. We're too close to the fire here."

Max led her to the front steps of a building and helped her to sit. She nestled close to him on their stone perch, her arms rigid bands about his chest. Her frozen mind knew only one thing: as long as she held on to Max she was safe. She concentrated on that fact, shying away from her anxiety about the others. Without them she was truly alone in the world.

"Your friends are well." Somerville had returned. "I saw Nancy and she says everyone escaped."

Something loosened in her chest and she burst into dry, overwrought sobs, unable to stop while Max and Somerville talked and the latter disappeared again.

"We've managed to find you a carriage," Max said. "Only a hackney but they are hard to come by in this maelstrom. The others will make their own way back to your hotel."

She clung to him as he led her into the throng milling in the thoroughfare. For some reason the crowd drew back, parted to make way for them. She heard scattered applause, her name called out in praise.

That was odd. She'd sung well, of course, but she hadn't finished the aria and it seemed likely they'd have forgotten, what with the excitement of the fire. She turned around to face the crowd and gave a slightly wobbly curtsey and a cheer went up. How polite people were.

It was Max they should applaud. He was the hero. He'd saved her life.

CHAPTER FIFTEEN

"The Tavistock Theatre was last evening devastated by fire."

The Times

THE SITTING ROOM at the Pulteney seemed another world, refined and still. Max had kept his arm about Tessa all the way to the hotel and up the stairs to her suite of rooms. When he disengaged she made an incoherent protest.

"Hush," he said, and with infinite tenderness, as though she were a precious and fragile egg, settled her on the sofa. Was he leaving her alone? He must not abandon her when she could still feel the heat and smoke coming for her, the certainty of death. But when she tried to ask him to stay, nothing emerged from her throat. Dazed, she watched him leave the room and heard him speak to a servant in the antechamber. He wasn't gone long. "Drink this." He held something to her lips.

Water, with a hint of brandy. She seized the glass, gulped the cool liquid, and asked for more. The drink soothed her ravaged throat and her fear. As though the water traveled through her veins, her body awoke from its paralysis.

She was alive. More alive than she had ever felt in her life. Max's expression turned from anxiety to his rare smile, teeth gleaming in his sooty face. She wanted to laugh with joy.

She leaped up and flung her arms around his neck as vitality suffused every inch of her flesh, every sinew. She was omnipotent, immortal, because she'd faced down death and survived.

Acting on heedless instinct, she pulled his head down for a

hungry, open-mouthed, ravishing kiss. As they kissed, wild and greedy, the cool water in her veins turned into fire, a wonderful reviving blaze.

The heat intensified and concentrated itself in a single place where she ached, empty, ravenous to be filled. She welcomed the ache, the hunger, and clung tighter, rubbing herself against Max and the evidence of his own desire, stiff beneath the fall of his trousers. Releasing her hold on his neck, she plucked with impatient hands at the buttons and sensed him smiling through their kiss.

"Shall we take this a little slower?" he murmured.

"No!" Her voice didn't produce much sound so she lent it all the force of her passion. "Now! I want you now!"

"Shouldn't we at least undress?"

"No!" She didn't want to wait even a second. Neither did she dare wait. At the back of her mind she knew she couldn't risk the loss of this delicious hunger, the return of fear. She must have him now, without thought or a moment's delay. She groped at his buttons with trembling, clumsy fingers, tore off the last one, reached in and found him, hot and hard through—astonishing she still wore them—her gloves.

He winced and removed her hand with his own. "This should come off, at least, I beg you," he said, tugging at the bracelet on her wrist. His voice was full of laughter beneath unmistakable urgency.

False diamonds glinted against the elbow-length gloves, once pristine white satin streaked with black. Tessa clawed at the jewelry without effect but somehow Max undid the catches and she pulled the bracelets off and flung them to the ground, then ripped off her gloves as he worked on the fastenings of her gown.

"Hurry," she rasped. His hands on her neck stoked her hunger. Unable to wait even another second, she spun around and shoved him so he sprawled clumsily on the sofa behind them. She landed on top, straddling his hips.

Now.

She pulled up her velvet skirts, pushed aside her fine linen drawers, seized his member and impaled herself. He slid easily into a passage slick and ready and aching to be filled and stretched.

What relief, what bliss, to have Max inside her at last.

A thrust of his hips toppled them from the edge of the seat onto the floor. Now he was on top, taking her hard. She kicked her legs free of her skirts and wrapped her legs about his hips, exercising muscles she'd forgotten she owned to draw him in deeper, to clench him to her so she'd never let him go, to assuage the agony of longing that was building inside her. Their joining was fierce and elemental as she celebrated her escape and her passion for the man she'd never forgotten. And at last she found blessed liberation, melting into a pool of joy she hadn't experienced in years. Perhaps ever. With a few powerful thrusts he followed her into release with an incoherent shout and collapsed, his face buried in her neck.

They lay side by side on the floor. Every nerve in her body buzzed happily and her senses seemed to function at a heightened pitch. She was intensely aware of his breathing as it subsided from panting gusts to a more regular respiration. She explored the texture of the skin over his hipbone, the contours of a muscled thigh, and heard the diminishing beat of his heart where her head rested on his still-clothed chest. His neckcloth had disappeared, whether during their fevered coupling or the escape from the fire she had no idea. A vee of skin and a tuft of dark hair showed where his shirt buttons had come loose and she shifted up to press her lips there, closing her eyes to savor Max's scent.

"Ew!" Her voice had returned sufficiently to speak at a low husk. "Max, you smell awful, like smoke." She raised her head. "And you're black and filthy all over."

He tipped his head up. "You think you're in any better state? Is this a new perfume? *Eau de Théâtre Brûlant*?"

She replaced her head on his chest and snuggled closer. His

arms tightened around her and she lay quiet, enjoying his closeness and a sense of peace.

"How do you feel?" he asked after a while, stroking her head.

"Very well." Her laugh sounded ribald to herself.

"I meant," he continued, "how do you feel after the fire? Any injuries you hadn't noticed before? Were you hurt?"

She shook her head. "Thanks to you, no. You saved my life, Max. How can I thank you?"

"It was my very great pleasure."

"Mine too." They both laughed softly.

"You'd probably like to bathe," he said. "Will the hotel provide water at this hour?"

She rose to her knees and took his hand. "Come with me. The best thing about the Pulteney is that it has the best baths in London."

Tessa loved the bathroom adjacent to her bedchamber. In all her travels on the continent she'd never come across a facility with a constant and immediate supply of hot water. Perhaps it was why she'd stayed on at the Pulteney long after the state of her purse dictated a removal to cheaper quarters.

"I've heard of these but I've never used one," Max said when she showed him the big marble tub, partly sunken into the floor. "How does it work?"

"I have no idea. You turn it on, so, and water comes out."

But he seemed to have lost interest in the wonders of modern plumbing. Once more he went to work on the back of her gown. In no time the mangled velvet had fallen to the ground, and his fingers attended to her stays with equal expertise. The unusual design, which raised her breasts while leaving her midriff free to breathe, gave him no pause. Of course, he'd had plenty of experience undressing opera singers.

She cast aside the thought. She was the only opera singer present and she was going to enjoy the moment. Kicking off her stockings, she began to climb into the bath.

"Wait." He turned her around to face him. "This needs to come off too."

Her shift hit the ground and she stood naked before him. *Oh God*! She knew men found her body alluring, but that was clothed in garments designed to entice. Would he find her breasts too large, her hips too broad? Her curves were nothing like the sylphlike slenderness Parisian fashions demanded. Domenico had constantly complained about it.

A hitch of breath encouraged her to look up. From the hot glint in Max's eyes he wasn't disappointed. He smiled slowly and picked her up.

With hardly a splash she found herself immersed to the chest in warm water while he stared down at her with an appreciation that took her breath away.

"Join me," she said, holding out her hand but looking away lest shyness overcome her bold impulse.

One invitation was enough. Within minutes he was as naked as she and climbed into the tub behind her, his chest hard against her back, thighs cradling her own, legs entwined, all muscle and heat with the faint tickle of rough hair. The addition of his bulk sent the water up to her neck. Cocooned by warmth and strength, she sighed blissfully. Had she ever felt better than at this moment?

He plucked the few remaining pins from her hair and smoothed the long waves over her shoulders, disentangling Angela's skillful braids with his fingers. With a movement that send a cascade of water over the edge of the brimming tub, he reached for a cake of pink soap, splashed water over her head, and began to wash her hair.

"Hold this," he whispered, handing her the bar.

She inhaled deeply, the scent of roses mingling with steam. Drawing the humid air into her lungs soothed her smoke-scarred throat and assuaged the concern for her voice that always floated at the back of her mind. Sinking further into Max's comforting embrace, she lost herself in the relaxing massage of her scalp.

One male kneecap peeked through the water. Taking the soap she washed the little island of bone and skin with infinite care, then continued down his leg, as far as her arm extended, and back again, kneading his skin and feeling his muscles ripple beneath her hand. Then the other leg, his hips, as much of his torso as she could reach. A small smile curved her lips as she felt his erection grow and press against the small of her back. Her *fica*, just inches away, began to throb in response.

She felt like purring—perhaps she did—as slow torrents of water, poured from a small jug kept beside the bath, rained over her head, washing away the soap. It never felt this good when Angela did it.

His hand found hers in the now foamy depths and removed the soap. "Just relax."

His touch rendered her boneless. Unhurried fingers worked her neck and collarbone, the warm lather silk against her skin. Every nerve quivered as he attended to her arms, her shoulders and her midsection, laving every inch with engrossed care. When he cupped her breasts she quivered with pleasure. For a moment he held them up so the tops appeared like hillocks above the water. With an approving murmur he closed those large, capable hands around them, squeezing her already stiffened nipples between his fingers.

A bolt of lightning flashed through her stomach and intensified the ache between her legs. She seized his hand and placed it over the entrance to her core. His fingers needed no further prompting to penetrate through the curls and her nether lips and give a jolt of pleasure. Oh, yes! She felt a surge of power in the certainty that the ecstasy of release could be hers once more.

HE WAS DAMN well going to take his time. Their frenzied coupling on the floor of the sitting room had been as exhilarating a sexual encounter as Max had ever experienced, but he wanted to savor every moment of this second chance, to enjoy Tessa at his leisure, to imprint the knowledge of her body on his soul and to ensure he did the same to her. He almost burst with joy at holding her, soft, wet and fragrant, in his arms.

His lips found the nape of her neck, tasting the clean, sweet skin. With a careful flick of his forefinger he brushed the nub of her desire, but only once. He plotted a long siege, to arouse her to the highest pitch before he lifted her from the floor of the tub and brought her down on him. His cock strained eagerly at the very thought, but it—he—could wait.

A knock at the door interrupted his plans.

"Signora!"

"Angela," Tessa whispered and lurched to her feet and out of the bath.

"*Aspette*, Angela," she said. She donned a silk robe that had been hanging on a hook and slid out the door, closing it behind her.

Double damn. As he left the bath, Max looked around the room and found neither a hiding place nor another dressing gown. He stared with disfavor at his filthy, rumpled clothing scattered on the floor and compromised by wrapping a towel about his middle. At least it concealed the throbbing evidence of their recent occupation.

Would Tessa even care if her maid knew of his presence? He had no idea if she was in the habit of entertaining lovers in her residence. He felt remarkably foolish as he listened, without comprehension, to a soft-spoken, lengthy exchange in Italian.

"I sent her to bed," Tessa said when she returned to the room. "They are all safe and well but they couldn't find a hackney and had to walk."

Though the edge of his hunger had subsided, Max was not unwilling to carry on where they'd left off. He glanced at the bathtub. It was a most unappealing sight, the water a dark gray with morsels of ash and soap scum floating on the surface.

He looked back at Tessa and noticed strain and fatigue in her face. Somehow their moment had passed, shattered by the restoration of reality in the form of the maid.

"You should go to bed too," he said gruffly. "You must be exhausted. I'll dress and leave."

She approached and took his hand. "Please don't go, Max. You are right, I am tired but I don't want to be alone. Stay with me. Sleep with me."

Devoid of cosmetics and framed by straggling wet locks, her face showed an innocence and vulnerability he hadn't seen in Teresa Foscari. She was suddenly the old Tessa, the girl of their youth. Of course it was an illusion. The fact that she had no qualms about sharing a bed with him while her staff occupied the other rooms in the suite had answered his previous question. Tessa wouldn't be embarrassed by his presence in the morning and it certainly suited his inclination to remain.

He raised her hands to his lips. "It would be my very great pleasure."

He followed her to the commodious bed and sat on the edge while she got under the covers. Without much talking, he used a towel to rub her hair. "I'm getting good at this," he said at one point. She chuckled, caressed his cheek tenderly, and yawned.

Once her head was dry enough to prevent a chill, he helped her remove her robe, tucked the covers up to her chin and joined her between crisp linen sheets. Gathered in his arms, she quickly fell asleep. For a minute or two he relished the rose-scented curls in his nose, her warm skin pressed along the length of his body. *My Tessa, mine at last* were his last thoughts before he joined her in slumber.

MAX AWOKE CONFUSED. He was not in his own bed. From the faint outline of a heavily curtained window and the distant sound of birdsong he guessed it was after dawn. A dry throat brought it back to him: the horror of the burning Tavistock and Tessa on the stage with the fire coming ever closer. He closed his eyes to squeeze out the memory of that falling beam but it seemed to burn his eyelids. Thank God he'd reached her in time.

And afterward...

A sense of wellbeing flooded through him when a sweet-smelling bundle stirred beside him in the bed. In the dim light he saw the outline of Tessa's head on the pillow beside him and heard her rhythmic breathing. He couldn't contain a grin, for his life had taken a most unexpected turn.

For a start he was now the principal owner of the only opera house in London. He and Simon would make a fortune and his mother could go choke on her eligible young ladies. And La Divina, Europe's greatest soprano, was in London without a stage. She had nowhere to go but the Regent and her genius would help fill its coffers.

And best of all and most importantly, La Divina, Teresa Foscari, *Tessa Birkett*, was his at last. And this time he would never let her go. To hell with her past and her countless lovers. Her future would contain only one lover. Him. And he'd make damn sure she'd never want another.

He couldn't wait for her to wake up so he could tell her. And show her too. But he wanted to tell her how he felt and hear from her that she felt the same way about him. Surely she did. They hadn't exchanged many words but he couldn't have imagined her response to him, a tenderness that went beyond simple passion. He tried to recall whether she'd said anything last night, any words to give assurance to his assumption. But she'd spoken little, a few inviting words in a husky whisper.

He froze. Her voice!

Smoke couldn't be good for a singer's vocal cords. Supposing the fire had damaged her voice beyond repair and ended her career? It would be a tragedy. But it made no difference to his own feelings and desires. He'd take care of her for the rest of her life.

Though he could hardly wish for the destruction of her talent, neither would he unduly mourn it. At least he wouldn't have to put up with other men ogling her on the stage and snakes like Edouard Delorme kissing her.

Listening to her light breathing in the dark room, he wished she'd wake up. He was anxious to start the rest of his life. Turning on to his side he reached for her lush breast, firm yet soft. Perfection. The scent of her in the dark warmth stirred his senses. He was ready for a little morning exercise, to complete the seduction he'd been forced to discontinue in the bathtub.

"Tessa," he murmured, kissing her temple and earlobe, searching for the pulse at the angle of her jaw. "Tessa, my love. Wouldn't you like to wake up?"

He played with her breast and felt a hardening nipple. She arched into him. "Does that feel good? I can make it even better."

He sensed her ascent into consciousness and leaned over to find her lips with his, showering her with shallow kisses, caressing her warm skin from neck to shoulder and downwards until he held the curve of her hips and pressed the weight of his chest over her upper body.

She felt like heaven. But in the next moment he discovered hell.

Fists pummeled his back, hands shoved hard against his shoulders. And he learned that Tessa's voice was intact. A trained soprano screaming at full force and close quarters was an agonizing experience for the eardrums.

"Angela, Angela. *Aiutto*!" The sleeping woman had turned into a dangerous weapon, writhing from side to side on her back, limbs flailing in every direction. Max disentangled himself with haste and scrambled off the bed where he landed on all fours, not before sustaining a few painful jabs in various sensitive areas.

"What the devil…?" Before he could rise from his undignified position, the door burst open and the maid rushed in brandishing a poker and yelling in Italian.

In the light from the adjacent sitting room he could now see Tessa, pressed back against the bed head, clutching her knees to her chest and wearing an expression of abject terror such as Max had never seen in his life, let alone caused. Her head shook like a demented metronome, sending long hair into Medusan coils. Tears poured down her cheeks and her shrieks subsided to a continuous, terrified keen.

His heart might have broken at the sight of such despair had he not been sprawled on the floor, stark naked, with a female Italian maniac threatening him with a dangerous weapon. His sense of self-preservation mingled with growing anger.

First deal with the immediate threat. Struggling to his feet, he held out one hand in an authoritative manner, using the other to mask his private parts. "Stop!"

Angela continued to advance, keeping up her incomprehensible commentary. It was hard to know if he was participating in a farce or a tragedy.

"Stop!" Then, turning to Tessa, "For God's sake tell your maid I wasn't attacking you." Lost in hysteria, she paid him no heed. He made a move towards her and she cringed, covering her face with her hands as though expecting a blow. The maid raised the poker above her head and Max jerked away from the bed, almost tripping over a footstool.

Just as the likelihood of tragedy gained the upper hand, the scene degenerated into farce when both Montellis appeared at the door, adding more Italian and some unpleasant-sounding German to the babble. At least neither of them was armed.

Mrs. Montelli said something sharply that arrested the onward march of the maid, though the poker remained poised for a strike, and the three of them stopped talking. For a few moments the scene froze: three figures clad in nightgowns glaring at Max who was horribly aware of his nudity and completely flummoxed by the turn of events. On the bed Tessa continued to weep.

"Mrs. Montelli." Summoning what dignity he could, Max

addressed himself to the only person showing symptoms of sanity. "I am in this room at your mistress's invitation. I brought her home last night and I was in the bathroom when you returned to thc hotcl. Had she wished to object to my company she had plenty of opportunity to do so then."

Mrs. Montelli looked over to the bed as though seeking corroboration from Tessa. Receiving none, she exchanged glances with her husband, thought for a second, then nodded.

"I have no idea why Madame Foscari is so upset," he continued with exaggerated enunciation. "But please believe that I did nothing to injure her and never would." What the devil did Tessa mean by it, weeping on the bed as though he had raped her?

Indignation made him sarcastic. "Since I take it that my invitation has been rescinded, I propose to retire, dress myself, and relieve Madame Foscari of my unwelcome presence."

"I think that would be best, my lord," Mrs. Montelli replied softly, with no hint of threat.

Keeping a wary eye on the poker, Max stepped around the bed and retreated to the bathroom. Wearing smoke-stained, reeking evening clothes put a cap on the disaster of a morning that had begun with such promise. Not even attempting to tie his black rag of a neckcloth, he stuffed it into his pocket and returned to the bedroom, wondering what on earth had happened and what to expect next. He found Tessa and Mrs. Montelli alone in the room, sitting on the bed. Tessa huddled in her companion's arms, sobbing piteously while the other woman murmured words of comfort.

They both looked up and Max bowed stiffly. Then Tessa buried her face in Mrs. Montelli's shoulder and cried unabated. If there was any sense to be found, it wasn't here. Max removed himself from the bedchamber, the suite, and the hotel without another word and with all possible haste.

He descended the stairs and stalked through the foyer, head held high but well aware of the curious stares of the hotel staff at the sight of a gentleman in soiled evening clothes. It was early enough that few guests were at large but he was a well-known figure. He would face further humiliation if gossip about his exit spread through fashionable London. At that moment he never wanted to set eyes on Tessa again. She was surely a madwoman.

And yet.

He stepped into the street and closed his bleary eyes against the sunlight, envisioning everything that happened after she woke up.

That last look on her face hadn't seemed insane. She had just been through a terrifying experience in the burning Tavistock and perhaps her nightmare had been reliving the fire. But that didn't explain the reaction of her staff, nor did it explain that look. Her expression had been one of fear, yes, but also of grief and deep despair.

CHAPTER SIXTEEN

"Only by the courage of Madame Foscari was the audience saved from the fire without loss of life. This singer, the marvel of our age, proved herself by her actions to be a True Englishwoman."

The Morning Post

TESSA SPENT THE next two days in her darkened room, sipping tea laced with lemon and honey, kept in constant supply by the devoted Angela, and refusing talk to anyone else, even Sofie. The particular excuse that she needed to recover her voice provided cover for a more general desire to bury her head under the blankets and never leave her bed for the rest of her life.

The third day after the fire Sofie marched into the room, stiff back exhibiting her descent from generations of Teutonic martinets.

"It's time to get up," she announced, yanking back the curtains and throwing open a window. "*Du lieber Himmel*! It stinks in here."

"What about my throat?" Tessa muttered, tugging the blankets up to her chin.

"A little fresh air won't make it worse. Besides, Angela says you were speaking normally this morning."

"I can't. I'll never sing again."

Sofie turned her attention to the bedcovers. Tessa fought her but Sofie was too strong, throwing them onto the floor and leaving Tessa exposed in her oldest and least becoming nightgown.

"Up, up, up!" barked Sofie. Then, in softer tones, "You're the heroine of London, you know. We've been besieged by callers wanting to congratulate you. You even have a letter from the Prince Regent. You saved the lives of thousands of people in that theater. You'll never hear another boo, that's for certain."

"I can't see anyone, ever again."

"Lady Storrington was here. She brought profiteroles," Sofie coaxed.

A faint flicker of interest stirred the leaden misery in Tessa's brain. She stood up, finding her legs shaky from disuse, and shuffled past Sofie into the sitting room. She was hungry. Ignoring countless bouquets of flowers, she stiffened like a pointer sighting game and made straight for a plate of pastries. She proceeded to eat all of them, at least a dozen, scarcely swallowing one before stuffing another into her mouth. Then she sat down.

"Feeling better?" asked Sofie, who had observed the display with folded arms.

"I think I'm going to be sick."

"So I should think." Sofie sat down beside her and took her hand. "*Liebchen*, I know you are upset but lying in bed won't help. There are decisions to be made and neither I nor Sempronio can make them without you. You are, you realize, without an engagement. The Tavistock Theatre no longer exists. It was burned to the ground."

Tessa said nothing. She knew there was only one other place for her to go in London.

"And Teresa, we must talk about Lord Allerton."

"I don't want to," Tessa muttered. If she talked about him she'd have to think about what she'd done and face her own shame.

"Don't you think," Sofie said with infinite gentleness, "that Lord Allerton deserves an explanation? Or at the very least an apology?"

Tessa wanted to cry but she'd spent all her tears in the days since Max had left her bedchamber. "I can't see him. And how can

I apologize? He can never forgive me for what I did, and even if he did what would be the use? I'm ruined, worthless to any man. Domenico has destroyed me."

She'd been so happy for a short time, but Domenico had once more returned to haunt her. She'd never be free of him. A single moment of joy, then the world had crashed about her again, leaving her worse off than ever. Before she'd merely suspected how hopeless it was to reach for happiness. Now she knew.

"You mustn't give up," Sofie said. "Give it time. Why don't I have Angela prepare you a bath? When you're dressed we can make plans."

The thought of the bath threatened to send Tessa into renewed hysterics. Luckily the entrance of Sempronio from the music room offered sufficient distraction to keep her uncertain serenity from disintegration.

"*Cara*! You are up. How are you?" His eyes fell on the empty plate. "What happened to those pastries? I wanted one."

"Teresa ate them," Sofie replied. "She has found her appetite at least."

"All of them?" A thought struck him. "They were stuffed with cream. What about your voice?" He glanced at Sofie who frowned at him. "Never mind. It will recover. Are you ready to try it? Angela says you are speaking normally."

"I don't want to."

"Just a few exercises. Nothing to stress it on the first day."

"I have nowhere to sing."

Sofie intervened. "You have half a dozen invitations to sing at private affairs, including one from Mrs. Sackville. Do you think you will accept that one?"

Even the prospect of a vengeful refusal failed to arouse Tessa's spirits. Neither did any of the letters of congratulation and praise, the floral tributes, the lavish encomia in every newspaper. Sofie had been right when she'd called her the heroine of London. The same scribblers who, a week before, had called her a grasping, heartless harpy, could hardly find the words to express their adoration for the woman whose courage had saved thousands.

Tessa simply didn't care.

One matter she could no longer ignore. For days Angela had bothered her about the diamonds. The tiara, necklace, and brooch from the Tsar's gift had been lost when she escaped the fire. Only the bracelets survived and thinking about the way Max had managed the clasp made her want to cry again.

"They're worth a fortune." Sofie said. "You must report their loss."

"Let them go," Tessa replied wearily. "They must have fallen off when I came down from the stage." It hurt to think of Max's brave efforts to save her, how he'd pulled her from the path of the burning beam. How much better if he'd left her to perish. "The fire will have destroyed them."

"Fire won't hurt the diamonds, even if the setting melted."

"They're not diamonds. They're paste."

The explanation of her recent discovery had Sofie clucking with horror and additional maledictions on Domenico's perfidy.

"I'm going back to bed," Tessa finally announced. "But I will rise for dinner."

Sofie thought to tempt Tessa's appetite by ordering all her favorite dishes from the Pulteney's excellent kitchen. She needn't have worried. Tessa sat in silence in the suite's small dining parlor eating her way through every course with rapt intensity. She even eyed the remains of a pair of ducklings and considered picking up a carcass and stripping the bones with her teeth. Instead she contented herself with three helpings of apple tart swimming in thick cream. She would have eaten more if Sempronio, catching her intent gaze on his plate, hadn't hurried to finish his own second slice.

With every mouthful Tessa expressed her hatred and defiance of her husband.

"Don't you think you've had enough?" Sofie asked.

Tessa glared at her and reached for a crust of bread that had escaped her attention. "You sound like Domenico. *You'll get fat. You'll ruin your voice. Don't eat sweets. Don't drink milk. Don't, don't, don't. No one will love you if you don't look beautiful.*" She stood up and glared at both Montellis who regarded her with mouths agape. "I don't care anymore. I don't care if I look like an elephant. No one will ever love me anyway so I may as well enjoy myself."

Flouncing out of the room she returned to her chamber, locked the door, and collapsed onto the bed, clutching her aching stomach as she stared at the ceiling. How badly she had behaved, taking out her emotional turmoil on her friends. The temperamental diva, the cliché invented by Domenico, had descended from the stage and become reality.

Domenico might be dead but he still dominated her life and she had allowed it. The expensive hotel suite, the indecent gowns, even her lack of capacity to manage her own affairs. It was as though Domenico was laughing at her from hell, taunting her with her inability to break away from his ascendancy and live without him.

The recollection that she'd controlled the urge to smash things buoyed her confidence for a moment. She might have eaten every crumb of food on the dinner table but at least she'd left the china intact. Then her heart sank further still. She might master her own reaction but the terror that provoked her panic remained, as demonstrated the morning after the fire. Her pleasure in making love with Max had been an aberration brought on by the greater fear of the fire and her relief at escaping it. The scene at dawn proved the impossibility of a sustained relationship.

How much worse it was now that she'd glimpsed the happiness that would forever elude her. She was doomed to be alone.

Repose was like a drug that calmed her body but did nothing to soothe her misery. Despite hours of sleep she felt little refreshed when she joined the Montellis for breakfast. They watched her warily but neither said a word beyond a banal morning greeting.

Her usual bread roll with raspberry jam was laid before her. "I'd like some cheese," she said, shaking out her napkin.

"Cheese?" asked Sofie faintly.

"Yes, cheddar cheese."

"English cheese!" Sempronio remarked with Italian scorn. "If you must eat cheese why not gorgonzola or parmigiano?"

"I like cheddar. I haven't had any since we came to London. Mr. Waring used to have it shipped to Oporto."

Seeing Sempronio about to argue, whether in defense of Italian cheese or in opposition to the danger to Tessa's vocal cords, Sofie silenced her husband with a brief shake of the head. "I'll speak to Angela."

"Are you ready to practice?" Sempronio asked.

The last thing Tessa felt like doing was singing. "I should do something about the diamonds. Suppose I lost them outside the theater? If someone found them I might get them back without anyone knowing they are copies. But if I don't report the loss they'd wonder why."

Sofie returned to the dining room. "Why are you so concerned that people know they are false?"

"It looks so bad to wear false jewels."

"At this point, my dear, you could have false teeth, false hair, and a corset stuffed with sawdust and no one would think the less of you."

"I don't want people to know about my lack of money." Perhaps she was irrational to fret so, but she couldn't let go of her pride. She didn't want it thought that she had sold the tsar's gift and she could hardly explain that her late husband had done so.

She continued to worry the problem aloud until Angela entered with a plate bearing a small, pale, yellow cube. Tessa cast Sofie a reproachful look but said nothing. She'd made the point that she could do whatever she wished, and it wasn't just about a craving for dairy foods.

Sempronio looked at this tiny serving of cheese and rose from his chair abruptly. "I'll be in the music room when you're ready," he said. A minute later she heard Scarlatti, played with exceptional force and rapidity. Such a display from the sweet-tempered pianist was unheard of.

"I'm sorry, Sofie." Tessa felt like crying again. "I've been a beast. You are all so kind to me."

"We worry about you, *Liebchen*. We know you are upset and we want to help. But there are things you can only do for yourself."

"Very well. What do you wish me to do today?" Tessa asked, praying Sofie wouldn't again raise the subject of Max.

"Mr. Coburn wants to see you this morning. He'll be here soon."

"Mr. Coburn?" Tessa was barely acquainted with the assistant manager of the Tavistock. "Why not Mortimer?"

"I didn't want to tell you before, but it seems that Mr. Mortimer died in the fire. He hasn't been seen since, but his office was completely destroyed and they fear his body may have been..." Sofie hesitated, biting her lip. "His body may have been burned away to ashes."

"Oh." Tessa had no affection or respect for Mortimer but she couldn't wish such a horrible fate on anyone. And believing the fire had claimed no victims had been one beacon in the gloom of her spirits.

When the assistant manager was announced she offered her condolences. "The loss of the theater is a terrible tragedy," she said, thinking that Coburn had lost his employment. "And of course I am much grieved about Mr. Mortimer's death."

Coburn, a slight man with the mild features of a slightly harassed sheep, looked more ovine even than usual. "As for that, Madame Foscari, it appears that our initial information was incorrect. We have reason to believe that Mr. Mortimer left the theater before the fire took hold."

"Thank God!"

"In fact there is every indication he started the fire himself." It was lucky Coburn worked behind the scenes. He had no idea how to make the best of his lines. So flat was his delivery that it took a few seconds for Tessa to comprehend him.

"Why on earth would he burn down his own theater?"

"Ahem. The fire safe in the office was empty, though a very large sum had been delivered from the box office at the beginning of the performance. Mrs. Sturridge's benefit drew a large audience."

"I'm sorry for Mrs. Sturridge. Does that mean she won't receive the money for the benefit?"

"Not only Mrs. Sturridge. There is no money to pay any of the performers. Including, I am afraid, you."

Tessa still didn't understand. "But I wasn't going to be paid for the evening."

Mr. Coburn cleared his throat again. "Investigations have revealed…Er…the long and the short of it is, that it appears Mr. Mortimer has…er…absconded with all of the theater's funds."

"But he owed me a great deal of money. Two hundred guineas for every night I've sung, and very likely more."

"I am aware, *madame*," Coburn said miserably. "I am in the unhappy position of informing you that we are not in a position to pay you."

Tessa felt her knees give way and she dropped into a chair, thinking furiously. "Bank accounts! Surely not all the money was kept in the office?"

"No indeed. That would be most imprudent. But all the theater's accounts were cleared by Mr. Mortimer earlier that day. The directors of the Tavistock company will declare bankruptcy."

"So there is nothing. Nothing for me at all."

Fully fifteen minutes after Coburn took his leave Tessa sat stunned, unable to comprehend this disaster. Then she stood up wearily. She could no longer afford to indulge her bruised emotions. She had mouths to feed.

"Sempronio," she called. "Let's see how my voice is."

"WE WON'T HAVE an empty seat until the end of the season." Simon Lindo was at his ease, leaning back in his chair behind the desk and grinning from ear to ear.

Max, not in the least at ease, stared morosely out of the window of the manager's office, tracing patterns on the dusty pane. After even a few weeks of London dirt the glass needed a clean. He was quite unable to share his partner's glee in the Regent's imminent success.

"Simon," he said suddenly, over his shoulder. "May I ask your opinion about a certain…situation? Not that this is something that actually happened, you understand."

"Of course not. I have two sons so I'm quite used to hypothetical questions. I shall don my fatherly mantle and advise you as best I can. Ask away, son."

Obviously Simon would guess the truth, but Max couldn't bring himself to talk about Tessa openly. "Suppose a man were…er…sharing a bed with a lady, a very willing lady. Then the next morning she awoke and started screaming and beating him. What would you think?"

Simon's eyes widened. "I don't," he said after giving the matter some consideration, "have your experience with womanhood in its infinite variety but I would hazard a guess that the lady was…surprised. And frightened."

Max had worked that out for himself. But he couldn't guess why Tessa had been surprised and frightened. Try as he could, when he considered the fervor of their lovemaking, the tender interlude in the bath, and the way she'd invited him to sleep with her, the morning's hysterics didn't make sense.

"Did that help?" Simon asked.

"No."

"I thought not. Wrong kind of question for me. Shall we return to business?"

Max nodded and took a seat next to the desk.

"Now that Madame Foscari has had three days to recover I think it's time to approach her."

Max stared at the desk. Of course Simon wanted her at the Regent. His own heart leaped at the idea of seeing Tessa again, but he feared it too. Many times over the past three days he'd set foot on the pavement outside his house intending to head for the Pulteney. Each time he ended up directing his footsteps elsewhere.

"I don't see why we need her," he said, "if you say we can fill the house without her."

"She's the best and we want to be the best. Our greatest problem has been the lack of a first-rate soprano and now the greatest of them all is available. I can't believe you even need to ask."

"We can do very well without her, and without paying her outrageous fees." A ridiculous excuse, but he couldn't tell Simon that the prima donna had taken him to bed and then virtually accused him of rape.

"For God's sake, Max, don't let's go through this again. You know what happened last time you decided La Divina was an avaricious harpy. She isn't. She's a charming woman and a great artist who will enhance the reputation of the Regent like no other." Simon peered at him suspiciously. "You seemed friendly—more than friendly—with her at Lady Clarissa's musicale and you saved the woman's life. What's going on?"

"I don't want to talk about it." Absently he noted that the finger of his buff leather glove was black. He stripped off both gloves and flung them onto an empty chair.

"So, don't talk about it. And don't hire her if you want to see her on stage at Covent Garden, filling every seat with her adoring admirers who regard her as the savior of thousands."

That brought Max up short. "Covent Garden? Tessa...Madame Foscari would never sing the nonsense they put on there. Pantomimes! Mozart in English with improvements by

Henry Bishop! Faugh!"

"She has to sing somewhere. If the rumors about Mortimer are correct she'll need to make some money."

"Do as you like," Max said. "But leave me out of it. You may speak to her about terms without my participation."

SIMON HAD AGREED to call on La Divina and politely refrained from calling Max insane. Thoroughly perturbed by the prospect of seeing Tessa again, Max went down to the theater, where a rehearsal was underway, and sat at the rear of the pit. Neither music nor singing had the ability to distract him.

Naturally the prospect of Teresa Foscari participating in such a rehearsal at *his* theater could hardly fail to please him. Simon hadn't been wrong about that, and four days ago Max would have been thrilled. As a businessman and a lover of the operatic art he rejoiced; as a rejected lover he was deeply reluctant.

Supposing Tessa, for what reason he couldn't imagine, did blame him for what had happened? If she had misinterpreted something he had done, how would their next meeting go? Would she even agree to sing at his theater?

Thinking of the tsar's diamonds, he guessed that she would indeed be looking for an engagement. Having her as an employee of sorts might make their meeting less awkward.

On stage, Edouard Delorme hit a ringing high note at full force, a quite unnecessary piece of showing off at a rehearsal. Max remembered his certainty that there was something between Tessa and Delorme. Singing with the Frenchman might be an enticement for her to choose the Regent Opera House. Max almost wished she'd go to Covent Garden after all.

He was mad. Quite, quite mad. Tessa had driven him to insanity.

Sitting in the theater was doing nothing for his state of mind. Perhaps a long walk would cure his lunacy. Naturally he would avoid Piccadilly and the Pulteney, lest he be tempted to tear upstairs and demand an explanation.

To perhaps find Tessa recovered and apologetic and ready to take him back.

Shaking off implausible hope, he rose to leave and found he'd left his gloves upstairs. Outside Simon's office, Max's heart thumped at the sound of a too-familiar voice. Hearing the manager outline the terms of an offer, he knew that La Divina had come calling. Had he any sense he'd leave, gloves or no gloves. He couldn't resist setting his ear to the door.

The woman made a complete hash of the contract. She was a mere infant when it came to tangling with a businessman of Simon's experience and vigor. Simon played her like a fiddle, giving in on inessentials and beating her down where it mattered.

"I'd prefer to sing only two nights a week, Mr. Lindo. And I insist on one hundred and fifty guineas a night."

"Madame," replied Simon at his most persuasive, "I already explained about the limitations we face with the size of the Regent. I cannot possibly offer anything like what a large house like the Tavistock could afford. One hundred guineas is as high as I dare go. And we must present opera six nights a week to cover our expenses. But I fully appreciate that it would be too much for you to perform more than four."

Simon exaggerated. *Come on Tessa,* Max urged silently. *Drive him up.* Simon expected to pay one hundred and twenty-five and would likely pay one fifty if she stuck to her guns.

Tessa sighed. "Very well, Mr. Lindo. I agree to your terms."

How could Max ever have believed her greedy? If she was a grasping adventuress she was a totally incompetent one. What she needed was a keeper. Max restrained the urge to intervene, smiling at Simon's likely reaction should Max burst in and take Tessa's side in the negotiations.

The final contract wasn't unfair or in any way dishonest, but they'd have paid much more. Tessa needed someone to look after her. Someone who had her interests at heart, unlike her scoundrel of a husband.

"I should like to receive two weeks' fees in advance," she said. She must bc short of money again.

"That shouldn't be a problem, *madame*. But before I issue payment, I'd like to have your voice evaluated. Naturally I accept your word that the fire hasn't affected it, but it would be rash of me not to be certain." Trust Simon to make sure he wasn't buying a pig in a poke.

"La Divina does not audition," Tessa said frostily, with more animation than she had yet expressed.

"Of course not. But perhaps you would indulge me for my own peace of mind."

"Very well. Arrange it for me with your vocal coach."

"As for that, let your own pianist accompany you. I shall listen myself. Signor Montelli is a fine musician, a superb pianist, and judging by the evidence of your own skills, a superior coach. I'd like him to work with some of the other singers at the Regent. If you can spare him, of course."

She agreed.

"He doesn't exercise his gifts to their fullest extent," Lindo mused. "He would be well-received in the concert hall, I believe."

Tessa sounded pleased that Montelli was receiving recognition. "No one knows better than I how fortunate I am to have Sempronio. Almost ten years it's been since he came to me. He is a man whose ambitions lag far behind his talents."

"That's settled then. I'll have the contract drawn up and delivered to you. Unless you'd prefer me to send it directly to your attorney."

"I'd like Mr. Butterworth to look at it. But Mr. Lindo, we haven't discussed my benefit."

"Benefit, Madame? Surely you don't expect a benefit performance after only a few weeks' work?"

"But I must! A full benefit. I'll wait till the very end of the season but I must have it." The sorrow, the hint of panic, in Tessa's voice cut to Max's gut. He reached for the door handle.

TESSA CLENCHED HER hands on her lap and tried not to let her alarm show. She'd done well with Lindo and was proud of herself. Proud but weary. The terms weren't quite what she'd hoped for but this time, at least, she would actually receive the money. She'd learned to appreciate the value of a bird in hand. Payment dates would be specified in the contract with no room for ambiguity. Lindo was straightforward about all terms. Negotiating with an honest man wasn't so difficult after all.

Yet the performance fees would hardly cover her expenses into the autumn. She relied on the capital sum from a benefit to lay the foundation of a regular income, independent of performing. Two thousand pounds she'd expected from the event at the Tavistock.

"I'm afraid that's quite impossible, Madame," Lindo said. "You can't ask the company staff to work an evening for no pay when you've been with them such a short time. It would cause resentment and endanger your relations with your colleagues. Next season will be time enough to discuss a benefit."

Next season! She could barely endure to finish this one. She was so tired. Tired of rehearsing, tired of dressing, tired of wooing the audience.

"Without a benefit I may have to reconsider our arrangement." It hurt to say it. Little as she relished the work, still less did she wish to look elsewhere, to enter negotiations with a strange management that might turn out to be of Mortimer's ilk. Lindo and the Regent suited her, even if it meant that she would have to face Max at some point. Not too often, she hoped. He appeared to be little involved with the daily business of the opera house.

The door opened and Max stood at the entrance. He looked pale, with a white, pinched look about the mouth and his eyes were grim. Yet Tessa's unruly heart jolted at the sight of him. Despite embarrassment and shame, the sight of his face, severe yet beautiful in the dim light, gladdened her for a moment. His attention was on Lindo but flickered to her, too quickly for her to avert her eyes and avoid meeting his black gaze.

"*Madame.*" He bowed. "I wasn't aware you were here."

She blushed deeply. "I was informed you weren't in the office when I arrived." The obvious corollary was unstated but understood. He knew she'd have left had he been here.

"I trust you are well. No ill effects from the fire? Your voice is well?" Of course that would be the only thing he'd care about now.

She murmured some platitude.

"You didn't tell me you expected a call from Madame Foscari, Simon."

The manager shrugged. "It was an unanticipated pleasure."

"I came on a whim," Tessa said quickly. "On my return from Bow Street. I had to report the loss of some of my jewelry in the fire."

"I can't imagine why you would trouble yourself," Max said.

Why had he said that? Oh God! He must know the diamonds are counterfeit. Was all of London aware? This was the final humiliation.

"We have been discussing having Madame Foscari join us for the rest of the season," Lindo said. "I am happy to say we have almost come to terms."

Tessa found it even harder to speak firmly with Max in the room, but she was determined not to capitulate in this all-important matter. "I cannot sign a contract without a benefit. It's quite impossible." Inwardly she quaked at the thought of having to walk out of the Regent without an engagement.

Max, at his most haughty, raised his eyebrows. "Is there a difficulty?"

Lindo repeated his objections; Tessa wanted to close her eyes and pray. She forced herself to appear as proud and unruffled as Max.

"An artist of Madame Foscari's stature deserves a benefit," Max said and she almost doubled over with relief. "It sits badly with me to see the Regent behave shabbily in refusing her request." He and Lindo exchanged some kind of silent communication and the manager nodded.

"Very well, *madame*. You shall have your wish," Lindo said, raising his hands in surrender. "The last performance to end our first season with éclat." His eyes gleamed and he sounded pleased.

She had been right to stand her ground. And meeting Max again hadn't been the embarrassment she'd dreaded. Although he hadn't shown any pleasure, he'd taken her side over the benefit. She was almost—not quite—disappointed when he didn't stay.

"I'll leave you to thrash out the details," Max said. "I only came back to collect my gloves. *Madame*, Simon." With a smart bow he departed.

WHAT HAD POSSESSED him? Max wondered. He'd committed himself, as Simon well understood, to fund Tessa's benefit. Moved by the sight of her, pale, distressed, and beautiful, a wilting hothouse flower in the workaday surroundings of the manager's office, he'd been unable to resist coming to her rescue again. Simon would have talked her out of the benefit while giving in on some less important matter. Yet Max had stepped in because he wanted to make her happy.

"Lord Allerton!" Mrs. Montelli stuck her head out of the window of a waiting carriage. Given that last time he saw the lady he'd been naked, exposed, and deeply embarrassed, his craven instinct was to pretend not to hear and decamp with all haste. She repeated her call and Max resigned himself.

"Madam," he said, his face heating as he stopped and looked in. She was alone, presumably waiting for Tessa.

"I realize some awkwardness is inevitable given our last encounter but if you won't regard it, neither shall I." The Austrian woman's accent always sounded no-nonsense but this was plain speaking indeed. Max nodded politely, feeling remarkably foolish. "I have something important to say to you," she continued. "First let me assure you that neither Teresa, nor any of her friends, hold you to blame for the unfortunate events three days ago."

"I'm glad to hear it, madam. Neither do I blame myself." Except for hours over the past three days and nights spent racking his brain to find the cause of Tessa's outburst, scrutinizing how his own conduct might have been the touchpaper of her hysterics.

"Teresa's distress had nothing to do with you, my lord, I assure you."

A knot of anxiety in his chest eased. "What was it then? For God's sake, what made her behave in such a way?"

"She was terrified because of something that once happened, a specter from the past." The theatrical phrase sounded odd, spoken in her precise German accent.

"Might I be permitted to know what you're talking about? I'd like to understand."

"The secret is not mine to tell. Teresa must do so herself."

"Is she likely to?" A fledgling hope batted its wings in Max's heart.

"She doesn't trust easily. Give her time, Lord Allerton." Mrs. Montelli looked into his eyes. "I think you might be the one who can help her."

"What can I do?"

Her mouth turned down at the corners. "I don't know, my lord. She may come out at any time and it is best if she doesn't see me talking to you."

Regally dismissed, Max headed for Piccadilly, a street that no longer held any terrors for him.

His head had cleared. What an idiot he had been. Nothing had really changed since the night of the fire, or, if he was honest, many weeks earlier. He wanted Tessa. For good and forever.

Because he loved her.

He loved her and all he had to do—all!—was find out how to win her trust and her damaged heart.

Now that she was to sing at his opera house he would have the chance to prove that she had no need to fear him. There were several weeks until the end of the season and he would give her the time Mrs. Montelli said she needed. By the final performance—her triumphant benefit which would take place, as was entirely proper, on *his* stage—he would win her for his own.

He invested a swagger into his walk and a smile on his lips as he tipped his hat to several acquaintances. The leafy expanse of Green Park loomed on his left and, on his right, the walls of Tamworth House.

Goddamn it, his mother!

Charging in to Lindo's office like a knight errant, he hadn't given her a thought. But by paying for Tessa's benefit he had violated the terms of their wager. He'd have to marry a girl of her choosing.

How was he going to avoid it? For avoid it he must. There could be no question of wedding anyone else when he knew with absolute certainty that he would love Tessa for the rest of his life.

CHAPTER SEVENTEEN

"This Present evening will be performed the Grand Serious Opera of LA SEMIRAMIDE at the Regent Opera House, the part of Semiramide played by Madame Foscari."

Advertisement

"WHAT HAPPENS TO a theater after it has burned down?"

"I imagine they clear away the rubble. Can't allow such an eyesore to remain in the middle of London." Simon knew that wasn't the answer Lady Clarissa wanted, but he was tired of her persistent questions about his professional qualifications and experience.

When asked—commanded rather—to call on Lady Clarissa Hawthorne, he'd thought she'd want to talk about her son. Something was going on between Max and his mother that Simon didn't understand. He was prepared to use his best stalling tactics while extracting the maximum information from his hostess. Instead he'd faced a series of piercing questions about the theatrical business in general and his own history in particular.

"Don't be foolish, Mr. Lindo. You know that's not what I mean. Will the Tavistock be rebuilt?"

"The company that held the lease and the license is bankrupt. I imagine the ground landlord will look for a new lessee."

"Someone with the means to build a new theater?"

"Or with the ability to attract investors."

Simon politely stood when she arose from her own chair and came over to stand close to him and look him in the eye, a feat requiring no great effort since he had scarcely two inches advantage in height. A subtle and undoubtedly costly scent tickled his nostrils. In fact her entire physical presence spoke of wealth. Her coiffure, without a dark hair out of place or a gray one permitted to intrude, arranged with an artless perfection that only high art could achieve. The flawless complexion of a woman half her age. Her fine, though not voluptuous, figure enhanced by a morning gown of olive-green sarcenet, which Simon, from his knowledge of costumery, could price by its very expensive yard. Unwillingly, he found she stirred him.

The perfection of her appearance complemented her surroundings—a sumptuous palace that existed only as a setting for this one woman alone.

Hardly alone, he corrected himself. Likely a hundred servants shared it with her, catering to her every desire. He mustn't let himself be intimidated by her power. He met her gaze squarely and found an expression of something—mischief perhaps, or gleeful anticipation—at odds with the arrogant dignity of her appearance and environment.

"How do you feel about shipwrecks, Mr. Lindo?"

"I can't say I've given the subject a great deal of consideration," he said with a straight face. "I'm glad I've never been in one."

"What about elephants?"

"Elephants, donkeys, dogs and cats. They're all the same to me. I'll admit I'm not an animal lover."

His nonchalance irked her. "Mr. Lindo, I believe you are trifling with me. I'm talking about animals on the stage."

"And shipwrecks too?"

"I once saw a shipwreck at the Aquatic Theatre at Sadler's Wells. Most disappointing. They had hardly enough water to drown a dormouse. I had hoped for a deluge."

"I infer that your dramatic tastes run to the spectacular."

"I always enjoy a visit to Astley's. Much more fun than the deadly serious stuff you and Max put on. Could you manage a display of that nature?"

"Though I have in recent years concentrated on musical performances, my theatrical experience is broad. I know the right people to mount a spectacle of the kind you describe. Should I be so inclined," he concluded repressively.

Lady Clarissa smiled. "Good. I have a mind to go into the theatrical business and you seem like a suitable partner for me."

Well, that was surprising. What was her game?

"I already have a partner. Your son."

"You and Max may continue to put on your little operas. I prefer to think larger. I want to rebuild the Tavistock."

Despite his suspicion of the lady's motives, Simon felt a gathering excitement. He'd always had large ambitions himself. "It's an interesting idea," he said, careful not to let his enthusiasm show.

"How long will it take? Can we have it ready to open next season?" she asked, undeterred by his lack of animation.

"Less than a year? A tall order, but it's astounding what can be achieved with plentiful money and the will to match."

"I assure you, Mr. Lindo, there is no deficiency of funds. And I always get what I want."

Simon could see himself carried away on the tidal surge of her will. An association with Lady Clarissa would be, he fancied, like riding a tiger. Frightening yet invigorating. If he lost his grip, the tiger would eat him whole. And that prospect was...arousing.

Where had that thought come from? He wasn't given to double entendre, even in his own mind. He wondered what he was getting himself into.

ENTERING TAMWORTH HOUSE a couple of weeks after promising to fund Tessa's benefit, the last person Max expected to find in his mother's drawing room was Simon.

"Max, my dear," she said, offering her cheek for a kiss. "What a lovely surprise!"

"Hardly, Mama, since you invited me."

"But I'm surprised you came."

"You told me you had someone for me to meet and promised me no females under the age of thirty." He glanced about the room, half expecting to detect a youthful beauty lurking behind a curtain.

"I want you to meet Mr. Lindo."

"Very funny."

"Mr. Simon Lindo, my new colleague in a theatrical venture."

"What?"

"I am so glad you persuaded me to engage Madame Foscari for that recital. I'd never have met such fascinating people, or discovered how interesting the theater is. We are going to rebuild the Tavistock Theatre and put on spectacles."

"Eyes beginning to give you trouble are they, Mama?"

"I mean dramatic spectacles."

The Tavistock fire had foiled her plan to make Tessa so popular it would empty the Regent. The soprano was comfortably settled in her spacious and very comfortable dressing room at the new house and had been drawing in the crowds for a week now.

"Not the operatic business, I trust?" he asked, casting Simon a reproachful look. Surely his mother wasn't so fiendish she'd steal his business partner and take him on at his own game?

"No indeed. For a start, everything we present will be in English so people can understand it. And we won't have ridiculous stories set in Spanish prisons."

Though he knew better, Max rose to the defense of his genre. "One opera set in a Spanish prison. One. Mozart and Rossini never set operas in prisons. Unless," he amended conscientiously, "you count a Turkish harem."

"A harem! I like it. A huge ballet with lots of beautiful dancers to attract the gentlemen."

"Mama!"

"Shipwrecks! Animals! Battles and fireworks!"

Despite his suspicions, amusement welled up. As long as the Tavistock didn't present opera, he didn't care. "Better make sure the building is fireproof."

"Mr. Lindo will see to all that. He's a most knowledgeable man."

"Simon?" Max turned to his partner, a little disappointed he'd succumbed to the temptations of Hawthorne gold. He'd had more respect for Lindo. "I thought you committed to the Regent."

"I assure you, Max, I can manage both concerns. Now that the Regent is well-established and has no rival, the management will be a simple matter." Simon grinned. "How can I resist the challenge of an enterprise to rival Astley's and Covent Garden under one roof?"

"You must do as you think best. I trust your judgment."

When it came down to it, Max wasn't that interested. He was pleased his interfering mother had found a project besides his matrimonial prospects. Happy, in fact, that she'd found a pursuit that amused her. Doubtless in the future the two of them would find pleasure in having dramatic productions in common. They were, after all, very alike. Aside from the fact that he wasn't a willful, imperious, interfering female.

Max had troubles of his own of the female variety, leaving him little time for other considerations. What should he do about Tessa?

Simon and Lady Clarissa chattered on in the background about the engineering feat of constructing a stage capable of holding a herd of pachyderms or enough water to reenact the Battle of Trafalgar. His mind was occupied by his own opera house and its new prima donna.

Following Mrs. Montelli's advice, he hadn't approached Tessa except as the concerned and admiring owner of her theater. He'd dropped by her first rehearsal to welcome her but he hadn't stayed, however much he wished to. By all accounts her behavior at rehearsals and back stage had been unfailingly gracious and obliging. He'd heard a comment or two that she seemed to have recovered from the horrible fire with remarkable speed.

He thought otherwise.

Whenever he glimpsed Tessa she looked forlorn. And worried too, as though she were Atlas responsible for gathering up the shattered remnants of the planet and holding them aloft on her frail shoulders. The audience offered its usual boisterous adoration but Max, watching every performance from his box, detected a strain, an almost undetectable disquiet in La Divina's stage presence.

"There'll be enough time," his mother was saying. "What do you think? Max! Wake up, Max!"

"When do you hope to open this new temple of wretched excess?" Max asked, wrenching his attention back to the present.

"Our goal is the beginning of next Season, straight after Easter."

A typically overambitious estimate. Absurd, in fact.

"You had better enjoy your little Regent's popularity while you may. Next year everyone will be coming to my new Tavistock."

That confirmed her game—to make the Regent fail and win her bet. It was a ridiculous notion, especially since they had La Divina and she did not. But there was the annoying truth he had already lost when he agreed to fund Tessa's benefit. Damn, he wished he hadn't made such a stupid wager. The only answer was to make sure she never found out. Dishonorable, of course, but the alternative was intolerable.

He didn't think Simon would discuss Regent business with Lady Clarissa, but he'd better warn him to keep his mouth shut.

"Is there anything else, Mama?" he asked. "I have an appointment. If you're ready to leave, Simon, we can walk together."

His mother waved her arm at him. "Go, go! You're no use here. But I need Mr. Lindo. We have much to plan about making my theater the greatest London has ever seen. How large an audience did you say we can fit in? Three thousand? Four?"

Max stormed out.

"YOU ARE A very wicked woman, my lady," Simon said as the double doors slammed, making a display of porcelain on the mantelpiece quake.

Lady Clarissa had the grace to look a little guilty.

"I don't enjoy being manipulated," he continued, "and I won't be used as a weapon in any battle you are waging against your son."

Privately, Simon wasn't unduly worried. Max could hold his own against his forceful mother. As for Her Ladyship, if her intention was to keep her son away from Teresa Foscari she was going about it the wrong way.

Nevertheless, there were things he needed to make clear to the willful heiress before he became irretrievably entangled with her.

"Do you wonder why I have worked in so many different theaters?"

"It's given you very wide experience."

He ignored her. "It's because I'm difficult to get on with. I like to have my own way and I don't take kindly to being ordered about and contradicted."

"You do very well with Max, apparently."

"I have enormous respect and affection for Lord Allerton and I believe the feeling is mutual."

"Max is a lamb," she allowed.

In Simon's opinion Max was a saint. And much tougher than he appeared to have survived a lifetime with Lady Clarissa without turning into a raving maniac.

"I repeat. Max and I respect each other and have found ways to resolve any differences that arise in a civil manner, but he is the only man I've ever worked with of whom I can say as much. If we are to be colleagues this is something you need to know."

"I'm very easy to get on with, Mr. Lindo." An outrageous statement delivered with a teasing smile.

"One of the first requirements of a successful association," he said sternly, "is trust. And that means you don't lie to your partner."

"Very well. I *can* be easy to get on with. I'm sure most of my acquaintances find me the most agreeable of women." He raised his eyebrows. "But not all of them," she admitted.

Simon sighed. "I can see this is going to be very interesting."

She wandered over to a large gilt mirror and adjusted some illusionary imperfection in her coiffure. A frivolity of lace and ribbon was its only adornment. Very different from the enveloping caps worn by respectable middle-class matrons of his own circle. Her straight back enhanced the discreet, elegant curves of her figure. Was she aware how much she appeared to advantage from across the room? Probably. Hastily he dragged his eyes from her body and met her eye in the glass.

She gave an enigmatic smile. "How old are you Mr. Lindo?"

"That's a personal question."

"Is it a state secret?"

"I'm forty-five. How old are you?"

"Thirty-nine," she said without hesitation.

Lady Clarissa had a way to go before she achieved a state of perfect frankness.

CHAPTER EIGHTEEN

"A scene of some dramatic interest passed at the Regent Opera House a few days ago. A lady of very estimable character, on entering the first row of boxes, was suddenly seized with a nervous attack, from seeing near her the mistress of her husband, who appeared disposed to insult her. For once the attention of the audience was distracted from the considerable charms of Madame Foscari..."

The Morning Post

RISING LATE, TESSA wandered downstairs and looked for Sempronio. Searching their new lodgings, a small house on Stratton Street, took only a minute or two. Sofie had done her best with the cramped quarters, demonstrating rarely used skills as a hausfrau. Her modest addition of throw rugs and table coverings drawn from shawls in Tessa's extensive wardrobe couldn't compete with the spaciousness, luxury, and modern plumbing of the Pulteney, but they lent a degree of elegance to a very ordinary—and mercifully cheap—abode.

Tessa wanted to get her daily vocalizations over. Dissatisfied with her performance the previous night, she had little enthusiasm for work, yet knew she needed it. The audience had been restive. While she might argue that her voice still suffered from the after effects of the fire, deep down she knew it to be an excuse. La Divina was losing her touch. And instead of feeling terror at the possible loss of her talent and livelihood Tessa was too listless to care.

Angela's entrance with a delivery of flowers and the morning mail aroused her attention—but only for a moment. Tessa flipped through the letters. There were several invitations, a couple of bills, and the usual fulsome tributes from admirers, most of them male and interested in more than her skills as a singer. But a quick glance at the arrangements had already told her not to expect anything better. Just about every glorious product of the English summer garden was represented in today's delivery from the florist. But no white roses.

They didn't arrive every day. The last bouquet, now two days old, still bloomed in a silver vase on the console, still filled the room with their unmistakable fragrance.

Why did he do it? The same roses, always white, arrived in her dressing room before each performance with Max's card and a polite note wishing her luck for the evening. Those ones were easy to explain, common courtesy of house management to the theater's main attraction. But why, every two or three days, did he send them to her home with a note? He never wrote anything very significant. The first note had been couched as a welcome to her new lodgings. Later missives enquired after her health or commented on the weather. One recommended a visit to Kew if she wished to see a fine variety of roses in bloom, but without any suggestion he should accompany her on the expedition.

What was the point? Sometimes she suspected he did it to torment her and wished he'd desist. For the appearance of the flowers always gave her a glimmer of hope that she instantly dismissed once reality intruded. Whether Max forgave her or not made no difference. The problem, the reason there could never be anything between them, lay within her and could not be mended.

An air of suppressed excitement hung around the Montellis when they returned, shortly after noon.

"What took you out?" Tessa asked Sempronio, never one of nature's early risers. "Sofie must have threatened you with some dire consequence to get you out of bed so early."

He looked sheepish and cast a pleading glance at his wife. Sofie appeared serene if also a little apprehensive.

"We have been meeting the directors of the Royal Philharmonic Society," she said. "Mr. Lindo introduced us. They wish Sempronio to play in a concert, maybe several."

"That's wonderful news!" Tessa cried, getting up to embrace Sempronio. "How kind of Mr. Lindo. But it's no more than you deserve and about time someone realized what a wonderful pianist you are."

"I am to play two concertos, one Mozart, one Haydn," he said, his endearing grin lighting up his face.

"And," Sofie said, "Mr. Lindo says he can find Sempronio some pupils."

"Splendid," Tessa said. Sempronio really didn't have enough to do. She needed him only for an hour or two a day unless she was learning a new role.

Sofie looked worried. "It means we won't be dependent on you for everything. You are too good to us and have supported us for too long, far beyond what we earn."

"I've never resented a single penny. You are my dearest friends."

"But you see, Tessa, we'll no longer be such a drain on your purse." Sofie took a deep breath. "We can afford our own lodgings."

"You mean, not live with me anymore? I'd miss you." She glanced around the small drawing room and grimaced. "I realize this place isn't quite what you are used to. We are rather cramped here."

"It's not that," protested Sofie. "But...but since Sempronio and I married we've never had a home of our own. If you need us, we'll stay with you."

"No." Tessa tried not to see their move as a desertion. She could understand Sofie's desire, had often felt the same way. "It's an excellent idea and I will be more comfortable here. I can turn your bedchamber into a dressing room."

"Sempronio will come every morning and work with you, just

as usual," Sofie said earnestly.

"Better make sure you don't live too far away or he'll have to get up early every day," Tessa teased, with a fond smile for Sempronio.

"Mr. Lindo suggested some rooms on Upper Brook Street he's heard will be available soon."

Sempronio broke in with a look of rapture on his cherubic features. "In the next house to where Handel lived in London. *Giusto cielo*! I shall be inspired!"

"When will you move?"

"Not before the end of the opera season," said Sofie. "The concert is at the beginning of July. Then there may be a few pupils. What shall you do for the summer, Tessa? You spoke of going to the country. Then when you come back for the autumn season at the Regent we shall see each other every day. You'll hardly notice the difference."

"I'm not sure I shall sing at the Regent again. Maybe I'll go back to Paris. Or Vienna or Berlin."

"But Tessa!" Sofie said in distress. "I thought you liked England. You said it was your home."

Sempronio gulped. "Wherever you go, we shall go with you, *cara*."

"Yes, indeed," said Sofie valiantly. "We'll never desert you."

How could she do this to her friends, drag them back to Europe when they were so excited about a future in London? Yet how could she remain in the same city, the same opera house, as Max?

"Not the autumn," she temporized, "but perhaps the spring. I'd like a long holiday. I could go to Italy. Angela would like that. I could stay six months and then decide. I might well come back here. After all," she said with a hint of her inner dejection, "it's possible no one else will hire me."

Under the cover of her friends' protests she considered her situation. Once they'd made the journey, she and Angela could live simply in Italy, but she needed money. She could only hope her benefit performance lived up to expectations.

GIVE HER TIME. Max repeated Mrs. Montelli's words on each occasion—and there were many during the final weeks of the season—that he felt the urge to dash over to Tessa's new lodgings. Instead he treated her with courtesy when he encountered her at the opera house but made no attempt at the personal conversation he longed for.

Why did you scream? A dozen times he bit his tongue rather than utter the words. Which left him lots of time to rack his mind for the answer to the question that obsessed him: What had happened to her that she reacted like that? He feared she had been hurt badly in the past, and the most likely candidate was her husband. By all accounts Domenico Foscari had been a worthless excuse for a man. More and more he bitterly regretted leaving Tessa to be exploited and abused.

His only overt advance toward her was the regular delivery of white roses. The accompanying notes cost him some struggle and a good many crumpled sheets of paper hurled at the waste-paper basket. Friendliness was the tone he sought, unthreatening banalities his subject matter. In ruthlessly suppressing the passion he wanted to express he feared he came across as cold and dull.

The greatest frustration in his decision to bide his time was the sight of her, night after night, on stage with and often in the arms of Edouard Delorme. His hatred of the tenor verged on the obsessive. Avoiding rehearsals because he couldn't bear to see them together, he fed his imagination with visions of Tessa and Delorme sharing much more than professional friendship. The fire between the two singers on stage couldn't possibly be all an act. He'd sensed something more in their relationship and he feared Delorme as his rival. If only the man weren't so damned handsome.

CHAPTER NINETEEN

"The London Theatre has seldom been gratified by a musical combination as notable as that of Madame Foscari and Monsieur Delorme."

The Examiner

"MA CHERE THERESE."

Tessa greeted the appearance of the tenor's handsome face at her dressing room door with a guarded lack of enthusiasm. Accustomed now to singing with him most nights and during rehearsals, she had learned to tolerate his company in the presence of others.

"Edouard," she said flatly and inwardly cursed the visit to her dressing room to find a pearl-headed hatpin whose loss Angela had been bemoaning all morning. Two minutes later and she'd have been on her way home.

"I heard you were to be in the theater this afternoon, planning your benefit. How fortunate you are to have a benefit when you have sung such a short time here." Delorme couldn't keep an undercurrent of resentment from his tone.

"You own benefit was well-received."

The tenor's chest expanded with satisfaction. "Every seat taken," he said.

"Well deserved," Tessa said. "I shall be late, so please excuse me."

Instead of letting her pass, Delorme came in and closed the door. "It is hard to find you alone." She made sure of that. "What will I sing at your evening?"

Tessa did a few breathing exercises and hummed a few bars of Mozart. As long as they stuck to business, she could survive ten minutes in a small room with him. "Because it's the last night of the season we have planned something *éclatant*. The company will perform two full operas and I shall sing both Leonore in *Fidelio* and Rosina in *Il Barbiere*."

Delorme whistled. "It has never been done. Will your voice survive until the end of the evening?"

She had her doubts and it was a huge risk, but she felt reckless. Perhaps she would fail dismally and the decision whether to remain in London would be out of her hands. "I can do it," she said, showing no weakness in front of Delorme. "As first tenor of the company you have your choice of which role you will take that night. I don't expect you to do both."

He huffed and puffed, torn between vanity and sense. Being a tenor, vanity won. "Naturally I will sing both Florestan and Almaviva. We will make operatic history."

"*Merci beaucoup*, Edouard. I value your support and I am glad for your sake that the soprano role in each opera is longer than the tenor's."

He looked for the barb in the remark and accepted her overly sweet smile at face value. Taking both her hands in his, he projected the full force of his shiny-eyed allure. "We were so good together, Thérèse, and we can be again. I shall never forget that night in Paris."

She backed away. Could he possibly be remembering the same episode?

"I have always wanted to have you again."

"You didn't have me then."

"But I would have. You wanted me. Now you are no longer married and we can enjoy each other without guilt."

He was coming for her again. "No," she whispered, terror clawing at her chest. "That was not why I refused you. It was a moment's madness that must never be repeated."

"But it must! Only you are a lover worthy of the world's greatest tenor." He seized her in his arms, silenced her with his mouth, and wrestled her onto the divan.

MAX STOOD OUTSIDE the dressing room door listening to the two voices speaking in French. Torn between the urge to interrupt whatever was taking place between Tessa and Delorme and dread at what he would find, he waited no longer when he heard a crash. Believing at first that he had burst in on violent lovemaking, the pain that howled in his brain was nothing to his red rage when he realized that she was struggling. With both hands he grasped the Frenchman by the collar, flung him to the ground, and stood over him with clenched fists.

"Get up," he roared, eager to knock him down again.

"Milord Allerton," Delorme said with an egregious smile. *"Il n'y a pas besoin de vous déranger."*

"Yes, there bloody well is a reason to be disturbed. You attacked a lady."

"Mais non. Dis-lui, Thérèse."

Tessa sat with tears in her eyes. She shook her head.

"Shall I hit him, Tessa?" Max asked.

She shook her head again. *"Va-t'en, Edouard.* Leave."

Delorme shrugged, bowed and complied. *"A bientôt,"* he said at the door, the picture of handsome insolence.

"Not if I see you coming," Tessa muttered and Max felt marginally better.

Pouring a glass of wine from a decanter on a side table, he brought it to her. He watched in an agony of disquiet while she took a sip of the drink. The wretched woman he saw was almost unrecognizable as the bewitching diva or the offstage beauty. Her eyes seemed to have sunk into her face, and no cosmetic art could have made her paler. He wanted nothing more than to take her in his arms but he didn't dare touch her, or even sit at her side.

She looked up and handed him the glass. "Thank you, Max," she said with a dignity that belied her haggard appearance. "I'm sorry you had to witness this ugly episode."

About Delorme, at least, he knew what to do. "He'll never sing at the Regent again," he said without any consideration of the business consequences of dismissing the popular tenor.

"Edouard is nothing." She dismissed him as though swatting a gnat. "He was troublesome, yes, but I wasn't in real danger. He is nothing but a voice to me and of no other importance."

Max had never guessed Delorme responsible for Tessa's profound unhappiness. While not ready to dismiss the tenor's attack on her so easily, he was glad to hear her call him insignificant.

"But," she continued, "we have a history."

"No history that justifies him forcing himself on you."

"No, not that. I think I had better tell you about it."

Painful as it would be to hear the confirmation that Delorme had once been her lover, he savored the fact that she was ready to trust him. He ventured to perch beside her on the low couch, his long legs hunched up. When he tried to take her hand she removed it, though not urgently. "I'm sorry," he said. "I have no right."

She swiped the back of her hand across her eyes and her nose pinched into an inelegant sniff. "You have the right of a friend but it's better not to touch me now. You will understand after you hear my story. To explain what happened today, and the night of the fire, I have to tell you about my life. The parts of my life that have not appeared in the newspapers."

"I am honored by your confidence and you may rely on my discretion."

"I trust you, Max. You deserve to know the truth."

His heart turned over at the naked vulnerability of her expression. She was no longer hiding from him.

She made a visible effort to compose herself but her hands, twisted together in her lap, gave away her anguish. Max guessed that her story would not be an easy one to tell.

"Don't speak of anything that upsets you," he said, longing to hear everything.

She shook her head and murmured something he couldn't make out. After a while she began, choosing her words carefully. "I told you how I eloped from Lisbon with Domenico Foscari. As an artist I made a good choice. He was an excellent manager for a young singer. He knew voices and made sure I had fine teachers in Italy. Had I stayed in Portugal I wouldn't have risen beyond the provincial. While I made my name as a singer, he created an image for me—the temper, the broken china, the gowns, the jewels, the lovers."

Was she saying what he thought? That there had been no lovers? That she had not lain with Napoleon Bonaparte after all? Max kept his mouth clamped shut and let her speak. Later perhaps he could ask questions.

"I didn't like behaving like a temperamental diva, or the rumors he spread about me, but I let him do as he wished as long as I could sing. La Divina was an invention of Domenico Foscari."

"Not your voice," he said firmly. "No one but God could invent that."

She smiled so faintly her face scarcely moved. Head bowed and shoulders hunched, unlike the confident, voluptuous goddess of the stage, she seemed fragile, as though she might break apart with the waft of the merest breeze. "The music and the performances were all I cared about. Domenico said if people read about me in the newspapers they would want to hear me, and the opera houses would engage me for the best roles. He was right. I became famous all over Europe and we became rich. He was very good at negotiating, unlike me." She glanced at him wryly. "Neither Mortimer nor your Mr. Lindo would have had my services for so little if Domenico was in charge. But no fortune was ever enough for him."

The words came more slowly as though enunciating them

was a task for Sisyphus. He hated to see her pain and would have told her to stop but he couldn't. He had to know. Unable to bear her nearness without offering physical comfort, he stood and put a little distance between them. From the sofa she looked up, her eyes dull.

"Performers often add to their incomes by coming under the protection of rich men, as I know *you* are aware. Domenico hinted that I should accept some of the lures sent out to me by noblemen, as long as they were rich. Many men wished to possess La Divina, but I refused them all. Even if I was tempted to give myself in a sordid commercial transaction, which I was not, I had made wedding vows and I honored them." Her lush mouth turned down in a grimace and her forehead creased. She had never looked uglier…or more beautiful to his eyes. "What a fool. I already knew Domenico was far from an ideal husband. We were happy enough at first. I believed I loved him. But he became unpleasant when he did not get his way. He lost his temper. And when I refused to let him be my pimp, he no longer troubled to cover up his own infidelities. Our marriage became a business arrangement only. I sang. He collected money. He spent money, far more than I knew."

Max nodded. Just as he had deduced. The man had ruined her in more ways than one.

"Then, last year in Paris, he began to woo me again. He said my coldness had driven him to other women. He made me believe that it had all been my fault but he wished to start again, have children, which he had always said was impossible for La Divina. I was wary but agreed. After all, we were tied to each other for life and I wanted a home and a family. I fooled myself that I could have them with Domenico. I let him convince me."

Her voice had dropped to a whisper and she bent low so he couldn't see her face. He sensed she was approaching the crisis in the tale and, as she had indicated, Delorme was not the villain.

"We began to share a bed again and once more he said I was

cold and had no idea how to please a man. He made a suggestion. He told me there were games we could play in bed that would make things more exciting for both of us. I was reluctant but I agreed." With her hands covering her face he could hardly make out the next part. "I had made up my mind to embrace our marriage so I let him—I let him tie me to the bed posts, bind my wrists and ankles, blindfold me. He left me for a while, telling me that the anticipation would increase my passion. I lay there for a long time, unable to move or see, and while I was waiting I knew that I did not love my husband and could never be happy with him. I heard his footsteps and the thought of him disgusted me. All I could think was that it would soon be over."

"Bastard." Max had indulged in some interesting bedsports in his time, but always with the full and enthusiastic participation of his partner.

Tears streamed down Tessa's cheeks. "He came to the bed and lay on top of me. Oh God, I knew it wasn't Domenico. He'd sent another man to take me. Larger, heavier. I couldn't move. I couldn't breathe." Horror written on her face, her eyes closed. *"I couldn't move.* I was so frightened and somehow I managed to scream. Angela heard me. She saved me from rape." Her voice was choked with tears and she bent over her knees. "He broke her nose."

FOR A YEAR or more, Tessa had tried to avoid reliving the terror of Domenico's ultimate betrayal. Angela and the Montellis knew, but she'd never described that night to anyone. She'd always locked the full horror away in an unexamined corner of her mind. Only in her dreams could she sometimes not control it. Hugging herself, she rocked back and forth, racked with sobs. Then a pair of arms came around her and drew her against a broad chest. The masculine touch should have terrified her. But this was Max and she knew he wouldn't hurt her. Instead she crawled onto his lap and curled up like a baby, crying out her grief for what Domenico had taken from her forever.

He murmured soothing words, rubbed her back, and pressed light kisses on her hair. Gradually she returned to consciousness and with it came shame and sheer embarrassment. "I'm sorry," she said with a giant sniff. "*Dio*, this crying will damage my voice. It's good that I'm not singing tonight."

"To hell with your singing," he muttered. He tightened his hold and suddenly she had to get away. Not from fear of Max but of her own reaction. She could not let herself weaken and allow him into her heart again. Indeed, it was likely too late for that, but the way ahead was paved with nothing but misery.

The moment she resisted he let her go and set her gently on the seat. She watched him stand and pace the length of the dressing room. She was glad she had told him. He deserved to know what had occurred when they shared a bed and why it could never happen again. Yet, what must he think of her now that he knew of her shame?

"Would you like some more wine?" he asked.

"No thank you. But I seem to have mislaid my reticule. Could I trouble you for the loan of a handkerchief?"

She dried her eyes on his large, clean linen square. He stood over her radiating tension, his brown eyes filled with concern.

"I'd kill Foscari if I could," he said abruptly. "Who was the other man?"

"A French *comte* who had earlier made his interest known. He paid Domenico a large sum for me to receive him according to his particular… taste. Once I convinced him that I was unwilling and not even aware of the transaction, he left."

"And Foscari?"

"I told him I wanted to live apart. We were still arguing about the terms of our separation when he was attacked and killed by footpads in a dark street."

"I wonder if the *comte* had anything to do with it."

"The police never found his assailants. As I learned later, there were plenty of others who wished him dead." The hordes of creditors who besieged his widow. "I couldn't bring myself to feel much sorrow but I didn't have him murdered."

"Of course not," Max said, shocked.

"The police questioned me and some of the Parisian newspapers hinted at it very strongly. The scandal made my performances more popular than ever and I detested it. I was glad to leave Paris when Mortimer came calling."

"I wish it had been I."

I do too. But she did not say it. "Certainly my association with Mortimer caused me nothing but trouble."

"I am not sorry you came to London." His intense gaze set off flutters—part pleasure, part regret—in her breast.

"You need to know one more thing," she said quickly. Perhaps the final confession would drive him away. "One thing that truly shames me. I told you that after the matter with the *comte* I demanded a separation from Domenico. But not only that. I was so angry that, for the first time in our marriage, I resolved to cuckold him. Not with a duke or an emperor, as he had always wished, but with a lowly singer who could give us no possible advantage. I didn't even like Edouard but I was prepared to use him for revenge."

Shaking her head, she remembered the decision that she had made during a duet on stage at the Paris opera. She had been a little insane at the time. Perhaps she still was. Max was waiting and she found this least important part of the story the hardest to relate, because she had certainly been at fault. "It wasn't hard to appeal to Edouard's vanity and entice him into my dressing room when I was alone. I flattered him, kissed him, drew him down onto the chaise longue. But as soon as I felt his weight my fear returned. I couldn't do it and sent him away. That is why I don't blame him too much for what he did today."

He rocked back on his heels and harrumphed. "I'm not sure

I'm ready to let him off so easily."

"As I said, he means nothing."

"I understand now why you panicked when I woke you that morning. I am sorry I frightened you."

"You couldn't have known."

"Listen, Tessa." He crouched at her feet, placed his hands on her waist, and, when she didn't shrink from him, wrapped them around her back. "I love you. I loved you years ago and I love you now."

She didn't doubt him. His strength, sincerity, and fundamental goodness were written plainly on features that she would never again see as harsh.

"Oh God, Max," she said, her voice breaking on a sob. "I wish you did not. Domenico has destroyed me. I am no use to any man."

"I refuse to accept that. When we made love on the floor you weren't frightened and you didn't fight me. It was only when I came to you when you were asleep and didn't know me. I could have been anyone and you panicked."

"The night before was different. I was not myself after the fire." She lowered her eyes. "Besides, most of the time I was on top. When you woke me I knew it was you. But as soon as I felt your weight I was terrified."

"We can solve this problem. We simply have to avoid those occasions. You can always be on top."

How like a man to believe logic and common sense could answer every difficulty. "I cannot argue away the fear because I wish it. Do you not think I have tried? Why do you think I threw that glass of wine at you?"

"You were *frightened* of me?"

"It is the only way I can be easy when my emotions become too painful." She placed her hand over her breast. "It comes from here, not from the head."

She could see him *thinking* while fear, misery, frustration, and too many feelings to catalog flowed through her veins.

"May I kiss you?" he said finally.

She sniffed. "If you wish."

"I will always wish it."

With infinite care he pressed his mouth to hers, as though she were something holy and precious. Physically his lips felt good, so familiar and dear, gently probing, inviting her response. Her heart wanted to open to his loving caress but it was locked tight and gave up the struggle. She shook her head and immediately he withdrew.

"It's impossible."

"If we love each other nothing is impossible. Do you love me, Tessa?"

"I trust you, and if I could love, I would love you."

"Is there no hope for us?"

"I don't know, Max. I will say this. The weeks I spent with you in Oporto were the last time in my life when I was entirely happy. If I could regain that joy I would."

"I was happy too, but I don't want that time back. I want now. We are different people. Older, I hope wiser, and richer in knowledge and experience. I loved the girl I first met but I adore the magnificent woman you have become."

"And who is she?" The question came from the depth of her soul. "Who am I? La Divina? Tessa Birkett? I don't know. Neither seems real to me."

"I know who you are. You are generous, clever, witty, beautiful, and my love. I am sure there is more, but it's enough to start and all I wish is to spend my life discovering the rest."

"Let me up, please," she whispered. His love was too much for her to bear. Against all reason it gave her hope. She couldn't allow herself to hope when disappointment, more acute each time, was the inevitable result. She needed, desperately, to be alone.

It wouldn't be fair to send Max away without explanation. She walked over to the washstand and splashed cold water on her face. Now as far from him as she could manage in the confines of the dressing room, she took a deep breath and forced herself to be strong and serene, as she would before a performance, even though her stomach was filled with lead.

"I will not complain about my life. I have friends, money—thanks to the Regent Opera House—and a talent I am proud of. Singing takes me out of myself and into a different world." He listened to her intently, which was more than Domenico did when she expressed her self-doubts. She wanted to weep for what could not be. "But when I am not performing, if I think too much about it, I am empty. I am afraid I don't exist. Am I English or French, Portuguese or Italian? Where do I belong? I have no home, no roots."

She didn't speak of her great fear, that she was doomed to wander from opera house to opera house until her voice was gone and she had nothing. Max would offer to ride to her rescue and that wasn't what she wanted. He did not deserve the empty husk of a woman she had become.

"I tell you this because you are kind enough to say you love me—"

"Kind! I have hardly been kind to you."

"Not always but from now on you will be. I know you and I trust you. But I cannot let myself love you. Now I must ask you to leave. I'm as tired as if I'd just sung an entire opera by myself."

What seemed a long time passed before he nodded and removed a piece of paper from his pocket and handed it to her. "This is for you. It's the reason I came to find you." He kissed her hand with punctilious gallantry, bowed, and left.

The paper bore the name and address of Mrs. John Birkett, Rose Cottage, Stoke Newton, near Bristol, Somerset and an addition in Max's handwriting. *I believe this lady is your grandmother."*

She had forgotten telling him about the mysterious J. Smith but Max had not. Ever practical, he'd handed her a potential solution to one of her problems. Perhaps in Somerset she would find something to fill the void inside her.

CHAPTER TWENTY

"Madame FOSCARI has undertaken to perform in TWO operas at the Regent Opera House tonight. Is this feat beyond even the powers of LA DIVINA?"

The Examiner

THE DAY OF her benefit Tessa did not speak. She hadn't sung a note or uttered a word since running through her vocal exercises with Sempronio the previous morning. With two heavy roles to perform she had to preserve her voice at all costs. For the past twenty-four hours she had sipped weak tea with lemon and studied the scores of the two operas, memorizing the places the works had been cut to shorten the evening and save the singers from exhaustion.

When she heard the door knocker she was alone, since Angela had run out to buy more lemons. Expecting a messenger from the opera house with further cuts, she opened the door to find Max, bearing the largest bouquet of white roses she had seen in a decade of extravagant accolades.

"Good morning, Tessa," he said breezily, as though she hadn't consistently avoided him since the scene with Delorme, exchanging only a few polite words when they met at the opera house and having Angela refuse his calls at home. "I've brought a letter from the musical director. May I come in? Upstairs, yes?"

She shook her head hard enough to make her teeth rattle. He ignored her, strode up the stairs of the rented house, through the open door of her sitting room, and went straight over to the table, where he deposited a letter and the flowers next to her open scores. She scurried after him and scrawled a note. *I cannot speak because of my voice.*

His years of keeping operatic mistresses clearly hadn't gone to waste. He understood her perfectly and smiled broadly. "Excellent. In that case you won't be able to refuse my invitation to supper tonight."

No, no, no, she scribbled furiously, but he wouldn't look.

"Naturally," he said, the picture of innocence, "the management of the Regent Opera House wishes to celebrate the end of a successful opening season and our future collaboration with our prima donna. I will fetch you from your dressing room after the performance." His air of insouciance slipped for a moment. The heat and affection in his dark eyes made her pulse race. "Don't worry about tonight, Tessa. You will be wonderful." He dropped a quick kiss on her gaping mouth and left without another word.

Don't worry about tonight was all very well, but which part? The benefit made her nervous, because of the vocal feat she was undertaking. Every seat had been sold and she would earn a splendid sum, enough to keep her for a year or more since she had reformed her extravagant habits.

But supper with Max she feared. Whenever she so much as glimpsed him, longing and misery crushed her. She'd been counting the days till the end of the operatic season when she'd no longer have to see him at the theater. Her body's eager reaction to his quick kiss filled her with hope and terror. Terror because of the certainty that her hope was only a delusion.

She prayed that by "management" he meant Simon Lindo as well as himself. If the supper was a purely business affair, she could just about get through it.

LEONORE WAS A breeches part and La Divina looked magnificent in breeches. Nothing like a boy, but that wasn't the point. The minute she arrived on stage the hoots and whistles from the pit were deafening. *Fidelio* was an opera of lofty ideals and noble music, but that wasn't what the benefit audience wanted. Tessa knew her job was to please.

Nancy Sturridge, who had joined the Regent company soon after Tessa, played Marzelline, the girl who is infatuated with the woman disguised as a youth. During the first act Tessa whispered to the other soprano. "Let's give them what they want." Nancy understood at once. When Marzelline tried to flirt, instead of fending her off at once, Tessa allowed a lengthy kiss on the lips and the audience, or at least the male portion, went wild.

After that nothing could displease the spectators, not even lofty ideals and noble music. By the time Tessa/Leonore rescued her husband from death and she and Delorme (without his shirt) performed their soaring love duet, there was scarcely a dry eye in the theater. By the end of the second opera, *The Barber of Seville*, no one could doubt that Teresa Foscari's benefit would be the talk of London for years.

When the curtain fell on her last bow, Tessa, delirious with pride and exhilaration, picked her way through the mounds of flowers thrown onto the stage and summoned enough voice to thank her fellow singers for performing at her benefit when she'd been in the company for such a short time. "That's all right, *madame*," said the bass who sang the roles of Rocco and Figaro. "It's always an honor to sing with you, especially since we were paid for our work tonight."

Smiling graciously, Tessa's mind worked furiously. If the company wasn't performing gratis, the management of the Regent had taken a huge loss on the evening. Her suspicions about the source of this largesse were confirmed by Nancy Sturridge. "Are we not fortunate?" she said on the way back to the dressing rooms. "Lord Somerville made up my loss after the Tavistock fire and Lord Allerton has done the same for you. A good voice is an excellent thing to have, but a generous protector is even better."

"Lord Allerton is not my protector," she said.

"Whatever you say," Nancy replied. "I didn't know it was a secret."

When Tessa finally drove away the mob of well-wishers from her dressing room and had a chance to change her clothes, Max and Lindo awaited her at the door. As luck would have it they emerged from the theater at the same time as Nancy, on Somerville's arm. Nancy winked at her.

Mr. Lindo is here too, she wanted to scream. Did everyone in London believe her to be Allerton's mistress? She was not pleased when the carriage stopped in Piccadilly to let the manager off, and she and Max proceeded alone to his house.

"I thought this was a party," she said huskily. Everything she would say all evening would be husky.

"A party of two."

"This isn't wise."

"I know you are tired and won't want to go out in public again tonight. Let me take care of you. I won't do anything against your wishes."

She knew that. He had never deliberately hurt her, except over the Chelsea Hospital affair. He had been angry at the time, repented, and made amends. Never at any point in their acquaintance had he given her reason to fear him. The terror came from within.

A quiet supper in Max's comfortable house sounded perfect. She was safe with him, trusted him. It was herself she did not trust.

"I have a bone to pick with you. You paid the singers for my benefit."

"Just a matter of business," he said evenly. "You wouldn't agree to sing at the Regent without one."

It *sounded* reasonable. "The entire company believes you did it because I am your mistress."

"Not a very good mistress, if you don't mind my saying so. You've barely spoken to me in weeks." Unwillingly her lips twitched at his teasing tone. "I'm glad to see you smile. *I* haven't been at all amused by your neglect."

"What nonsense you speak." Enjoyable nonsense, she had to admit. Relieved at getting the benefit and the season over with, she felt more cheerful than she had in ages.

"I'm sorry about people having the wrong idea, Tessa, but there will always be talk, whatever the truth of the matter. You know that better than most."

"It's true. And I needed...well, thank you, anyway." Although Max probably had guessed her financial straits, she still preferred not to discuss the matter.

A stately butler admitted them to the house in Upper Grosvenor Street and showed them into the library where a supper table had been set up. Embossed leather wall panels of dark orange polished to a high gloss complemented the gilt spines of the books stored in bookcases with gilt trellis doors. The curtain hangings were of red velvet, as was the upholstery. She was glad she had dressed simply this evening, in a pale blue silk evening gown that didn't compete with the splendid surroundings. Max seated her at the table and the brush of his fingers on her back when he pushed in her chair made her shiver.

"Are you cold? Do you need your shawl?"

"No, thank you. It's quite warm in here."

She turned down champagne in favor of Madeira because the sweetness of the wine soothed her throat. A pair of footmen served a series of delicious light dishes, perfect for a tired singer who'd eaten nothing since breakfast, then withdrew.

"I must thank you, Max, for finding my grandmother. I wrote to her and she has written back. I have an aunt too. I'm so happy to have discovered that I have some relations."

"Did you learn why your father lost touch with them?"

"Apparently he and *his* father had a disagreement about his profession. It doesn't seem a good reason for estrangement but Papa went abroad and married my mother in Paris before moving to Portugal because of the Revolution. Perhaps they didn't approve of him marrying a Frenchwoman. Anyway, when my grandfather died, my grandmother tried to find him. He had died, but she learned he had a daughter who was a singer and married an Italian. I wish Domenico had not denied her inquiries. I realize now he wished to keep absolute control over me."

"That's why you never sang in London, you know." Max explained about Mortimer's earlier efforts to lure La Divina to England. Another tale of Domenico's perfidy.

Alone with Max, she felt relaxed and well cared for, just as he had promised. Eating a meal *à deux* was something they'd never done together and it was enticingly comfortable, even cozy, like having dinner with a friend.

"I'm enjoying myself," she said, and flushed when their eyes met and he gazed at her with a heat that wasn't at all friendly. "I'm glad we can meet as friends," she said hastily, to convince herself that there was nothing more.

FRIENDS!

The last thing Max wanted was her friendship. Or rather he wanted much more. He wanted Tessa for life. Still, if she could only offer friendship for now, he'd accept it as an invitation to change her mind.

He poured more wine and leaned back in his chair. "I'm honored to be your friend. What would friends like to talk about over supper?"

"Anything at all and I would be grateful if you, as my friend, would talk about yourself. My voice won't last much longer. Tell me about your childhood. I enjoyed meeting Lady Clarissa very much." Her mouth twitched. "Was she a comfortable mother?"

"Excuse me, but were you by any chance asleep when she spoke to you? Comfortable, no, but I am immensely fond of her even while I have to resist her efforts to run my life for me. She had her parents and grandparents twisted around her finger." The fact that he was in violation of the terms of their wager weighed on his mind, but not much. Such a trifle wouldn't stop Lady Clarissa from going after what she wanted and it wouldn't stop her son. Max had other plans for his future than wedding the girl of his mother's choice.

He told her about life at Tamworth House in Piccadilly and Tamworth Hall in Staffordshire and how much he disliked the pomp of the former and loved the beauty of the latter.

"I've always wanted to live in the country," she said dreamily.

You will.

Then, because it was a topic that could not be avoided forever, he told her how his love of opera, sparked by meeting her, had turned into an obsession that culminated in the creation of the Regent Opera House. "I had to grease a few palms to get a license for a new musical theater. My influence was useful too. I aim to make it the greatest opera house in the world, an easy thing when Teresa Foscari sings there."

"Don't forget Edouard Delorme. He would be desolated not to be named."

He took it as a good omen that she was able to make a joke about the tenor. He talked on about his fascination with the art they shared. She didn't say much, but he basked in her rapt attention and warmed beneath the appreciation in her limpid blue eyes. He did not mention the succession of singers he'd taken to his bed. Max might not have Somerville's savoir faire when it came to women but nor was he a fool.

"Tell me about Isabella Cavatini," she said. "A good voice but a small bosom, according to Sofie."

Damnation. Of course she knew. There were no secrets in the theater.

Throwing caution aside, he met her eye squarely and told the truth. "Every woman I ever took to bed was a substitute for you. No one could truly satisfy me because she was not you."

"There is only one La Divina," she said softly.

"There is only one Tessa Birkett. I didn't want a goddess but my sweet girl." He pushed back his chair and removed something from his desk drawer. "I bought this for you in Oporto as an engagement gift, or so I hoped."

She gazed at the piece of ancient ivory with the dancing couple. "It's beautiful," she whispered.

"It makes me happy that I can finally give it to you as a token of my love."

She fell silent for an age and he feared every moment that she would demand her cloak and leave. He'd spoken too soon.

"Max," she said, so softly he could barely hear her. "Will you take me to bed?"

IN CONTRAST TO the opulent library, Max's bedchamber was almost monkish. Expensively but simply furnished, it was a place for sleeping and Tessa took comfort in that fact.

"I've never—er—entertained in this room," he said, as though reading her mind.

More importantly, nothing could be further from the sybaritic luxury of the Parisian apartment where *it* had happened. Instead of embroidered hangings and gilt cherubs, Max slept among dark woods and subdued hues. A few quick breathing exercises calmed Tessa's jitters as she faced the enormity of her decision to try again to be a normal woman. She desperately wanted to be normal.

He stood holding her shoulders, as grave and somber as his surroundings, but his medieval face no longer seemed grim, merely serious, and very beloved. He looked down at her with eyes that were intense, ardent, and a little concerned.

"Do you know what is unfair?" she asked.

"Many things."

"I have the reputation of a *grande amoureuse* and none of the joy. I *want* the joy."

If it were possible his eyes grew darker. "I want to give it to you."

She touched his cheek and her heart leapt with faith. "Will you do something for me?"

"Anything."

The words came as quickly as the idea had entered her mind. "Will you blindfold me?"

For a moment he seemed struck dumb and she was too. "Why?" he asked finally.

"I thought if I was helpless again, but with a man I trust, I might get over the fear."

He turned his head to kiss the palm of her hand and his eyes were like polished coal. "Are you sure?"

"Please, Max. Let's try it."

He nodded and then he kissed her, long and sweet, making her doubts melt away with the pleasure of his lips on hers, his arms about her, proving to her that she was Tessa and not the body of a famous singer that men wished to possess. When they drew breath they clung to each other, panting a little.

"How shall we go about this?" he asked. His cheeks flushed adorably. "What do you want to wear? Aside from the blindfold, I mean."

"I was naked," she whispered.

"Much as I would enjoy that, you may feel better if you keep your shift on."

She swallowed. "I shall wear a blindfold so I won't see my nakedness. I considered having you tie me up too, but I think that's going too far. Unfasten my gown please." She turned around.

"Wait," he said. A few seconds later he returned with a broad strip of starched white linen. "You deserve a clean neckcloth." He folded it in half lengthwise and held it over her eyes. "How's that?"

"I can almost see the room in a blur."

He folded it again. "Now?"

"Good." She couldn't see, but neither was she deprived of all light as she had been by Domenico's black mask.

"Now for those buttons. Damn, they are small."

His complaint made her smile. It was so *normal*. It was impossible to be frightened with Max grumbling as he fumbled with the loops and silk covered buttons. "If you tear them you can sew them on again for me," she said.

"My needlework studies never progressed that far. All right, that's done." He slipped the silk down her shoulders, helped her step out of it, and went to work on her stays.

The slight chill as each layer was removed made her shiver with anticipation, more so when he kissed her shoulders. Blindness lent a frisson to the act of being undressed. As her shift, the final garment, came over her head she was exposed in a delicious vulnerability.

Fingers, light and faintly abrasive, ran over her breasts. Masculine fingers. "I never saw anything so beautiful. I wish I had the brilliance of a Mozart to express my awe."

She leaned into his touch but it was the wonder in his voice that affected her most. Lack of sight enhanced her already acute aural perception.

"I'll get onto the bed now." She longed for and dreaded what was to come. And feared the discovery of which emotion would endure.

"You can call a halt at any time," he reassured her. "I sent my servants to bed so you may scream as much as you like without fear of embarrassment."

"You are very funny. You know this evening I can only manage a croak."

She could almost hear his smile. "If you croak I'll stop at once. Why don't you go and lie down while I—"

"Don't tell me." She gathered her courage. "Let me wait a little."

Once she heard him leave the room she extended her arms and found the bed. Climbing onto the high mattress, she stretched out on her back. Max had removed the counterpane and blankets leaving only soothing linen to rest against her skin. A man was coming to her and she could not see him. He could be anyone: a footman, a chimney sweep, a *comte*. He would get on top of her, crush her with his weight, and take her. Beneath her blindfold she squeezed her eyes shut to exclude the memory of long minutes when she had waited for Domenico and known she loathed him. The man who would come to her wasn't her vile husband, or any of those others. It was Max, whom she trusted and loved.

She wanted him to return and dreaded his coming.

Vorrei e non vorrei. The line from *Don Giovanni* drifted into her head. *I would and I would not*. How perfectly Zerlina, a role she'd sung often early in her career, expressed the ambivalence of seduction. She hummed a few bars and as always music calmed her, but only for a short time. *I could be happy, but he could betray me again.*

She was naked, defenseless. No, her hands weren't tied. She could escape. But she wouldn't need to. She need only croak and she would be free. Supposing he didn't hear her? She experimented and nothing came out. Had the long night of singing destroyed her vocal cords so she would be helpless? Max didn't mean to hurt her but supposing he did and she couldn't stop him?

Breathe, Tessa.

A few breaths and the knot in her chest loosened a little. She wanted Max to arrive and put an end to her panic. Unless he made it worse.

Come, don't come.

I desire it and I don't desire it.

I love you, I can't love you.

Where *was* he?

She missed his footsteps on the carpet.

"Good Gracious! There's a naked woman in my bed."

Her croak became a chuckle. How could she fear him when he made her laugh? The dip of the mattress hardly disturbed her.

"Max?"

"Yes."

"I knew it was you."

"Who else? I certainly haven't invited anyone. In fact I have had the entire male population of Upper Grosvenor Street placed under guard."

She wanted to touch him but kept her hands flat on the bed, remaining physically still so that she could concentrate on her emotional responses, and perhaps control them.

"I'm glad you are here," she said.

"Thank God. I'm going to kiss you now."

The only thing frightening about his kiss was how much she enjoyed it. He must be kneeling on the bed and leaning over her because only their lips touched. She grew feverish. It wasn't enough. Neck, shoulders and every other inch of her throbbed in vain, but he made no further move. Her breasts yearned for him and her sex grew warm.

"Touch me," she whispered.

"Was that a croak?"

God no. She shook her head vehemently, groped for his hand and brought it to her breast.

"I can do better," he said. "Lie still and don't think about anything."

Emptying her mind proved impossible but her teeming thoughts slowed to a low hum of delight while he caressed her body with his hands and lips. Holy St. George, he felt good. Better than anything ever. Better than a hot bath at the Pulteney or whipped cream or hitting a perfect high D. Or hitting a high D after eating whipped cream in the bath. She'd like to hit one now. Her back arched when he sucked hard on a nipple and a lightning bolt streaked down through her belly and set her on fire. Never once did he lean his weight on her.

The man had *una lingua di genio*, as she learned when he kissed and licked his way down the sensitive skin of her midriff, giving her hot shivers and making her sway her hips in desperate pleading. Longing centered on her *fica* and again the deprivation of sight enhanced the physical sensation.

Touch me there.

Yet she was shocked when his hands and then his mouth found it, for she'd never been caressed thus. He hushed her gasp and thrust his tongue into her *buco*, finding the *perla* with unerring skill, stroking and lapping and driving her near to wondrous insanity.

"We should stop this," she whispered after a while, though her senses were soaring and it was the last thing she wanted.

"Why?" he said, with quick concern. "Are you alarmed?"

"That was not a croak. But this isn't what I planned. I must know if having you on top will make me panic."

"Time enough for that later. Now I wish to give you pleasure. Do I please you?"

His obvious anxiety turned her heart over. "Of course you do."

"In that case…"

He returned to driving her mad until her mind could think of nothing but the genius of his *lingua* and then nothing at all as her body followed her into the heavens in great shudders of joy. His head lay on her stomach and she played idly with his hair as she returned to herself. "Thank you, Max."

"It was my very great pleasure."

She wished she could see him, for she was sure he wore his infrequent, heartbreaking smile. She almost suggested he remove the blindfold. He crawled up the bed and lay beside her, taking her loosely in his arms, and they rested there for a while, murmuring appreciative nothings and nuzzling each other with lazy kisses.

"I want you to know," she said, feeling as though she was leaping into a dangerous void with no known end, "no matter what happens, that I love you."

She'd sung those words in several languages a hundred times

on stage and when she was in character she always meant them. This time she believed them in real life. She, Tessa, loved him, Max. Now at this minute, whatever the future held. It was a moment of such perfection that she felt she could die happy.

"Then nothing else matters. We can find our way."

A couple of quick, shallow breaths pushed aside a momentary flare of anxiety. She embraced his optimism and thought only of pleasure ahead. Lying blind on her back, she let his presence permeate her senses: the light odor of soap and sweat, the heat of his body, the faint rhythm of his beating heart. Her skin prickled with renewed desire and her *fica* glowed and clenched.

When, without warning, he moved over her, and she felt his legs rasp hers, the heft of his lean torso against her belly and breasts, his thick *cazzone* seeking entrance, she opened to him without a hint of disquiet. They joined together with scorching heat and melting tenderness and when they had both achieved fulfillment they fell asleep in each other's arms.

MAX WOKE UP happy. Tessa loved him and he'd passed the most glorious night of his life. At some point her blindfold had come off. He gazed at her face, artless in sleep, beautiful in the dim light. *His*.

But he'd been happy that morning at the Pulteney too, so he took nothing for granted. With trepidation he stroked the golden hair from her forehead and called her name.

She stirred. He tensed. She smiled.

"*Tutto va bene*, Max," she said. "I am fine. I am *normal*." Her glee was infectious and they lay in bed chortling like children.

"Sit up," he said, arranging the pillows and covers so she could lean against them comfortably. "I have something important to say."

"Are you making me an offer for next season at the Regent?"

"Not that kind of offer." He was absurdly nervous, like the

youth who had wanted to marry Tessa Birkett eleven years earlier. He knelt before her, naked and vulnerable, both literally and because, even more now than when he'd been nineteen, she had the power to break his heart.

"Will you marry me, Tessa?"

Her mouth gaped in a perfect oval. "Holy Saint George, I wasn't expecting that."

"Did you think I wanted you as a mistress?"

"Why not? You are a lord. I am an opera singer. I am not a suitable match for you. Think what Lady Clarissa would say. Think what she did last time you took it into your head to marry me."

"I am no longer nineteen years old and my mother does not run my life. I don't want you as mistress and I do not believe you would accept me on those terms."

She nodded. "You are right. I have this odd wish to be respectable, finally."

"Marry me! Not only for that reason but because we love each other. We should wake up every morning together, read the newspapers at breakfast, have children if we can, and live in the country."

"Max. I am a *singer*."

"We don't have to live in the country. We'll be in London during the season, or anywhere else you wish."

"That was not my point. You can't marry a singer who has bedded Napoleon Bonaparte as well as half the nobility in Europe."

"You haven't."

"What's the difference? Everyone believes I have. I will never be fully accepted."

"I don't care. We'll put it about that it was all an invention of the French newspapers. The English love blaming the French for anything. And I don't care. All I want is you." The last was true. Her other arguments had some merit but he welcomed the challenge to overcome them. There would be talk and even scandal when Lord Allerton married the notorious La Divina. There'd be the devil to pay with his mother, but after a horrendous row he'd bring her around because she cared for him.

"I have influence," he said. "No one will dare to snub you."

"I'm not sure I want to be accepted by people like Sir Henry Waxfield, who despises a delightful, intelligent man like Simon Lindo because of his race."

"I'm certainly not giving up Simon's friendship. Waxfield is a buffoon and we won't have him in our house." *Our* house. How immensely satisfying it would be to have Tessa here all the time. In this bed, but also in his library and dining room and entertaining guests of all kinds, chosen for their characters and abilities, not merely for social position.

"He is hardly alone in his prejudices."

It had never occurred to Max that his place at the highest pinnacles of the English aristocracy, which he took for granted and never thought about, could be a disadvantage. What Tessa said was true—he'd thought of it himself in the past as a reason not to marry her—but he wouldn't admit it aloud. He wasn't going to let any obstacle, let alone the petty opinions of other people, get in his way. He had a lot of Lady Clarissa in him.

"Tessa, my darling," he said, taking her hand and holding it against his chest. "Please marry me. I can't bear to lose you again."

Hope beat a tattoo in his heart as she examined his features. She touched his cheek, then an elegant finger traced the line of his brow, his too-prominent nose, sealed his lips as though to silence further argument. Tears gathered in her beautiful, expressive eyes. "I wish I could, Max. I wish others didn't matter but they do. I'm too famous to ignore the world because the world will not ignore me. I don't have the strength to face more notoriety. I cannot be Lady Allerton."

"I'll protect you from the scandalmongers. You told me you didn't know where you belong, that you felt empty because you had no home. Let me be your home and belong with me. We'll make our lives the way we want them and to hell with everyone else."

She fended off his movement to embrace her, descending from the bed, glorious in her nakedness, and snatching up the same silk dressing gown she'd worn the day they were caught in the rain.

"I didn't tell you earlier," she said, "but I am leaving London tomorrow. I am traveling to Somerset to see my grandmother."

"Good idea. I shall escort you."

"No." She buttoned the garment with an air of finality that matched her voice. "I must go alone and find my father's family."

"Don't give me an answer yet. I'll wait."

"Maybe I will decide to be a proper country lady like the characters in the novels by the author of *Emma*. I shall live out my life in happy obscurity."

Max refrained from snorting. Despite the natural charm and simplicity that lay beneath the public face of the operatic diva, Tessa hadn't spent years in the theater without acquiring her share of dramatic foolishness.

Happy obscurity? *Pah*!

First it was ludicrous to think of a musical genius like Teresa Foscari rotting in a provincial English village. Secondly, he wouldn't let her. If she wasn't tired of it and back in London within two weeks, he was going to fetch her.

CHAPTER TWENTY-ONE

"It has come to our attention that a Lady of Rank will purchase the lease of the Tavistock Theatre."

The Times

SIMON LINDO HAD become accustomed to the baroque grandeur of Tamworth House. He'd visited the Piccadilly mansion many times since Lady Clarissa Hawthorne made her offer to buy the Tavistock and employ him as its manager. As he made his way up the grand staircase, his conscience pricked him. He wasn't sure Max had taken his mother's plans seriously; Simon had scarcely believed the willful lady would go through with the purchase and construction of a brand new theater in the middle of London. Since Max had other matters on his mind, Simon had decided not to bother him.

Which was nonsense and Simon was not in the habit of lying to himself. He'd wasted his time with Lady Clarissa Hawthorne because he couldn't keep away. By the time she convinced him her plans weren't castles in the air, it was too late. He couldn't warn Max about the Tavistock Phoenix Theatre, as its owner had fancifully decided to rename it, because he might not be able to disguise the dismaying fact that he was in love with Max's mother.

A fact that he intended to keep a secret, especially from the lady herself. Not drowning in her whims took all his resolve, without giving her any other advantage. For his inconvenient passion could come to nothing. Any connection, beyond a business one, between a Jew from the City of London and the richest and most aristocratic woman in England was too ludicrous to even consider.

His palms were damp, like that of a very young man instead of a sober middle-aged father of two grown sons. He stopped in front of a massive Chinese-style mirror at the top of the stairs to make sure his features were composed and suitably inscrutable for engaging in the final stages of a negotiation with a woman who would maul him to death if she could. Love had spared him any illusions about the character of the beloved.

Lady Clarissa was seated at the table in the splendid library, papers arrayed before her on her colossal desk, an ormolu-encrusted French masterpiece that must have cost his year's income. Impeccably attired and coiffed as ever, she stood up and smiled at him.

"Simon! I have all the papers prepared for the final purchase of the Tavistock site, the architect's designs, and your contract."

"I shall read them with care," he said, giving her a hard look. "I will not sign anything unless it's all in order."

"My attorney is in the house to make necessary changes. I sent him downstairs to wait so that we can talk in private."

He wished the lawyer were present. She insisted on leaning over his shoulder as he read and her proximity made it difficult for him to think clearly.

When he finished, he put away his spectacles and told her to sit down.

"Come and sit by the window. I don't like the hard chairs at the desk." The hard chairs she used every day while attending to the affairs of her fortune. She moved purposely to a sofa and patted it. "Here."

For once he allowed her to address him like a dog; she wasn't going to like what he said next. "Before we go any further, my lady, I want to know something."

"Yes?" She fluttered her lashes in a doomed attempt to look innocent.

"What has the new Tavistock to do with Max?"

"Why, nothing. He scarcely knows about it."

"That is my concern. I have a nose for chicanery and something doesn't smell right. What are you up to? Max was my patron and colleague before you, and he is also my friend. I won't have any part in a plot to harm him." He punctuated the statement with a stern frown.

"Max is my son. Why would I harm him?"

"Because you like to have your own way. And because you may not think of it as harm, though you are almost certainly wrong."

Her eyes narrowed and she pouted—both affectations adorable to his infatuated gaze. "Very well, I will tell you. I had a bet with Max that he couldn't run the Regent Opera House for two seasons without spending more of his own funds than his initial investment."

Interesting. It explained a few times when Max had not offered money when Simon expected it. He decided not to mention the small matter of Teresa Foscari's benefit. "And what was the stake?"

"Max's marriage. If I win, I choose his bride. If not, I stop nagging him."

Simon nodded and kept his mouth grave. "Very wise of you," he said. "I married a young woman chosen by my parents and we were happy until the day Leah died." She beamed at him. "And really the point is moot. If you should win, by no means a certainty regardless of what happens at the Tavistock, you will choose the bride he wants."

"I will?" With satisfaction he noticed that his answer surprised her.

"He wishes to marry Teresa Foscari and you will embrace the match."

"I will not!" She folded her arms.

"Of course you will. He's madly in love with her. You want your son to be happy and no other lady will do. She is a brilliant talent and of excellent character. I happen to know you like her. That is important between mother and daughter-in-law."

"But she's a singer! Her reputation!"

Her face set into a stubborn look, reminding him of her son when he'd tried to persuade Max to offer a contract to a second-rate baritone. He'd lost that battle but he knew just how to handle the mother.

"I didn't think you cared for the opinion of the vulgar. I'm a little disappointed to hear that Lady Clarissa Hawthorne would sacrifice her son's happiness and her own wishes because she is afraid of what people will say."

"Never! I can do anything I want and other people be damned."

He raised a skeptical eyebrow and waited, letting her puzzle it out for herself.

"I am going into the theatrical business," she said.

"True."

"And it would be useful to have the most admired performer in the world in the family."

"I agree."

"It's not as though she's an ordinary singer. Her mother belonged to a French noble family."

"You make excellent points that I hadn't even thought of myself. We are agreed, then?"

"I suppose." She still looked sulky but he knew she'd keep her word. He was pleased to have done a favor for Max, whom he liked almost like another son. Also because he was a little guilty about the Tavistock.

In one of the mercurial changes of temper he found so fascinating, she settled down and regarded him with an inquisitive look. "Why did you never marry again?"

"I never met a lady I wanted to marry. And you, my lady? You've been widowed longer than I. You must have had many offers."

"Dozens, but they all wanted my money. Like my husband."

"Surely not all," he said, struck by an unwonted vulnerability behind her eyes. "You are a very beautiful woman. You've been alone for a long time."

"I had Max but then he moved out of this"—she indicated the vastness of their surroundings—"and into his own house." She pinched her lips together. "Once I tried a less formal arrangement for a while but for one reason or another it didn't satisfy."

"Not the right gentleman, eh? And none of the others tempted you even a little?"

"If they aren't fortune hunters they are frightened of me. Am I so terrible?"

"I'm not frightened of you."

"That's why I like you so much."

He gazed at her strong, handsome face. Very like her son's but in a softer, feminine version. She wasn't strictly beautiful but she possessed an animalistic quality, a vigor and lust for life that he found endlessly appealing. She was headstrong and spoiled but possessed a core of decency that she did her best to hide, the same way she disdained to show fear. Max had told him a little about the scoundrel who had married her and sired her son. By all accounts Hawthorne's death had been a mercy and the risk of finding another such man might have kept her from remarrying.

Age cannot wither her, nor custom stale her infinite variety. Simon was far gone to compare her to Cleopatra, but Shakespeare's famous words expressed the fascination he had for her. Desire stirred, something he usually kept under control. He was not a religious man, but he did regard himself as a moral one.

"Simon," she said, reminding him improbably of a shy girl. She lowered her eyelids and tilted her chin a little. If he didn't know better he'd think she was inviting him to kiss her.

Incredible.

She swayed a little.

She *was* inviting him. An invitation impossible to refuse or resist. He had no idea what he was letting himself in for and he didn't care.

As soon as their lips touched all resemblance to a girl, shy or otherwise, vanished and the tigress returned. Five minutes later—or ten or an hour—they were horizontal, breathing hard with clothes in disarray.

Needless to say his insane love was not discomposed for long. She sat up, patted her hair and smiled at him, a new happiness in her voracious eyes that found an answer in his heart. "Shall we marry?" she asked.

Would she always have the power to astonish him? He hoped so.

"No," he said. "You are mad to even think of it."

"Why?"

"I'm a Jew."

"You told me you left your synagogue."

"Like my friend Isaac Disraeli, I had a disagreement with the Bevis Marks congregation. Also like him, I had my sons baptized so they could go to university. But I have no desire to renounce Judaism for Christianity and see no need to do so. If I ever remarry, which I will not, it will be to another Jew."

"That's not fair."

"Let us not argue about an irrelevancy. Even if I became a Quaker or a Methodist or a member of the Church of England I'd still be a Jew in the eyes of the world. For me to wed someone like you would be a scandal beyond description."

"Lady Clarissa Hawthorne can do anything."

"And my people have not survived the centuries by looking for trouble."

"Yet you would have me accept Foscari as a bride for my son?"

"Max and Teresa are young and in love."

"I'm in love with you." The dear termagant had no idea of the realities of life.

"And I, God help me, am in love with you. Luckily our arrangement in running the Tavistock gives us reason to meet alone that no one will object to, beyond Lady Clarissa's eccentricity in conducting such a venture."

Her eyes widened and her lips formed an eager O. "We can be secret lovers. How delicious."

"Where are you going?"

"To lock the door."

CHAPTER TWENTY-TWO

"Many notables have now left Town, including the PRINCE REGENT and Madame FOSCARI."

The Morning Post

TESSA'S POST CHAISE rattled up the narrow street of Stoke Newton, her spirits matching the gloomy day. The hard labor and emotional turmoil of her months in London had left her exhausted. The pretty village, so unpretentious, so English, posed no threat to her tranquility. She looked forward to a few weeks devoid of alarms and crises.

The final triumph of her benefit had been put behind her. Its miraculous aftermath was harder to forget but she managed. Whenever she thought of Max she returned to her book. She had spent the two-day journey reading *Emma* again, the anonymous author of the novel her only companion.

At Rose Cottage, which did indeed have pink roses climbing up the stone front, two ladies hurried out, fluttering with excitement.

"You must be Tessa," said the elder, a neat little lady with tidy gray curls covered with a delicate lace cap. "You look just like Jonathan. You may call me Grandmama." She embraced her tenderly and introduced Aunt Hester, who was about sixty and quite unlike her dainty mother.

"How was your journey?" Aunt Hester, tall and raw-boned, lurched more than she fluttered. "You must be very tired. Such a tedious drive from London, not that I've ever been there. Did you stop at an inn? Of course you did. I hope the sheets were dry. Did you have a good dinner?"

"Hester," Mrs. Burkett said quietly, laying her hand on her daughter's arm while keeping hold of Tessa's hand. "You are quite right that Tessa must be tired. Let us go inside."

Over teacups in the tiny, perfectly tidy parlor, they exchanged stories. Her grandfather had been vicar of Stoke Newton and his widow and daughter had moved to the cottage after his death. They did not appear to be prosperous. Tessa guessed that it must have taken a good portion of their resources to trace the long-lost black sheep of the family. She could improve their fortunes, she thought, then remembered that unless she returned to the fatiguing round of endless performances she would not be able to do so.

"You see, my dear," Grandmama said, "Jonathan was studying for the church but he became infected with *French* ideas." Her genteel voice dropped to a whisper. "*Atheism*. His father told him to leave and never come back, but a son is a son and I never stopped missing him. Perhaps it was disrespectful to Mr. Birkett's memory but I had to find him." Something in her voice told Tessa that the vicar had not been a pleasant man, also that his widow was far too loyal ever to say so. "We were distressed to learn of his death in Portugal. And equally so when we had the letter from Mr. Foscari saying that you were not our granddaughter. Was that a mistake? Perhaps your husband didn't understand English."

Tessa muttered a vaguely worded agreement. She didn't want to explain Domenico's falsehood, or his many crimes. She was putting that part of her history behind her. "The important thing is that I have found you." Tears pricked her eyes. She had a grandmother and an aunt. She belonged somewhere. "It means so much for me to have found my family. I have no one else, apart from my cousin Jacobin in London. Her father and my mother were first cousins."

Aunt Hester dropped a biscuit on the floor. "So sorry. I am always clumsy," she said cheerfully, then hissed an aside. "Better not to talk about the French. We are so glad you speak English."

"I grew up in the English colony in Oporto so English is my first language. Later I often sang in Paris, of course."

"I thought you lived in Italy," Grandmama said. "I believe you are quite famous and I daresay you are very good to have been hired to sing in Paris and London."

"Also St. Petersburg, Berlin, Munich, and many other places besides."

"Dear me, what an adventurous life you have led. Was it quite comfortable?"

Tessa sank into the soothing company of people who had little notion of opera. They never read the London papers and knew nothing of her recent disasters and triumphs. It also meant they were ignorant of the less respectable rumors about her. These sweet provincials would no doubt faint if they heard she'd even met the Emperor Napoleon.

"You must sing for us although we do not have a piano. None of our family has ever been at all musical and I don't know where you inherited it." With that, Grandmama put a period to the discussion. "Are you fond of raspberries, Tessa? We have plenty in the garden."

"And fresh cream sent by Mrs. Keith at the Hall," Aunt Hester added. "So obliging of her."

"I adore raspberries and cream," Tessa said. "Will you show me the garden, Aunt Hester? I would enjoy some fresh air and it's a beautiful afternoon. How happy I am to have found you. I want to learn everything about you."

IT WAS LUCKY Tessa had read *Emma*, else she would have found life at Rose Cottage incomprehensible. Accustomed to the theater where emotions were displayed like jewels and there was always a drama, off stage as well as on, she found it hard to adjust to a household where politeness ruled absolutely and dissension was avoided at all costs. At first they spoke of her father, but his mother and sister were too pained by the family quarrel to revisit anything but uncontroversial stories of his youth. Tessa would have liked to hear about his "French ideas" and match them with her recollections of him and her French mother.

She enjoyed Aunt Hester's cheerful friendliness despite the inanity of her conversation. She admired the way her grandmother, an intelligent woman with all her faculties intact despite her advanced age, tolerated the mindless chatter of her daughter without anything more than a tactful turning of the subject. What she couldn't understand was the resistance to any topic that wasn't firmly rooted in the mundane activities of Stoke Newton, varied by a rare shopping trip to Bristol.

If she found her father's family strange, they were baffled by Tessa. Much too courteous to say so, her life appalled them. Even the mildest of theatrical anecdotes made them blush. She hoped they never discovered that she had quite often appeared wearing breeches.

By the end of the fifth day the small size and number of the rooms had begun to seem stifling. Since there was no way to escape the constant company of her new relations without going outside, it gave her a new appreciation of the English passion for walks. The fresh air and green fields did her good, and her energy revived.

The disruption of years of ingrained discipline gnawed at her brain. She had never gone so long without exercising her voice, yet inflicting the tedium of vocalization on the inhabitants of the tiny cottage seemed an imposition. She missed Sempronio and Sofie, and Angela who had remained in London because there wasn't room here for her personal maid.

She missed Max, quite desperately. What he'd done for her, what they'd done *together*, was wonderful. The greatest weight of Domenico's legacy had been lifted and she was free again. Free to love. But why couldn't she have fallen in love with an ordinary man? Why did he have to be a member of one of the richest and most famous families in England? She wanted a quiet life without the infamy that had dogged her for years. The thought of living with Max in a sweet little country cottage made her soft with longing. Hosting a grand ball in the Piccadilly mansion or presiding over the grandeur of his country estate filled her with dread. People would be looking at her and judging—not for her performance but for herself. She knew she would fail.

They had been invited to dinner at Stoke Hall, a very large house according to Aunt Hester, home of Mr. and Mrs. Keith who were the neighborhood grandees. Since this was precisely the milieu Max inhabited, she looked forward to it with trepidation. These people would have heard of her and most likely knew some of the more shocking stories. Determined to behave like an impeccable English lady, she prepared to stem any attack of panic.

"How very fine you look," Aunt Hester said as she helped Tessa into her gown. "This lace must have cost ten shillings a yard or more. I'm sure Mrs. Keith has nothing finer though she has her clothes from Madame Tillault in Bristol who came from London."

"Am I not correctly dressed?" Tessa asked anxiously. It was one of the new gowns she'd bought in London after being engaged at the Regent. They were modest, both in cost and design, compared to her old wardrobe. She had thought she looked very proper and countrified.

"Mrs. Keith and Miss Keith usually outdo us all, but I daresay they won't mind."

THE KEITH LADIES did mind. Though they received Tessa with great condescension, she caught them eyeing her ensemble with disfavor.

"You are from London?" Mrs. Keith asked. "We prefer the country." She then proceeded to almost ignore her. Most of her remarks were addressed to her own family, and occasionally to the

Birketts, who were expected to praise everything. Stoke Hall didn't seem particularly large or splendid to Tessa, compared to the country palaces of kings and emperors, but she dutifully admired the new Wilton carpet when haughtily asked for her opinion.

Mr. Keith talked about hunting and farming; his daughter boasted of the assemblies in Bristol; the hostess went into raptures over everything either spouse or daughter said.

Tessa amused herself by comparing the company to the characters in *Emma*. Mrs. Keith bore an uncanny resemblance to Mrs. Elton, the self-satisfied vicar's bride. The Birketts were, of course, Mrs. and Miss Bates. And who was she? Who else but the mysterious Miss Jane Fairfax who played the piano so very well? She wished Miss Woodhouse and Mr. Knightley were there to enliven the evening.

After dinner, they repaired to the drawing room and Mrs. Keith asked her daughter to entertain them with a song. The young lady sang an English folk song with reasonable ease. Her voice was weak and occasionally off key, but pretty enough and not bad for someone who had been, as Mrs. Keith condescended to whisper to her, trained by the best singing master in Bristol.

"What a pleasure you have given us, Miss Keith," Aunt Hester said. "We haven't heard Tessa sing yet since we have no piano."

"I haven't practiced," Tessa said, having the good manners not to wish to embarrass her hostess's daughter. "And I don't generally sing straight after a meal. I would prefer not to."

"Oh but you must," Mrs. Keith said, scenting an opportunity for her daughter to vanquish the London interloper. "You will find our pianoforte superior, I believe, and I daresay we have the music for something you know."

"I am no great pianist," Tessa replied, thinking of her Broadwood and wishing for Sempronio. "I will choose something simple that I know well and can play from memory." Truthfully, she ached to sing. Her voice was an instrument begging to be played.

She decided on the popular *Caro mio ben* that she'd performed at Jacobin's musicale. In a room this size if she sang at anything like full voice she'd blast her listeners' eardrums with the force of an explosion. Taking a few breaths she launched into the Italian love song almost sotto voce. It was a lovely tune and she couldn't but recall the last time she'd sung it, just before she saw Max again for the first time.

Senza di te languisce il cor. Without you my heart languishes.

And so it did. She always sang from the heart but never more truly than now. She sang for Max, pouring her love into the tune, aching for his presence. This subdued performance was one of the best she'd ever given.

She bowed her head with the last heartrending phrase and you could have heard a pin drop. Nothing was as satisfying as the silence of listeners so affected they must recover themselves before they break into a rapturous ovation. She knew that silence well and she waited with her usual anticipation for the love and admiration of the crowd to wash over her.

Calling the applause a smattering would be almost too much. Raising her head, she saw nothing but indifference and perplexity.

"Very nice, I'm sure," Mrs. Keith said.

"I know that song," from Miss Keith.

The gentleman of the house yawned.

Only Aunt Hester displayed enthusiasm but she'd clapped equally for Miss Keith. Grandmama smiled at Tessa. "That was beautiful. You have a lovely voice. It is very loud."

Something came to life inside her, a volcano erupting and spreading heat and vigor through her veins. What was she doing in this provincial backwater? Was she to waste the talent that God had given her and she'd sweated, wept, and suffered to perfect? Who were the people of Stoke Newton to scorn what had delighted tens of thousands of others in a dozen countries? And filled her with joy too. For the all the pain her fame had caused her, she wasn't prepared to renounce it because her celebrity was earned and merited. Not as a beauty or a wearer of jewels or an object of desire, but as an artist.

She was La Divina, the greatest soprano in Europe. She was also a woman in love. If she could be both she would.

CHAPTER TWENTY-THREE

"The theatres are closed for the summer and London is very dull."

The Examiner

MAX HAD BEEN prepared to give Tessa a fortnight to wallow in rural tranquility. After less than a week he had had enough. First he had to tackle his mother and address his violation of the terms of their bet. He'd been avoiding her since the benefit.

He found her in the library at Tamworth House with Simon Lindo. Both seemed self-conscious at his arrival. Something to do with her idiotic plan to rebuild the Tavistock, most likely. He didn't much care.

"Max, darling," Lady Clarissa said. "Simon and I were just discussing the opening of the Tavistock Phoenix Theatre. All the papers have been signed and the plans are made. Building starts next week."

"Congratulations, Mama. I wasn't sure you were serious. You're going to be busy, Simon."

Simon cleared his throat and looked nervous. "Managing both houses is quite within my capability."

Max would have brushed aside the whole matter since it was the last thing on his mind, when Lady Clarissa interrupted. "And of course we must have Madame Foscari for our opening."

That got his attention. "We'll see about that." Enough was enough. His mother had taken Tessa from him once and he was not going to allow it again. Come to think of it she *owed* him.

"But, Max, La Divina is the most popular performer in London and I must have the best."

Simon intervened to prevent an unseemly brangle. "The kind of show we envision for the new Tavistock, my lady, is hardly Madame Foscari's cup of tea."

"No indeed!" Max said. "I can't see her prancing around in *Harlequin Gulliver or The Flying Island* or whatever nonsense you mean to present in the name of entertainment. Tessa is a serious artist. A great artist! You want her to share the stage with an elephant?"

"Elephants. Plural," Lady Clarissa snapped, then continued with a deceptive air of innocence. "She's good with animals. Being bitten by a chicken didn't bother her in the least. And she's such a magnificent creature. Imagine her surrounded by the light of a thousand fireworks."

Max could imagine it only too well and it made his blood freeze. Rockets and Roman candles raining fire on Tessa's head. "When is this opening, anyway?"

"I wanted to be ready for the spring season but Simon says there isn't time." She didn't appear upset about the foiling of her plans. Simon must have exerted a calming influence, for which her son could only be grateful, given the news he had to break. "It means," she continued, "that your little opera house will have no competition to speak of until then and I am sure you will make lots of money. Lucky for me that I already won our bet."

Max braced himself for war. "I don't know what you mean," he said in a vain hope that Simon hadn't let the cat out of the bag about Tessa's benefit.

No such luck. "You had to dip into your own pocket to persuade Madame Foscari to sign a contract." Yet his mother smiled at him, her dark eyes devoid of malice or triumph. Lady Clarissa in a gentle mood could only be coiling for attack. She looked over at Simon, the snake in the grass, who raised his brows and nodded.

"Since I win our bet by default, I have chosen a bride for you."

"I won't marry her. I'll choose my own, thank you, in fact—"

"Don't you even want to know her name?"

"Not especially. You've doubtless picked someone like Lady Mary Greville but I can tell you—"

"Lady Mary? Goodness no. She wouldn't suit me at all. I've thought of someone much better." She examined her amethyst bracelets—even in the morning Lady Clarissa had no use for subtlety in adornment—and muttered something about getting them cleaned, all the time casting Max sideways looks to see if she'd driven him insane yet. He considered sitting down and pretending to fall asleep, just to annoy her, but decided against it. He let her enjoy the moment. She'd be disappointed soon enough.

But, damn it, the moment was taking too long. "Can we make a little haste? There's somewhere I need to be." Somerset, or rather Marlborough, where he intended to spend the night on the way.

"I insist that you marry Teresa Foscari."

Max had to sit down after all. "Tessa?" he said faintly.

"Simon says you are in love with her and I want you to be happy." When she leaned over and kissed him on the cheek Max saw that her eyes were shining.

He seized her hand. "I came to tell you that I am going to Somerset to propose to her."

"Very naughty of you, but I forgive you this time." She sat beside him and held both his hands. "I won't apologize for separating you years ago. At nineteen and seventeen you were too young to know your minds. Now you are grown up. I like her. A namby-pamby daughter-in-law wouldn't suit me."

Max thought they would get on very well. Lady Clarissa and Tessa were *not* alike, thank the Lord, but he could see them as friends, especially if he and Tessa had children.

"One more thing," Lady Clarissa said. From her tone he gathered her attack of sentimentality had passed. "I expect her to sing at my first night. As her husband you must insist."

"Tessa will make her own decisions about where and when

she sings. However—" He gave Simon a stern look. "—I will advise her on her contracts. Now I must be off. I have sixty miles to travel today."

"Make sure you accepts you," his mother called as he reached the door.

When he turned back she was standing next to Simon near the hearth.

"I will."

He wished he felt confident in his powers of persuasion.

TESSA WAS SORRY to say goodbye to the Birketts and promised to visit them again. She had made up some nonsense about a wobble in her voice that required the instant attention of a vocal coach. They found the excuse plausible if perplexing. She didn't blame them for finding her performance less than enthralling; they simply had no comprehension of either her life or her art. She had come to Somerset to find out who she was and now she knew.

She was not an English country lady and she couldn't wait to get back to London. What if Max had left town? He might have given up on her and her lack of decision. Perhaps he'd thought better of his eccentric wish to marry a notorious soprano and found himself a suitable young lady. Why did London have to be so far away, requiring that she spend the entire night at Marlborough? She might miss him by a day. Panic clawed at her stomach.

She breathed a little, hummed a few bars, and looked out of the window of her private parlor into the courtyard of the Lamb Inn. An elegant traveling carriage drew up, the kind built especially for a family of means. She'd owned such an equipage herself once; it had been sold along with the house in Italy and so much else to pay Domenico's debts. The hired vehicles in which she'd journeyed from London and back had almost rattled her teeth out.

At first the gentleman who alighted seemed a product of her

hopes and imagination. Then her head filled with an orchestral crescendo heralding a soaring operatic climax. She tore out of the parlor, out of the inn and hurled herself at Max.

Trumpets and horns sounded as she pressed herself shamelessly against his long, lean body, burying her face in the wonderful Maxness of his chest. His arms came around her and now she was home.

"Why are you here?" For a terrible moment she wondered if their meeting was a coincidence he hadn't sought. "Are you on your way to Tamworth?"

"My darling, your grasp of English geography is abysmal. I was on my way to find you."

"And I was coming to London...." She could scarcely speak for joy so instead she pulled his dear dark head down and kissed him passionately.

"We have to stop doing this in an inn yard," he said, putting her aside with obvious reluctance five minutes later. "There are grooms and Lord knows who else staring at us."

Tessa, unable to summon an iota's care for the opinions of Lord knows who, shrugged. "I am accustomed to performing in public."

He threw back his head in an infectious, full-bodied laugh from deep within his chest and they continued to make a spectacle of themselves, clinging to each other in mirth.

"Shall we continue this inside?" he said. "I trust this unseemly demonstration means you are going to marry me."

She took his arm and led him to the parlor. He looked about the small room with disfavor. "Not the setting I had envisioned for our reunion. All the furniture is hard and looks uncomfortable."

"There are things we need to discuss," she said.

"Be warned. I am prepared to counter every argument with sound reasoning."

"Reason? I am a creature of high flights and emotion."

"Then all I will offer you is my love, now and forever."

"That's my favorite kind of reason." She sighed because there was still a world outside this pokey little parlor, much as she'd like to surrender to love, hard furniture and all.

"Are there any others?"

Taking her place on a hard little chair, she indicated that he should sit too. "Not too close. We need to speak seriously and I'm not sure I can do that if you touch me." He obeyed, fixing her with a gaze that threatened her resolution. "And don't smile at me either. My grandmother lives in a cottage that could fit into your mother's housekeeper's room. The family at 'the Hall' barely speak to them and I doubt Lady Clarissa would speak to *them*. I have discovered my family and I am not ashamed, but there is nothing about them that would make me acceptable to the nobility where you belong."

"I cannot believe we are having this conversation again," Max said. "If it matters to you, my mother has given us her blessing. Quite happily so, I may add."

She digested this unexpected news. "There's still my reputation. And I cannot give up singing. If I had to settle down and be nothing but Lady Allerton I should shrivel away. Sometimes I think I never want to sing another note, but after a few days the music calls me. I need it. I need to share it with an audience as long as I am able."

"My darling Tessa. What have I ever said to give the impression I would want you to stop? I own an opera house. I revere your genius. To me talent is the true aristocracy, far more important than birth. You may sing as often or as little as you like. If you want to perform in Paris or Venice or Vienna, I ask only to come with you."

An enchanting vista opened. No longer tied to the demands of an opera house contract that required her to perform three or four times a week for months at a time, she could sing when and if she wanted, or not. And she would have Max at her side.

"You said," he continued, "that you wanted children. If I can give them to you I will. If not, or if you decide you'd rather not, I shall accept your choice." He leaned forward and held out his hand.

"Are you a saint?" she asked in wonderment, accepting it. "After all these years can Providence have let me love the one man who offers me everything?"

"I am definitely not a saint, especially where you are concerned." He brushed a kiss on her knuckles, his eyes filled with an unholy invitation.

Ready to accept, she was shocked when he stood and put on his hat.

"Where are you going?"

"I have a long-neglected appointment I need to keep. Will you meet me at the churchyard in half an hour? It's only a few minutes' walk."

"I will!" she cried, her heart singing an aria. "I will." The words answered every question he'd ever asked her.

When she reached the church he wasn't there. Ancient dismay gripped her, but only for a second. Max wouldn't let her down again and it wasn't raining. She sat on a bench to wait, turning her face to the evening sun that cast shadows from the gravestones. She breathed the scent of a flowering shrub and lowered her eyelids to enjoy birdsong and the hum of bees. For the first time in years she was completely at peace.

"Tessa."

She opened his eyes and he was there, looking anxious.

"I'm sorry I kept you waiting."

"I knew you would be here."

The tension in his shoulders relaxed and he smiled his beautiful smile, went down on one knee and took her hands in his. "Tessa Birkett, will you marry me?"

"Yes," she said. "A thousand times yes."

"Will you marry me now?" He nodded at the church door where a man in clerical dress had emerged. "The vicar took a little persuasion, despite the special license I brought. He wanted us to wait until the morning."

She raised her brows. "I suppose we could wait."

"Have you ever stayed in a respectable inn with a man who was not your husband?"

She shook her head.

"Such a virtuous lady. Let me tell you, innkeepers don't like it. They might ask us to leave."

"Should we go elsewhere?" Tessa wanted him very much, now. Her blood thrilled at the idea of going to bed with Max without the least doubt about her ecstatic response.

"Not at all. The Lamb is the best inn in Marlborough and the mattresses are excellent. But first we must go to church."

She took his arm like the proper English lady she could be and let her love lead her to the altar.

EPILOGUE

"The First Night of the TAVISTOCK PHOENIX Theatre was graced by the long awaited return of LADY ALLERTON. The former Madame Foscari's voice has lost none of its radiance during her absence for Private Reasons. The company was exceedingly numerous and brilliant. Among the fashionable circle were the Prince Regent, The Duke of Clarence, The Duchess of Richmond, Lady Jersey, The Earl and Countess of Storrington [etc. etc.]"

The Times

Upper Grosvenor Street, two days before the performance

JACOBIN BURST INTO the drawing room of Tessa's and Max's house. "There isn't a ticket to be had. We could have filled our box six times over with people who have suddenly decided that we are their dearest friends. No one wants to miss the return of La Divina." She skidded to a halt and kissed her cousin on both cheeks. "You look nervous, Tessa, but I know you will be as superb as always."

"I am worried about my voice, though I've been working hard with Sempronio for a month. I am also concerned about whether the *ton* will accept me off the stage, at Lady Clarissa's supper party."

"My dear, they can't wait for you to be going out in company again. The invitations will pour in. They are all counting their sons and grandsons of the right age and thinking about little Despina's dowry. We should arrange a betrothal with Augustus now, before she is beset by dukes and so forth."

"I'll have Max turn away every other suitor."

"Besides, they are all too frightened of Lady Clarissa to make trouble. There are always a few high sticklers but they don't speak to me, either, so we can disregard them."

Tessa had scarcely suffered a moment's panic since her marriage. A few pangs during her pregnancy, a flutter or two when Lady Clarissa was being particularly acerbic. Now she was terrified—afraid of failing herself, and even more of failing her husband. Rationally she knew nothing she did would disappoint him, but not even a happy marriage could turn an operatic soprano into a creature of pure reason.

"Will you come upstairs and see Despina?" The sight of her daughter, now three months old, never failed to calm her.

HARDLY A DAY passed without a visit from Tessa's mother-in-law. Enchanted by her granddaughter, she hadn't objected to Despina being named after the role Tessa had sung the first night she met Max, when he brought her white roses in Oporto. In fact Lady Clarissa wanted to change the program for the Tavistock opening to *Così fan tutte* in the infant's honor, until convinced by Simon Lindo that even she couldn't turn that intimate opera into a grand spectacle.

The day of the opening, Lady Clarissa and Simon arrived at the house just as Tessa had finished her vocal exercises in the second drawing room, which Max had converted to a music room. Although her mother-in-law usually treated her with an exhausting excess of kindness, both as mother of the grandchild and leading attraction, Tessa was not pleased.

"You may stay exactly fifteen minutes," Max said, without even intercepting his wife's pleading look. "Tessa needs absolute rest and quiet until she goes to the theater."

Lady Clarissa pouted. "But I want to hear what Despina has done today."

"Since she is a small baby I doubt she's done much that was different from yesterday," Simon Lindo said. "Do you wish to upset your prima donna?"

Lady Clarissa cast wide, reproachful eyes on her manager, smiled, almost simpered, then returned to the charge in another direction. "Don't you think it would be splendid if Tessa made her second big entrance on a horse? A white horse?"

"No," Simon said. "We have quite enough animals."

"Spoilsport. A camel?"

Simon shook his head and laughed and the conversation moved on.

"Thank God for Simon," Max said when the manager had managed to make his willful partner leave. "They're like an old married couple, those two."

"More like bickering lovers," Tessa replied.

"Nonsense. Mama had merely found someone who stands up to her, and about time too. It's lucky for her, because this theater would never have got off the ground without Simon to talk her out of her more ridiculous ideas."

Tessa shook her head at her husband's naiveté. This wasn't the first time they'd had this argument and she always let it rest, understanding that Max might not wish to acknowledge his mother's liaison, even to himself. Tessa, however, saw what she saw.

"Lady Clarissa's ideas may go too far, but she has an instinct for the theater. Tonight's performance will be spectacular, even if my voice is not at its best."

"I heard your practice and I haven't the slightest twinge of concern. London will be as enthralled as ever. Come," he said, offering his hand. "You need rest and quiet and I intend to make sure you get it."

How lucky she was to have a husband who knew and enforced her wishes. Her preference was always to be alone on the day of a performance, but now, on the first such day since the long ago benefit when she'd uttered not a single word, she wanted something different. "Will you come upstairs and keep me company?"

"Are you sure?"

Grasping his shoulders she wiped away his uncertainty with a soft kiss and elicited a happy smile with a deeper one. "A little exercise before a nap could become my new habit. But of course I must be very, very quiet."

That, as they both knew well, might be the difficult part.

LIKE THE REST of the theater, the principal dressing rooms at the Tavistock Phoenix had been furnished without regard to expense. Still, it was a theater, instantly familiar to Tessa, as was the atmosphere of gaiety and gossip and first-night nerves. She ran through her warming-up exercises, then Angela helped her into the magnificent costume of black gauze and net scattered with stars, and a parure of enormous diamonds. Paste of course. Not even Lady Clarissa possessed jewels big enough for the Queen of the Night.

Sempronio and Sofie came in to hug and kiss her and wish her luck. Tessa had a new *répétiteur* now, one who was able to stay in the country for long periods, Sempronio being in constant demand in London for concerts and as a singing teacher. She saw them almost every day now she was in town again, and they would always be her dearest friends. Knowing her well, they didn't stay long. She needed quiet to prepare her mind for the challenge ahead. Even Max had been banished to his box. Only Angela was permitted to remain with her.

As a result of her new performance-day regime, she felt absolutely splendid: confident, powerful, invincible even. She fingered the white roses on her dressing table, inhaled their fragrance, and kissed them.

Then she forgot everything but the evil queen and the fiendishly difficult music Mozart had written for her.

MAX HAD REFUSED to sit in the stage box with Lady Clarissa and Simon. Since Tessa was on stage he preferred his own company, so he could admire her without distraction and think how lucky he was to have such a talented wife. And luckier still to be the one to take her home afterward.

He had every faith in Tessa, but nervousness was inevitable. He fretted. About her voice, which he knew was as good as ever. But what if giving birth had affected it so she could not be heard in this grandiose theatrical palace his mother had created? Or perhaps some unmannerly yahoos would remember the old controversy over the hospital and boo her? He'd have to jump down to the pit and fight them. Or, and this seemed the most likely of all terrible eventualities his brain could dream up, a massive piece of scenery would fall on her?

She had sent him away when he escorted her to her dressing room, saying she needed quiet before the performance. But what if she needed him to help soothe her nerves? He should go back at once.

His exit at the back of the box was blocked by the appearance of the Marquess of Somerville. "What do you want?" he asked rudely.

"Always a pleasure to see you, Max. You look calm."

Max grinned sheepishly at the man's perception. "I'm more nervous about tonight than Tessa."

"How is the lovely Lady Allerton?"

"Lovely and all mine, thank you."

"Yes, you won that one. Don't worry. Domesticity has never been to my taste, but I do look forward to hearing La Divina again. Lady Clarissa has promised something spectacular."

Max groaned. "She hasn't let me into the theater for rehearsals since I own the rival house, but I hear things. I don't think you need to worry about insipidity and good taste this evening."

"Excellent. While we're on the subject, will your wife be returning to the Regent? Nancy is anxious to know." Somerville's mistress had been promoted during Tessa's absence and was doing well in the leading soprano roles, though not, of course, as well as Tessa.

"Tell Miss Sturridge that she is safe, though Lady Allerton may return for particular operas from time to time. She does not intend to perform regularly. She has accepted an engagement in Italy so we shall take the whole family to spend the winter in Naples."

When Somerville had departed, Max dwelled on the many advantages of life as husband to a singer—private concerts at home, winter in a warm climate—if only he could control his nerves. Tessa said any agitation she felt always disappeared once she appeared on stage. Max hoped it would work for him too. Perhaps he'd better do some breathing exercises. He inhaled a time or two, in the way he'd watched her prepare so often. The absurdity made him feel better.

The opera was about to start. In *The Magic Flute* Simon had found the ideal vehicle to combine first-rate music with Lady Clarissa's passion for the sensational. There would be a dragon, other fantastical creatures, and plenty of live animals, including, yes, an elephant. Tessa was quite excited about her own entrance but had refused to spoil the surprise. Every form of persuasion he'd attempted, many of them quite inventive, had failed.

The overture began and he fell under the spell of Mozart's music. Much of the audience was less easily enchanted and fell silent only when the curtain went up and the giant proscenium arch revealed a magical forest. The dragon was splendid, the singing adequate—though not, to Max's satisfaction, up to the standard of the Regent. As thunder announced the approach of the Queen of the Night, a dark curtain fell. The orchestra played the thrilling music that heralded her appearance and a collective gasp went up from the vast auditorium when the curtain reopened. A rocky island rose from beneath the stage, surrounded by water. From within a cave Tessa emerged, gorgeous in black and silver.

The scenery did not collapse and every word could be heard. Each soaring note was perfect, and the end of the aria was greeted with rapture. La Divina was back.

No one in the audience could be happier than the diva's husband whose eyes were damp with love and pride.

Except, perhaps, the husband's mother. Although she hadn't managed to fit a shipwreck into *The Magic Flute*, she had insisted on an ocean.

AUTHOR'S NOTE

Opera singers, especially sopranos, were celebrities in the eighteenth and nineteenth centuries, comparable to rock stars now. In creating Teresa Foscari I drew on incidents from the lives of two of the period's most renowned, Angelica Catalani and Maria Malibran. The soubriquet La Divina I borrowed as an homage to the twentieth century's greatest diva, Maria Callas.

The Regent Opera House is an invention inspired by the short-lived Pantheon Opera, built in the 1780s. I trust the Regent lasted longer. The Tavistock is based on the King's Theatre in the Haymarket, which was the home of Italian opera in Regency London. In the British Library I found a treasure trove in the form of three volumes of newspaper clippings from press reports, gossip columns, reviews, and advertisements concerning the King's Theatre. Many of the press reports that head each chapter are taken, with appropriate adaptation, from those volumes. Among the reports was a furor over Catalani refusing to sing at a benefit for a hospital and having her donation returned. Without knowing the reason behind the controversy, I adapted the incident for my story.

Tessa's solo operatic debut at the age of seventeen was not unusual. Catalani's was at sixteen while Malibran was seventeen when she stepped in for a sick prima donna—shades of Forty-Second Street! The enormous sums earned by the top singers challenged the incomes of aristocrats: One year Catalani was estimated to have earned over £16,000. Like Tessa, she had trouble collecting money owed, as well as having her fortune frittered away by a gambling husband.

I set my story in 1818, the year that Rossini's *The Barber of*

Seville was first performed in London. Beethoven's *Fidelio* premiered in 1805 so there is no reason it couldn't have been performed in 1818. In fact, it didn't reach London until 1832. All the operas, songs, and arias mentioned in the book were staples of the period and can be found in multiple performances on You Tube if you want to hear them.

My eternal gratitude goes to Louisa Cornell, professional opera singer and Regency romance writer, for her invaluable information about the habits of sopranos, current and historical. Any inaccuracies are mine, not hers. Thanks to Edie Danford for her stellar editing and to Megan Mulry, Anne Calhoun, Stacey Agdern, Janet Mullany, and many other writing friends for their suggestions, support, and encouragement.

Secrets of a Soprano has been a long time in gestation. Originally it was intended as a follow-up to my debut novel *Never Resist Temptation*, the story of Tessa's pastry cook cousin Jacobin and Anthony, the Earl of Storrington. Instead I put it aside and began the Burgundy Club series. But I always loved the half-written story so last year I decided to revise and finish it. I hope you enjoyed it.

Miranda

ABOUT MIRANDA NEVILLE

Miranda Neville grew up in England, loving the books of Georgette Heyer and other Regency romances. Her historical romances include the Burgundy Club series, about Regency book collectors, and The Wild Quartet. She lives in Vermont with her daughter, her cat, and a ridiculously large collection of Christmas tree ornaments. Miranda loves to hear from readers and can be reached through her website, Facebook, or Twitter. To hear about future releases, sign up for her newsletter at her website www.mirandaneville.com.